MODERN
SOUTH AFRICAN
STORIES

MODERN
SOUTH AFRICAN
STORIES

EDITED BY
STEPHEN GRAY

REVISED SELECTION

AD DONKER PUBLISHERS
JOHANNESBURG & CAPE TOWN

Originally published as *On the Edge of the World*, 1974
Revised and expanded edition under the title *Modern South African Stories*
    published in 1980
Reprinted 1981, 1983, 1987, 1990, 1993
This new revised edition, 2002

Published in 2002 by
JONATHAN BALL PUBLISHERS (PTY) LTD
P O Box 33977
Jeppestown
2043

ISBN 0 86852 226 0

Front cover painting by Keith Alexander
Design by Michael Barnett, Johannesburg
Typesetting and reproduction of text by Alinea Studio, Cape Town
Reproduction of cover by Triple M Advertising & Design, Johannesburg
Printed and bound by CTP Book Printers, Caxton Street, Parow, Cape

CONTENTS

INTRODUCTION

From modest, embattled beginnings.

Since 1974, when the first edition of this anthology appeared, the conditions under which South African authors were producing short stories have profoundly altered. When Ad Donker agreed to my proposal that we produce *On the Edge of the World*, a liberated South Africa was hardly even in view; rather, the censorship system of a quarter of a century ago was the pervading factor in all attempts to enlarge freedom of expression.

By then the exuberant and accomplished wave of the Sixties in South African literature in English had been driven into exile (Es'kia Mphahlele, Bessie Head) or otherwise dispersed. Yet, arising from within it seemed, was an irresistible new wave of practitioners. They were publishing especially within South Africa as a more outspoken and daring group of independent publishers girded themselves to promote their work (besides Donker, there was David Philip, Ravan Press and others). There were also several now defunct but once outstanding review outlets, so that part of the intention of *On the Edge of the World* was to pay tribute to the seedbed conditions they afforded the rising generation: *The Classic* returned as *New Classic* (represented by Mongane Serote here), *The Purple Renoster* (Ahmed Essop), *Contrast* before it became the present-day *New Contrast* (Yvonne Burgess) and even *Drum* and still more. My own experience of publishing a review was as part of *IZWI/Voice/Stem* for twenty numbers over 1971-74, where in No. 17 Lionel Abrahams's 'The Messiah' first appeared ... and has come through proudly to maintain its place here.

The tactic of *On the Edge of the World* was to summarise those little mags in a cross-section: from Nadine Gordimer and Alan Paton as they had appeared in the best reviews with recent and topical examples, through to a typical new work by the rising figures like Sheila Roberts, Sipho Sepamla (then still Sydney Sepamla), Adam Small, the late Barney Simon. Keith Alexander, sadly also now departed, walked into the Donker office in Craighall Park and volunteered an apt cover of a broken aqueduct leading across a desolate plain towards extinction: the probable fate of the book, should the censors buck up and move in on it. Common sense in those days decreed that such a risky venture be produced cheaply to minimise the financial risk and hit the shelves fast. The subtitle told how it was meant merely to catch a moment: *Southern African Stories of the Seventies*. A collector's item now.

So it was produced inside South Africa as a holding action to demonstrate that, before the outlawed diasporans of the literature could return to the unnaturally divided land, the new inside wing was not going to remain creatively silent. Predictably the work was attacked for its stance – understandably by the proscribed abroad on grounds of lack of solidarity, and unforgivably by the Afrikaans-language writers at home who felt they had been excluded from the lists of those marginalised English-speakers cliffhanging from the end of *their* continent.

On the Edge proved to be a chipper product, even if a mere part of a far larger movement gathering towards its showdown in 1976. With Donker I was able to continue my disposable surveying with the equivalent selection for the poets, *A World of their Own: Southern African Poets of the Seventies* (which in 1984 was expanded as *Modern South African Poetry*), with a sequence of low-priced playscript clusters: *Theatre One* (1978), *Theatre Two* (1981), *Market Plays* (1986) and so on. All appeared following the same criterion: broadly sampling an otherwise ephemeral activity, cheaply produced, handy.

But by 1980 *On the Edge of the World*, with its solid cargo of varied and unbeatable short stories, attuned to those times as perhaps no other items were quite so well, was the one which had proved itself. Donker felt we could go for a more enduring version of it, expanded to include a broader range – for example, Mphahlele controversially returning from exile and still unbanned, a fresh Richard Rive really pushing the envelope in the new *Staffrider* and even some younger shockers: for example, the young Chris van Wyk and the then much-taboo Pieter-Dirk Uys.

Donker intended to move with what we now boldly called *Modern South African Stories* into the league of the big post-war anthologies: David Wright's *South African Stories* of 1960, Mphahlele's *African Writing Today* of 1967, a large proportion of which was South African (banned in South Africa), Gordimer and Abrahams's *South African Writing Today*, also of 1967 (banned in South Africa). There to fill

the gap the now twenty-seven pieces appeared, strictly in alpha-
betical order to show no favour or bias towards celebrities (or any
other form of discrimination).

By the Nineties those stories of the Seventies and Eighties were
even being performed in South African public spaces – for instance,
by Soli Philander. For two decades and more, in its various jackets
(by Erik Laubscher and by Nicholas Combrinck) and printings,
Modern South African Stories came through, reliably and unscathed.

But now, in the altered world of South African English-language
affairs, and fallen over into the twenty-first century, another wave
of our literary story is undoubtedly upon us. Some items in the
1980 collection frankly have passed their sell-by date and become
fine period pieces, while others have taken on a renewed interest
now that the historical tissue out of which they were born may be
revalued.

Here I have decided, with the chance of a revised edition, to pre-
serve for reprinting the best ten of the old selection as a foundation. Some of them have achieved anthology-favourite status in
the interim, all of them have become 'classics' in their own ways,
so that in the first part any new reader is assured of a tried and
tested quality read.

Numerous selections of more specialised groupings of work have
succeeded *Modern South African Stories* since 1980 (can the present
work be the only one on the market that does not include Gcina
Mhlope's wonderful 'The Toilet' and Njabulo Ndebele's equally
dazzling 'The Music of the Violin'?). But for the second part here
(17 items) it was a matter of returning to first principles (and without repeating available material): as ever, a cross-section of the
best work being done by South African authors in English, across
the threshold of the millennium – work hardly known outside the
obscure pages of so few journals, nowadays often only on computer
printouts, not yet famous.

For us the switchover occurred on one particular day – 27 April
1994 – superbly summarised here by Elleke Boehmer in her piece
so entitled. As everything in the second part post-dates that transi-
tional, magical moment, her contribution acts as the appropriate
prelude. From there on read post-apartheid literature.

Two of the now older contributors – Van Wyk and Roberts – have
taken the opportunity to refill their assured slots with brand-new

works; and I have thrown out a makeweight story of my own for a leaner one of today. Other contributors are included in the Donker surveys for the first time: Shaun Levin making his debut in his home country, Rachelle Greeff, Phaswane Mpe, Deena Padayachee, Farida Karodia, and also Dennis Venter with his first appearance ever. As the notes on each item make clear, at least half a dozen other stories are reproduced here for the first time.

Stephen Gray
Johannesburg, 2002

ES'KIA MPHAHLELE
A BALLAD OF OYO

Es'kia Mphahlele (previously Ezekiel, always Zeke, b. 1919). The doyen of South African writers, author of the now classic *Down Second Avenue* (1965). To the augmented *Modern South African Stories* of 1980 he contributed 'A Ballad of Oyo' as representative of his work in the short story form. As it was first published in his collection *In Corner B* (East African Publishing House) in 1967, it is the earliest story included here.

Ishola (also called Mama-Jimi because her first son was Jimi) found a tramp on her counter slab at Oyo's central market, where she took her stand each day to sell vegetables and fruit. Furiously she poked the grimy bundle with a broom to tell him a few things he had better hear: there are several other places where he could sleep; she sells food off this counter, not firewood – like him; so he thought to lie on a cool slab on a hot night, eh? – why does he not sleep under a running tap? And so on. With a sense of revulsion she washed the counter.

These days, when market day began, it also meant that Ishola was going to have to listen to her elder sister's endless prattling during which she spun words and words about the younger sister's being a fool to keep a useless husband like Balogun in food and clothing. Off and on, for three months, Ishola had tried to fight against the decision to tell Balogun to go look for another wife while she went her own way. Oh, why did her sister have to blabber like this? Did her sister think that she, Ishola, liked being kicked about by her man the way Balogun did? Her sister might well go on like this, but she could not divine the burning questions that churned inside Ishola.

That is right Ishola, her sister, who sold rice next to her, would say. You are everybody's fool, are you not? Lie still like that and let him come and sit and play drums on you and go off and get drunk on palm wine, come back and beat you, scatter the children – children of his palm wine-stained blood, (spitting) like a hawk landing among chicks then you have no one to blame only your stupid head (pushing her other breast forcibly into her baby's mouth for emphasis). How long has he been giving you so much pain like this? How long are you going to try to clean a pig that goes back into the mud? You are going to eat grass very soon you will tell me and do not keep complaining to me about his ways if my advice means nothing to you.

And so goes the story of Ishola, Ishola who was called Mama-Jimi, a mother of three children. Slender, dark-and-smooth-skin with piercing eyes that must have seen through dark nights.

Day and night the women of Oyo walk the black road, the road of tarmac to and from the market. They can be seen walking, riding the dawn, walking into sunrise; figures can be seen, slender as twilight; their feet feel every inch of the tarmac, but their wares press down on the head and the neck takes the strain, while the hip and legs propel the body forward. A woman here, a woman there in the drove has her arm raised in a loop, a loop of endurance, to support the load, while the other arm holds a suckling child in a loop, a loop of love. They must walk fast, almost in a trot, so that they may not feel the pain of the weight so much.

The week before the week before Mama-Jimi started for Oyo Market, her body feeling the seed of another child grow that had not yet begun to give her sweet torment, bitter ecstasy in the stomach. The night before her husband had told her he was going to the north to see his other wives. He would come back – when? When he was full of them and they of him, Mama-Jimi knew. When he should have made sure that the small trade each was doing went well, he said.

Mama-Jimi looked at his shadow quivering on the wall in the light of the oil lamp as he stooped over her, and loneliness swept over her in a flood. They loved and they remained a promontory rising above the flood. And Mama-Tunji again took her place in the order of things: one of three wives giving all of her to one she loved and taking what was given by her man with a glad heart. Oyo will always be Oyo whatever happens to it, the market will always be there, come rain, come blood, come malaria.

It was the week before only the week before when the rain caught the market women on the tarmac to market. The sky burst and the rain came down with power. It rumbled down the road in rivulets. Mama-Jimi felt the load inside become heavy knotting up beneath her navel. Her feet became heavy, the hips failed to twist. But she tried to push on. She could see the others way ahead through the grey of the rain. Mama-Jimi's thoughts were on the market, the market of Oyo: she must reach it. For if she should fall, she thought, or feel sicker, other women were there.

But the woman sagged and fell and dragged herself out of the road. She felt the blood oozing, warm and cold. A life was running out of her, she was sure of it. A life dead just as soon as born and sprouting in her ...

Two women found her body on the roadside: cold, wet.

Whispers bounced and rebounced at the market that Mama-Jimi was dead, dead, Mama-Jimi was gone, gone in the rain.

Did she know it was there?

Ehe, she did she told me so.

And her man gone to the north, a-ah? So it is said.

Are they going to call him? They must. Only yesterday night we were together and she was glad she was going to give her man a second child.

To die when your people are far far away from you, a-ah!

We are most of us strangers here.

It is true.

This was a week before, and the market at Oyo jingles and buzzes and groans, but it goes on as it has done for many years before when the first Alafin came here.

You know what the market is like every morning, not so? Babbling tongues, angry tongues, silent tongues. Down there a woman was suckling a baby while she sold. Near to Ishola a woman was eating gari and okaran and gravy out of a coloured enamel bowl. Someone else next to her handled her sales for her. As the heat mounted a lad was pouring water on bunches of lettuce to keep them from wilting and thus refusing to be sold. But the lad seemed to be wilting himself, because as soon as he leaned back against a pole, sleep seized him and his head tilted back helplessly like a man having a shave in a barber's chair.

The mouth opened and the lettuce lost its importance for a while. Mostly oyingbo – white people – came to buy lettuce. On and off while he slept, someone sprinkled water on his face. This seldom jolted him out of his stupor. He merely ran his hand over his face, stared at the lettuce and then poured water on it. Some fat women opposite Ishola's counter were shouting and one seldom knew whether they were angry or simply zealous. They also splashed water over the pork they were selling so as to keep away blue flies that insisted on sitting on it. All the would-be buyers who stood at the pork counter fingered the pieces: they lifted them up, turned them round, put them back, picked them up again. There was no exchange of smiles here.

Ten shillings, said the pork woman who herself seemed to have been wallowing in grease.

Four shillings, suggested the customer.

Eight shillings last.

Five (taking it and putting it back as if disgusted).

Seven las' price.

With a long-drawn sound between the teeth to signify disgust, the customer left. The pork woman looked at her fellow-vendor, as if to say, 'Stupid customers!'

Oyingbo women did not buy meat at these markets. They said they were appalled by the number of hands that clutched at it. They bought imported meat in the provision stores at prices fixed seemingly to annoy expatriates. One missionary woman had been known to bring a scale for the vendor to weigh the meat in order to get her money's worth. What! she had exclaimed, you don't weigh meat in this market? Ridiculous! The meat women had looked baffled. The next time the missionary brought her own balance. This time *they* thought something was ridiculous, and they laughed to show it. Even after weighing a piece, she found that she still had to haggle and bargain. Enthusiasm had flagged on her part, and after this she came to the market only to rescue some of the lettuce and parsley from continual drenching and to buy fruit.

So did the other white women. One of them turned round in answer to a shout from a vendor, Custumah, customah! She approached Ishola's counter where there were heaps of carrots and tomatoes. She was smiling, as one is expected to do from behind a counter.

Nice car-*rot*, madam.

How much?

Shilling (picking up a bunch).

Sixpence.

No madam, shilling (smiling).

Sixpence.

Ha-much madam wan' pay? (with no smile).

All right, seven pence.

Ni'pence.

Seven.

No, 'gree madam (smiling).

The customer realised that she had come to the end of the road. She yielded, but not before saying, 'Ninepence is too much for these.'

A-ah madam. If not to say madam she buy for me many times I coul' 'ave took more moni for you.

Towards sunset Ishola packed up. She had made up her mind to go to Baba Dejo, the president of the court of the local authority. She firmly believed that the old man had taken a bribe. Either her father-in-law or Balogun himself, her delinquent husband, could have offered it. This, she believed, must be the reason why the court could not hold a hearing of her case against her husband. Twice Ishola had asked him to hear her case. Each time the old man said something to delay it. The old fox, she thought. This time, she fixed simply on putting five pounds in front of the president. He cannot refuse so much money, Ishola thought. But go back to that animal of a husband, never – no more, he is going to kill me one of these days I do not want to die I do not want to die for nothing I want to work for my children I want to send them to school I do not want them to grow old on the market place and die counting money and finding none. Baba Dejo must take the money he must listen to my case and let the law tell Balogun to leave me alone with the children and go his way I will go mine I know his father has gone and bribed him to keep the matter out of the court and why? – because he does not want to lose his son's children and because – I do not know he is very fond of me he has always stood up for me against his son – yes he loves me but I am married to his son not to him and his love does not cure his son's self-made madness. Lijadu loves me and I want him let my heart burst into many pieces if he does not take me as his wife I want him because he has such a pure heart.

Ishola was thinking of the day Lijadu came to fetch her in his car and they went to Ijebude for that weekend of love and heartbreaks: heartbreaks because she was someone else's wife someone who did not care for her and even then had gone to Warri without telling her. Now Lijadu was ready to give Balogun the equivalent of the bride price he had paid to Ishola's parents and so release her to become his wife. Balogun and his father had refused Lijadu's money.

Just what irritates me so, Ishola thought. I could burst into a hundred parts so much it fills me with anger. So they want to stop me from leaving their useless son, useless like dry leaves falling from a tree. Just this makes me mad and I feel I want to stand in the middle of the road and shout so as everyone can hear me. That man! – live with him again? He beats me he leaves me no money he grows fat on my money he does not care for the children the children of his own blood from his very own hanging things …

I wonder how much the old man will want? The thought flashed across Ishola's mind, like a streak of lightning that rips across the milling clouds, illuminating the sky's commotion all the more.

If your father-in-law Mushin were not my friend, says the president of the court, Dejo, when Ishola tells him the business of her visit, I should not let you come and speak to me on a matter like this. It is to be spoken in court only.

You do not want me to bring it to court sir.

I would do it if, if –

How much, sir?

Give me what you have, my daughter. He looks disdainful in the face as he says so. It does not please the young woman. He takes five pounds in paper money from her hand.

What is this I hear from your father-in-law, that you want to leave your husband? Ishola feels resentful at the thought that her case must have been chewed dead by these old men. But she presses the lid hard to keep her feelings from bubbling over. I beg that you listen, sir, she says. Balogun beats me he does not work he eats and sleeps he does not care for the children of his own-own blood, sir, he drinks too much palm wine this is too much I have had a long heart to carry him so far but this is the end of everything no no this is all I can carry.

Is he a man in bed?

Not when he is drunk and that is many times sir. She was looking at the floor at this time.

Hm, that is bad that is bad my child, that is bad. What does he say when you talk to him about his ways?

Nothing, sir. He just listens he listens and just listens that is all.

A man has strange ways and strange thoughts.

There is silence.

So he drinks himself stupid. I know there are certain places in Oyo where you can hear the name of Balogun spoken as if he were something that smells very bad. So he drinks himself stupid until he is too flabby to do his work in bed, a-ah! How many children have you by the way?

Three, sir.

The youngest is how old?

Two years, sir.

If a man gets too drunk to hoe a field another man will and he shall regret, he will see. He seems to be talking to himself. But a man who comes home only as a he-goat on heat, the old man continues, and not as a helper and father is useless. I will tell him that I will tell Balogun that myself. Animals look for food for their mates and their brood, why cannot a man?

You have talked to him twice before, sir.

Oh yes oh yes I have my child I know.

Silence.

But your father-in-law Mushin loves you so much so much my child.

I love him too but I am his son's wife not his.

You speak the truth there.

Silence.

It would break his heart all the same. Look at it whichever way you like. You fill a space left in his heart by the death of his wife and often defiled by the deeds of a worthless son. Dejo's face is one deep shadow of gravity.

I do not like that boy Balogun not one little moment, he goes on, but his father will weep because he holds you like his own-own daughter.

Ishola's head is full of noises and echoes of noises, for she had heard all this a few times before. She has determined her course and she shall not allow her tender sentiments to take her out of it, she mustn't, no, not now. Perhaps after, when tender feelings will be pointless. She still bears a little love for Balogun, but she wants her heart to be like a boulder so as not to give way.

Let me go and call my wife to talk with you more about this, old Dejo says as he leaves the room. As he does so, he stretches out his hand to place a few crumpled notes of money in Ishola's hand, whispering, 'Your heart is kind, my child, it is enough that you showed the heart to give, so take it back.'

Ishola feels a warm and cold air sweep over and through her. She trembles a little and she feels as if something were dangling in space and must fall soon.

Old Dejo's wife enters, round-bellied: the very presence of life's huge expectation.

But – such an old man! Ishola thinks ...

I can see it in her eyes Balogun I can see it in her eyes, Mushin said in his son's house one morning. Ishola is going to leave us.

She is at the market now, Papa. She loves me too much to do a foolish thing like that.

When are you going to wake up you useless boy. He gasped, as he had often done before. What kind of creature was given me for a son! What does your mother say from the other world to see you like this!

Balogun poured himself palm wine and drank and drank. I can see the blade of a cutlass coming to slash at my heart, the older man said, I can feel it coming.

Go and rest father, you are tired.

And Balogun walked out into the blazing shimmering sun, stopped to buy cigarettes at a small stall on the roadside and walked on, the very picture of aimlessness.

When are you going to stop fooling like this with Balogun I ask you? Ishola's sister said rasping out as she sat behind her counter. Her baby who was sucking looked up into her face with slight but mute concern in its eyes.

She does not know she does know this woman she ... will never know she will know what I am made of ...

I would never allow a man to come stinking of drink near me in the blankets (spitting). I told you long ago to go to court and each time you allow that old Dejo with his fat wife to talk you out of it. Are you a daughter of my father?

Oh what a tiresome tongue sister has ... You wait you, you just wait ...

Just a black drunken swine that is what he is. A swine is even better because it can look for rubbish to eat. Balogun does not know what people are he would not go a long way with me no he would not he does not know people. Eat sleep and lay a pile of dung, eat sleep and lay a pile of dung while men of his age group are work-ing: the woman who gave birth to that man ...!

Sister! Leave that poor woman to lie quiet in her grave!
I will but not that wine-bloated creature called Balogun.
Lijadu must not forget to send Mushin's money of the bride-price ...
That piece of pork? a customer asked.
Ten shillings.
Five.
Nine.
Six.
No 'gree.
Six and six.
No 'gree. Eight, las' price.
Seven.
No 'gree.
And the market roar and chatter and laughter and exclamations and smells put together seemed to be a live symphony quite independent of the people milling around.

Black shit! Ishola's sister carried on ...

Ishola was out of Oyo in the evening, going towards Oshogbo with her three children. Lijadu would follow the next day and join them in a small village thirty miles out so as to make pursuit fruitless. Lijadu joined her at noon the next day, looking pale and blue and shaken.

What is it with you Lijadu? Why are you so pale? Are you sick?
Silence.
Lijadu what is it?
He sat on the ground and said Mushin has passed away. He passed away about midnight. One of the neighbours found him lying cold in the passage. People say they heard him cry the last time: Ishola, my grandchildren!

Ishola could not move for a few moments. She seemed frozen cold cold cold.

At break of day each morning you will see the women of Oyo with their baskets on their heads. You can see them on the black tarmac going to the market, their bodies twisting at the hip the strong hip. You can see their feet feel their way on the dark tarmac as they ride the dawn, riding into daylight. The figures are slender as twilight. You can see Ishola, too, because she came back, came back to us. She told us that when she heard of the death of her father-in-law she thought, This is not good for my future life with Lijadu I will go back to that cripple.

LIONEL ABRAHAMS
THE MESSIAH

LIONEL ABRAHAMS (b. 1928 in Johannesburg, founder editor of *The Purple Renoster*). 'The Messiah' first appeared in *IZWI*, No. 17 in August 1974 and was incorporated into the eighteen-story sequence called *The Celibacy of Felix Greenspan*, first published by Bateleur Press in 1977 and subsequently in an American edition.

On Sunday mornings and Wednesday evenings there was Service, run by a member of the committee or a real priest, in the Big Play-room. Being Jewish did not stop Felix from attending. He learnt that only faith was needed to save one's soul – faith in Jesus, who was so good and had such powers, and who was a Jew on top of everything else. The parts about him suffering and being crucified – by Jews – made Felix less comfortable. He wished those parts could be left out. Then Service would just be interesting and enjoyable to go to.

But those parts wouldn't be left out. They came into the thing every day, in a way, even when it wasn't prayers at school or grace at table or anything that was supposed to do with God. He was 'Jewboy' and had to hear about Jews having long noses and being stingy and cheats, all because Jesus got crucified by those old Jews – even though it was the Romans who really did it.

The old carpenter boy, Moses, who had a wonderful workshop opposite the kitchens near the end of the drive where he would do anything from fixing a crutch or the wheel of a wheelchair to sharpening a pencil, old Moses who walked with a limp because one of his thick muscly legs was shorter than the other, who was so clever with his hands and so kind that everybody loved him and he seemed like someone out of the Bible even though he was black – he said one day, while Felix could hear him: 'No, I don't like Jews. They killed Jesus.' The boys were always saying that and Felix felt half cross and half ashamed. But when Moses said it, it was much worse: it seemed to be true, and Christians and Jews had to hate each other.

All the same, Felix went on going to Service. He learnt there about the lamb that had been lost being more precious to the shepherd than the ninety-nine that were never lost and somewhere he heard about converted Jews. He decided to be a converted Jew and to believe in Jesus and love him. He said prayers in bed every night and he knew that good Christians, apart from forgiving everyone who hurt them, had to try to save other souls by converting them too. So when he was home on holiday, one night he told his mother the parable about the one lost lamb and begged her to be converted also. But she wouldn't be. She seemed uncomfortable about what he was saying, but she only laughed a little and went on not even believing in God. All the same, Felix hoped that he would be able to convert her one day. He knew that his father did believe in God because he sometimes said Jewish prayers; he did not try to covert him.

Once Felix heard something wonderful. It was about the Messiah. The Jews believed that one day the Messiah would come to the world from heaven to save everyone. The Christians believed that the Messiah had already come and was Jesus. But they also believed that one day, any day, he would come again. When that happened, surely Christians and Jews would all believe the same thing and wouldn't need to hate each other any more.

The Messiah, when he came, must be Jewish, a Jewish Christian. So any Jewish boy, any day now, could be Him. Felix, loving Jesus and believing in him with all his heart – as the ministers always begged everyone to (Felix's favourite was the committee member, Mr Cooper, who told wonderful stories and made him feel it would be lovely to go to exciting places with him) – believing so much in Jesus and always managing not to do the things that the naughty ones among the children did, and caring so much about Moses and all the other Christians hating the Jews, began to think that it might, it could, it must be him. The Messiah. Although nobody knew it yet, and he wasn't ready to tell anyone – he would know when it would be the right time to let the secret out – he, Felix, was that special Jewish boy who was Jesus back in the world for the second time to make the different people love each other, and to cure all the cripples and blind people and do all sorts of miracles that would make everybody believe in God.

He loved it on Sundays and Wednesdays when the ministers told about the miracles Jesus had done and the stories he had told, or about people who had got converted in wonderful ways or been helped by God when they were in trouble or had been very brave about doing what they knew God wanted them to do or about going on having faith when something was making it very hard. He wished he had a chance to show his faith like those strong believers, and he longed for the time when he would be able to do miracles that would be better than any of the tricks that he had seen magicians do at concerts and parties. Waiting for the day when he would show everyone that he was the Messiah, he didn't mind so much any more what the other boys said about Jews, or when they said things like: 'Don't try to Jew me' when someone wanted to make a bargain that wasn't fair. They were only the chaps at the home, and they didn't know his secret yet. Anyway, one of the things Christians had to do was to forgive those who trespassed against them, so it proved that he had faith because he was always forgiving the other boys for all their insults.

Mr MacDavid was the Chairman of the committee and he came up to the home much more often than any of the other members. Sometimes he came to show special visitors around, and sometimes to inspect with Matron if anything had to be done to the building. Once or twice when some of the biggest boys had done something extra naughty, Mr MacDavid came and shouted at them in his big voice in a terribly angry way. He also came very often to be the minister at Sunday morning Service.

He was a big, oldish man with grey hair who spoke and sang in a strong Scotch accent. He always seemed to wear the same greyish-brown suit and, just like Moses, the old carpenter boy, he walked quickly but with a deep limp. He did not make his preaching as friendly and interesting as Mr Cooper, who came quite seldom and always looked as if everything he wore was brand new. But Felix could tell by the loudness of his voice when he preached ('Oh, yes, boys and girls, I can tell you that our Lord Jesus today ...') and sang the hymns and prayed that he had very strong faith.

Felix also sang the hymns and choruses ('Build on the Rock' was the one he liked best, because of the bang they had to make for 'earthquake *shock*'), as loudly as he could so Mr MacDavid knew that he was there at Service. Mr MacDavid also knew – because Felix had been at the home for years already – that he was Jewish: there were hardly ever any other Jewish children.

One Sunday morning Mr MacDavid preached the Bible story of Joseph and his brothers. He was at the part where the jealous elder brothers had put Joseph into the pit and were getting ready to kill him when the traders from Egypt came by. 'When the eldest brother, Reuben, saw the traders,' said Mr MacDavid, 'he said to the others, "Why should we kill Joseph, when we can sell him as a slave to these traders?" Well, Jews, you know, are always ready to sell anything, even their brother – so they agreed to do as Rrrueben said …'

Felix gave a little jump. The boy on the bench next to him nudged him and he saw two other boys turn to look at him with quick grins on their faces. He heard nothing more of the preaching or prayers and did not join in the singing of the last hymn.

On Wednesdays Service was after supper, so all the children had to go because there was nowhere else to be. It was always the same minister, Mr Harty, who was not a committee member but a real priest who wore a black shirt with a stiff white ring collar that none of the children could guess how he put on or took off. Mr Harty was telling them a long story like a serial, about the adventures of a man named Christian and his friend Faithful. Even after what had happened that Sunday morning, Felix didn't have to miss the rest of the story.

But on the next Sunday morning at Service time, instead of being in the Big Playroom with all the others, Felix was sitting outside on the lawn looking at *Pip, Squeak and Wilfred's Annual*, and hearing the hymns and the preaching without being able to make out the words. It was Mr Cooper today, but that didn't matter.

No one else was outside until Nurse Verster came past on her way to the dormitories. When she saw him she said, 'Hello, Felix. Why aren't you at Service?'

Felix tried to look up at her, but the sun shone into his eyes. 'Because I'm Jewish,' he said.

YVONNE BURGESS
IF YOU SWALLOW YOU'RE DEAD

YVONNE BURGESS (b. 1936 in the Eastern Cape). Her 'If You Swallow You're Dead'
is a condensation of the first novel she wrote and first appeared in Cape Town's
Contrast in August 1969. Her most recent novel, *A Larger Silence*, won the
Sanlam Literary Award for Fiction in 2001.

Seven days after Mr Labuschagne's visit the hearse, adorned with
four wreaths and followed by two cars, wound its way slowly past
the Mercedes Benz showroom.

At Berry's Corner, where the traffic is always heavy, it went
through against the red light, and on, past the neat grass verges of
the factories, past the General Dealer's, Gent's Tailors and Star of
the East Fruit, painted in dry, scratchy, childish strokes on boards
nailed to the communal dirty-brown verandas, past the shanties
huddled incongruously under the bright new Gold Dollar sign,
and on to the cemetery where the prickly pears and headstones are
a uniform sooty-grey from the smoke of the shunting trains, where
the khaki-coloured trees lean crookedly, their naked boles turned
like camels' backs to the wind, where a bedraggled brown donkey,
having wandered in through a hole in the fence, was snuffling at
the sour scrub for food.

There Alida Slabbert was, as the dominee put it, 'laid to rest'.

And afterwards when her husband Kobus, her children Chrissie,
Ivy and Susie, her brothers Chrisjan and Pieter, her sister-in-law
Hester and Marie and her lodger Luigi Sersoni had returned to the
house in Uitenhage Road, they sat solemnly, still in a state of shock,
around the kitchen table where Alida had so often sat peeling
potatoes on *Die Vaderland* and reading as she peeled those bits and
pieces of news she had missed the evening before.

The Slabberts had moved into the house in Uitenhage Road
shortly after Alida's father, Oom Chrisjan Koen, had died leaving
the farm near Graaff-Reinet to her and her two brothers. They had
bought her share between them and the money had come just at
the right time when the room in the boarding-house in Myrtle
Avenue had become oppressively small, when the children were

beginning to play in the street, and Alida and Kobus to bicker and snap.

On the very first evening Alida shivered and rubbed at her thick forearms because the hairs on them, she said, were 'standing straight up'. She looked around into all the shadowy corners and up at the mottled ceiling. She walked from room to room with the children holding hands in their excitement and apprehension following her, and Kobus wondering what it signified, this search, when houses were not so easy to come by and they had already put the deposit down.

From half-way up the stairs that led to the attic Alida called out urgently: 'I can feel it now.'

'Oh Alida ...' Kobus said, stroking his bald patch in exasperation.

'A ghost. Up there,' Chrissie whispered down to Ivy who passed it on to Susie.

The front part of the attic which had been converted into a bed-room with ceiling and floorboards was empty, but in the part that had been partitioned off Alida found tied securely to a strong beam a rope with its edges hacked off and frayed just above the place where the knot of a noose may have been.

She came down then, her bluish lips puckered into a thin line of satisfaction. In the kitchen the children crouched down in front of the stove.

'Is it up there?' Chrissie asked loudly, seeking not so much con-firmation as reassurance in the brash sound of his own voice.

Alida took a handful of rice out of the tin on the kitchen dresser, poked vigorously at the coals in the grate and sat down grinding a few of the grains between her false teeth. At last when she was ready she nodded.

'What is it?' Ivy quavered.

'A ghost, man,' Chrissie said.

'How do *you* know?'

Gently Susie touched her mother's knee. 'Did Mammie see it?'

'Shhhhh ...' Ivy said.

Alida loosened her top plate with her tongue to retrieve a grain of rice which had stuck underneath.

'A ghost!' Chrissie said, raising his arms menacingly. 'Up there! A big ghost with long yellow teeth and eyes like turnips – *booooooh!*'

The girls jumped.

'Ag no man,' Ivy said.

Unperturbed, her jaws moving sideways like those of a ruminating cow, Alida chewed.

'Is it a bad one?' Ivy, filled with ghost-lore, knew there were good ones and bad ones; that the good ones had a white light shining around them and the bad ones a red light like the glow from a fire.

'A bad one,' Alida said. 'I won't see it. Not this one. But I can feel it in the ringing of my ears. And the tickling in the soles of my feet.'

They waited for her to go on but she sat stolidly staring at the fire and chewing her rice, her rough hands kept warm under her unconfined spreading bosom.

'But *why* does Mammie feel it?' Ivy asked. 'Why are *all* the houses haunted?'

'I was born with the caul,' Alida said contentedly. 'I told you. And my mother, your late ouma, before me. *She* was the eldest daughter just like I was the eldest daughter. Just like *you* are the eldest daughter.'

Chrissie and Susie looked at Ivy with some envy.

'It's funny, but I also feel funny,' Ivy said.

'You weren't born with it,' Alida said regretfully.

'And what sort of a thing is a cau-au-l supposed to be?' Chrissie asked, irritated as he always was to discover something he did not know.

'It's a skin over your face that you are born with,' Alida said.

'Where is it then?' he scoffed.

'The doctor pulls it off,' Alida said. 'And when he does that a person's eyes are opened onto the other world. That person has got second sight for the rest of her life.' She leaned back yawning and tugging at the spiky black hairs that sprouted from the mole on the side of her nose. '*That's* why. *They* know when a person can see them and feel them. Ghosts. And premonitions too. I know when someone is going to die. Sometimes I *see* them, sometimes I just know. I look at them and I can feel it, I can *smell* it, like the flowers at the funeral ... a sick sweet smell just like the flowers at a funeral ...'

'Like Tannie Louisa,' Susie reminded her.

Alida sighed. 'Poor Tannie Louisa. Before your poor late Tannie Louisa was taken away ... I still remember as if it was yesterday ...' Alida closed her eyes and putting the last few grains of rice into her mouth wiped her slightly floury hands off on her apron.

'Yeeees ...' Chrissie encouraged.

'Tell us,' Ivy begged.

'But haven't I told you already?' Alida asked, knowing that she had, several times.

'No,' the children cried, 'no, but we've forgotten.'

'Well then. It was still on the farm. I was sick, lying in bed. It was a Sunday morning. I was sick with …'

'Mumps!' they prompted. 'Mumps!'

'Was it mumps? I don't know any more … but I must have been feverish it was so hot in that feather-bed although it was winter and your late Tannie Louisa came in and said to me: "Sister," she said, "can I borrow your hymn-book, sister?" She always called me sister because I was older than her, and she was dressed for church. I remember that dress as if it was yesterday. Your late ouma made it for me but she made the sleeves too tight so your Tannie Louisa got it. And later when your ouma came in I said to her: "Mammie," I said, "why is Louisa still here then? She will be late for church." And your ouma looked at me and her face went as white as this apron and she said: "But Louisa went to church hours ago," she said. "What are you talking about?" But she knew. And it was only three weeks after that. And your Tannie Louisa had three flowers on her hat that Sunday morning.'

The children were silent for a while, savouring the unimpeachable precision of the premonition. Then they began to coax. 'Tell us about the dog, the big black dog!'

'The ball of fire!'

'No, the stones that fell …'

'The thing that said "shh, shh, shh" behind you and Tannie Louisa like chasing chickens!'

Alida tugged absent-mindedly at the hairs on her mole, her blue eyes vague, fixed upon that time eons ago when she was a child …

'The piccanins around the fire,' the children pleaded.

Alida got up. 'Go wash your feet,' she said. 'It's school tomorrow.'

When Mieta came into the kitchen, as she did at eight every morning, having wiped her fawn felt slippers on the folded sack at the back door and hung her shopping bag made of coloured patches of leather on the hook behind the door, she went at once to the sink where Alida had stacked the breakfast dishes in a basin because the 'old Miesies' had always used a basin and Mieta had, like Alida, a respect for tradition.

While Mieta washed the dishes Alida made the beds, folded the nightclothes and emptied the chamber pots just as her mother had done, and if she had thought to question it she would have discovered as the reason that white man's pride – so deeply instilled in her – which precluded the leaving of any tasks as intimate as these to a servant.

By the time Mieta was ready to go into the house to sweep and dust, Alida had begun to tidy her lodger's room.

This matter of taking in a lodger had occasioned one of the few really bitter quarrels in the Slabberts' married life, and it was, moreover, one of the very few Kobus had won.

They were still struggling to furnish the house when he suggested that they offer a room to Luigi Sersoni who worked at the factory with him and was looking for a place to stay.

Alida had set her thin lips tightly and refused. He was a bachelor, she had said, and worse, a middle-aged bachelor. Bachelors were the same the world over, especially middle-aged bachelors. She had two young daughters and her heaven-invested duty lay in protecting them from the crudities of life and, she gave Kobus to understand, there was nothing on earth more crude, if only potentially, than a middle-aged bachelor. He would have women there at night and he would drink.

Nevertheless it was true that the extra money would come in handy. School-books, blazers and shirts cost the earth; and then, as Kobus had argued, what difference would there be in making meals for one more as long as the payments on the house remained the same?

Sersoni therefore came and he was given the best room in the house, the front room with its white fireplace and large window looking out across the street at the wood-and-iron fence of the Showgrounds, the room which would have been the living room, kept locked with its curtains drawn to be used only for special visitors like the dominee and the members of the Mothers' Union who came once a year with their lists to inquire what Alida would be willing to contribute to the bazaar in the way of jellies and puddings.

To Alida's consternation Sersoni appeared to be a model lodger. He took all his meals in his room and hardly ever ventured out except to go to work and sometimes to issue a formal invitation to Kobus to come in and play draughts with him.

He did not have women as far as Alida could tell, and she had risen in the middle of the night for several weeks to listen at his door for suspicious sounds. He did not drink either; or if he did she had yet to discover evidence of it.

A less determined woman would have given up but as far as Alida was concerned there were simply too many factors pointing towards secret vice: Sersoni was a middle-aged bachelor – that anomaly on God's earth worse only than a middle-aged spinster and twice as unnatural – he was a foreigner and a Catholic and the foreigner who was a Catholic as well could not exist, in her opinion, without being guilty of some profligacy or other. She had even considered the possibility of indecent pictures and had rifled through every book in his room without finding anything but holy pictures; Papish pictures, that is, of doll-like Virgins and chubby Infants but these, even if the Infants were rather too obviously naked, could hardly be called indecent.

Convinced as she was that she would one day unearth proof of Sersoni's secret vice, Alida not only made his bed and folded his pyjamas (he was not in the least bit nervous about going to the bathroom of that haunted house at night and so would not have a chamber pot) but swept and dusted there as well, for worse than that he should have some secret vice would be Mieta's discovery of it. Alida never forgot that although a bachelor, a Catholic and a foreigner, Sersoni was a white man still and that her duty therefore lay in hiding whatever weakness he might have from the eyes of a native servant.

Never knowing what she might find, Alida experienced a little flutter of excitement whenever she went into Sersoni's room and it was while she stood there one morning with her slightly startled curious blue eyes surveying it, the strange man's room, that she heard the click of the bottom gate. She rushed to the window and saw the visitor, a man and certainly not the dominee, just before he opened the second gate at the top of the steps and disappeared behind the wall of the stoep.

Alida whipped her apron off and ran to her room to dust her face with the musty powder which she kept in a plastic bowl. Quickly she twisted a turban around her head, but as she daubed at her thin blue lips with the drying tube of Pond's Natural, her old affliction, *hartkloppings* – the shivering and shaking instead of a regular beating of her heart – brought on no doubt by the presence of a strange man on her stoep, caught at her breath and forced her to go to the triangular wall-cabinet where she kept among other remedies, the *groenamare* for her cramps, the *versterkdruppels* for her nerves and the *rooi laventel* for her heart.

By the time she opened the front door just a crack and holding on to it firmly because one never knew with strange men, Alida's heart had quietened down sufficiently for her to say impassively as though strange men called every day: 'Good morning?'

The man raised his hat to reveal a scalp shaved clean to the tuft of greying hair right on top.

'Listen Mrs,' he said, 'I'm looking for a Mrs Slabbert.'

'Yes,' Alida admitted cautiously. 'That's me.'

'Oh,' he said. 'Well look. I come from Graaff-Reinet. Labuschagne's the name.'

'Graaff-Reinet!' Alida's heart began to thump.

'No,' Mr Labuschagne said. 'It's nothing. I'm just bringing greetings from Chrisjan and Pieter.'

'Chrisjan and Pieter.'

'And a chicken. A rooster. From Chrisjan and Pieter.' He gestured towards the old black Dodge parked in front of the house. 'I was coming to the Bay.'

Her fears allayed with Mr Labuschagne's credentials thus satisfactorily established, Alida invited him in.

'But don't look at the house,' she said.

'I'm early,' Mr Labuschagne apologised, and he followed her in, looking, out of politeness, neither left nor right. In the kitchen Alida asked him to sit down and distantly instructed Mieta to pour coffee.

'Have sugar,' she said. 'You come from Chrisjan and Pieter?'

'Yes.' Mr Labuschagne, sitting stiffly in his black town suit and hard collar, took small polite sips, carefully keeping his elbows off the table.

'From Chrisjan and Pieter.'

'And how are they all then?'

'I must say all right,' Mr Labuschagne said.

'You can tell Chrisjan and Pieter that we are also all right.'

There was an awkward silence, broken only by the sound of Mr Labuschagne sipping his coffee through politely pursed lips.

'And you brought a chicken, you say?'

'In the car outside. Yes.'

'Well,' Alida said, pushing her cup aside, 'you can tell Chrisjan and Pieter and Hester and Marie that we are also all still well.'

Mr Labuschagne tilted his cup to catch the last grains of partially melted sugar and wiped his mouth on the back of his hand. 'Yes,' he said. 'Yes, yes, I will surely tell them that.'

After he had put the small crate containing the rooster next to the shed in the backyard Alida took him down the narrow lane at the side of the house to the front gate where he gripped her hand hard, scratched the back of his head, put his hat on firmly and said: 'Thank you for the coffee. It was a pleasure to meet you and I will tell Chrisjan and Pieter that you are all still well.'

'And thank them for the chicken,' Alida said.

'Not at all,' Mr Labuschagne answered for them.

That afternoon Alida went to lie down as she usually did, tucking her feet in under the old moth-eaten kaross which had come down to her from her grandmother. It was then that she heard, quite distinctively, five loud knocks on the floor next to the bed.

She knew at once what they portended. Poor Mrs Labuschagne, she expressed silently and in advance her sympathy for the soon-to-be-bereaved. Poor man. Poor widow and how many orphans? And how long? Five months, five weeks, five days, even, heaven forbid! five hours – on the road back, perhaps, to Graaff-Reinet?

'We've got a chicken,' Alida told the girls when they came in. 'From your uncles Chrisjan and Pieter. I want you to put some bread out for it and some water.'

'Alive?' Susie asked. 'A live chicken?'

'Dead chickens don't eat bread.' Alida swung her legs down and felt for her slippers under the bed. 'I better come,' she said. 'You'll only take the fresh bread.'

The girls ran out to stare at the little rooster. He stared back at them pertly through the netting which covered the top of the crate.

'Oh the lovely thing,' Ivy said. 'Oh, what a lovely thing.'

'Look,' Susie cried rapturously. 'The tail so dark blue like purple.'

'*Koo-koo-koo*,' Alida crooned as she crumbled a crust of stale bread over the rooster. '*Kooo-koooo-koooo* … Get some water.'

'Oh our lovely chicken,' Susie said, clapping her hands with joy.

Ivy lifted a corner of the netting wire and put a tin of water into the box. The rooster looked at it suspiciously.

'It's clean,' she assured him. 'It had some polish in but I washed it clean.'

'Why don't you drink then, little chicken?' Susie asked plaintively.

The rooster scratched at the breadcrumbs and the girls laughed in delight at the way his bright comb flopped from side to side.

'What's his name?' Ivy cried. 'What will we call him?'

'*Cooked-chicken-and-gravy!*' Chrissie shouted close behind them.

'No man,' they chorused indignantly. 'You'll frighten our chicken.'

'*Your* chicken?' Chrissie poked his finger through the netting. '*Your* chicken? Where do you come from then?'

'Give us a name for him,' the girls begged.

'I told you. Cooked-chicken-and-gravy.'

'We don't want to call him *that*.'

'*You* don't want to call him ...' Chrissie laughed. '*You* don't want to ... oh help me, before I die. I'm just telling you. He will be Cooked-chicken-and-gravy, never mind what *you* want to call him.'

Ivy's eyes turned dark with anguish. 'It isn't true,' she said. 'Mammie, say it isn't true.'

'True?' Chrissie screeched. 'It's true as true as true! And you want to know how?'

'That's enough now,' Alida said. 'You're making my head sore.'

Chrissie skipped away beyond her reach. 'Mieta will take him *here* and she'll throw him down *there* and she'll take the axe and *bam!*'

'Chrisjan!' Alida warned.

'And the stupid body doesn't even know it's dead and it ...'

Alida lunged suddenly and Chrissie fell over backwards in trying to evade her, his small eyes wide with surprise.

Within a moment, her anger forgotten, and despite the girls' wailing, Alida began to laugh, holding her hand up to her mouth although she had got her false teeth six months before.

'Do you still remember your first chicken?' Alida asked Mieta as they plucked, squatting in the backyard with the fowl between them on a sack.

'Ag, Miesies,' Mieta said, 'I've cleaned so many already.'

'My first chicken,' Alida shook her head. 'Really you won't believe it.' She worked quickly and the beautiful speckled feathers came out in handfuls, to be dropped carelessly onto the sack. 'The old Miesies was away, I can't remember where but they were all away, for a funeral, I think, and only coming back on the Sunday and I wanted to surprise them – how old was I then, eight or ten, I don't know any more – but it was my first chicken. We had an old brown girl called Sannie and she was sick, she was always sick when the old Miesies was away, you know how these people are, but the chicken was already killed for the Sunday and Chrisjan, Baas Chrisjan and me, we were going to pluck it. We were in the kitchen I remember because it was late and dark outside so we lit the lantern and did it in the kitchen just like this on a sack. We didn't even know about the hot water, we just plucked and the skin was coming off with the feathers, but the funniest part, when the feathers were all off Baas Chrisjan took a blade to cut it open with, a blade! No, really! I don't know why. He was playing doctor again, I think, he was always playing doctor, so he cut a little V here and took the gut, not all together, just one end and he pulled and the whole lot came out, like crinkle paper at Christmas, spraying stinking water all over me, my dress, my hair, everything ...' Alida laughed briefly, nostalgically.

'Oh Lord, Miesies,' Mieta giggled.

'On the farm ...' Alida tugged fretfully at the feathers.

'On the farm ...' Mieta echoed. 'We had our own old jersey cow ...'

'Not only that,' Alida sighed. 'Not only that. But what if a person dies here in the Bay? You must lie in that graveyard there next to the shunting trains, in the middle of rows and rows of people that you don't even know ...'

'Ag, Miesies mustn't talk like that,' Mieta said.

'No, old soul, but really, they must take me back! They must take me back where I can lie with my own flesh and blood. These others they can lie where they like but they must take me back so that I can lie with my own people on the koppie behind the windbreak. I don't want the wind to howl over my grave ...'

The fowl lay between them, its pocked blue-white skin flecked with blood and its legs stretched out stiff and cold. On the sack the dark-blue tail feathers had already lost their lustre.

Alida heaved herself up. 'I'm not saying anything,' she said. 'But Baas Chrisjan must just understand that I want to lie behind the windbreak ...'

Alida stroked the old kaross and allowed the all-but-forgotten sights and sounds and smells to overwhelm her: the coffee in the afternoons, the Mazawattee tin filled with the slightly sour *soet-koekies*, the veranda sagging under the weight of the vine; the path down to the quince hedges which wound past the dam where the ground was always muddy and trampled and smelt of manure, the orchard, the fruit, and before the fruit, the flowers; the bedroom she had shared with Louisa, smelling of polish and methylated spirits, and always dim and cool, right through the hottest summer day; the big bed and cupboard which even at noon were little more than darker masses so that at night, when the lamps were lit, one looked at everything with interest, seeing them properly for the first time that day.

Alida remembered lovingly, longingly, even the inconveniences: the nervous trips to the outhouse at night with a candle and matches, the struggle to keep the candle burning in the draught and the stomach-squirming fear that one would be left sitting there, helpless and alone in the dark.

And the games, oh, the games they had played, she and Chrisjan, Pieter and Louisa, when the grapes were ripe and Chrisjan was the doctor and he squashed them, collecting the purple rivulets of 'medicine' which he squirted into their mouths so that it trickled and tickled down into their throats. And they weren't allowed to swallow. Not one. For if they swallowed they were 'dead' …

Alida pulled at the hairs of her mole until her eyelids turned red and her eyes filled with tears.

Was the vine still there? she wondered. Were the grapes ripe? But no, it was the wrong time of the year for grapes. It was the wrong time of the year for everything …

Aching all over with a sense of irreparable loss, Alida brought out the gramophone and the records she had bought long before she met Kobus. Her favourite, badly scratched and buckled as it was, wobbled round and round before the balladeer began, dolefully drawing out the vowels: 'Oooooo ek *Diiiink* weer va*naaaaaand* aan my *blouuu* oë …'

Alida sang with him in a high, reedy voice; and as she sang she thought not of Kobus but of Chrisjan, Pieter and Louisa and of the boys she had known as a young girl: of Joop Vermeulen, Marius van der Linde, and Attie Vermaak who had a motor-bike and looked like a film star.

'Didn't I say so?' Chrissie smirked as he ate his chicken. 'Isn't that your name, old Cooked-chicken-and-gravy?'

Ivy and Susie ate only their vegetables.

'What is it?' Kobus asked mildly. 'Are you sick?'

'They were stupid about this chicken,' Alida said. 'What do you think? Do you think a rooster can lay eggs?'

'It was so nice and *live*,' Susie said.

'And now it's *nothing!*' Ivy added, and at that both of them burst into tears.

'What do you mean nothing?' Chrissie asked. 'It's damn nice chicken and gravy! *Nothing!*' he snorted.

'You can *shut up!*' Ivy screamed.

'Well now dammit!' Alida said, losing her temper. 'Mustn't I give them something to cry about now? If I was so stupid about a chicken your oupa would have knocked me off my chair! It's too easy for you. That's the trouble. I didn't have it so easy.' She looked reproachfully at Kobus. 'I said their oupa would have knocked me off my chair!'

'Your chair?' Kobus stroked his bald patch.

'You're the *father* aren't you?' Alida shouted. 'You're supposed to be the *head!*'

But before Kobus could do anything to prove that he was the head, Alida clapped her hand to her heart, leaned back heavily, turned quite blue, and would have fallen if he had not caught hold of her in time.

'Louie!' he called in panic. 'Chrissie! Get your Uncle Louie!'

Sersoni hurried in, still chewing, and between them they half-carried, half-supported Alida to her bed.

There they stood around her, astounded by the suddenness of the collapse, Sersoni so embarrassed in the presence of the whole family at such a distressing moment that he could only beam in an effort to hide his discomfiture and pat the kaross they had put over Alida, as much to keep his hands busy as to soothe her.

'A doctor,' Kobus suggested helplessly. 'Musn't we get a doctor now?'

'The *laventel* ...' Alida begged weakly.

Weeping with fear, the rooster forgotten, Ivy knocked over the bottles labelled *Duiwelsdrek* and *Wonderlijksens* (which were, fortunately, empty, Alida having been unable to procure those remedies in Port Elizabeth) before she found the *rooi laventel*.

'Alida,' Kobus persisted half-heartedly. 'What about a doctor?'

But she, her face as stoically expressionless in pain as it was in pleasure, had already recovered sufficiently to ask: 'Now what can a doctor do?'

'Is there still some chicken left for my lunch?' Chrissie asked on Monday morning.

Alida gave him a pile of old newspapers to make the fire in the copper geyser for the weekly wash and said: 'No. Thank heaven. That chicken made enough trouble. That chicken had a hex on it.'

'A hex!' Chrissie whooped. 'Then the hex went into my stomach! I've got a hex in my stomach!'

'Don't joke about hexes,' Alida warned him sternly. 'A hex is nothing to joke about. Lettie Potgieter joked about hexes and look what happened to her.'

'What happened to her again?' Ivy asked.

'Her bladder swelled up like a balloon,' Alida said.

'Oh yeeeeees,' Chrissie said. 'You mustn't say that. Say ...'

'She wanted to be excused,' Ivy said.

'That's what *we* must say,' Susie said.

'Yes,' Alida said. 'That's nicer. It's nicer to say it like that ...'

To save water (although in the city there was no need) Alida always bathed on Monday mornings, afterwards putting the washing in to soak ready for Mieta when she came in.

By the time she had stripped the beds and gathered up the soiled clothing the old geyser was rumbling and leaking boiling water. Alida drew her bath and lowered herself carefully into the scalding water. She scrubbed herself hard all over and lay back, only to find that she could not move, could not get up again, could hardly hold her head up, for the pain in her chest.

'Mieta,' she whimpered. 'Kobus.'

She struggled to keep her head above water. Her children were young. She had told no one but Mieta where she wanted to be buried, and she had yet to discover Seroni's secret vice.

'The *laventel*,' she groaned; but even as she called for it Alida lost faith in the efficacy of the brew. Pneumonia and tuberculosis could be cured if the warm skin of a newly-slaughtered cat were applied to the chest of the sufferer; *uittrekpleisters* could draw out boils and even a cancer if it were not too deeply rooted; there was nothing like *rooi laventel* for *hartkloppings*. But what must be, must be. Five days had passed since she had heard the knocks on the floor, and there had been no bad news of Mr Labuschagne.

The water lapped against her jaw, washed over her blue lips and finally covered the mole with its stiff black hairs.

Alida let the water trickle and tickle down into her throat. The big black grapes, she saw through the steam and the grey-green water, were ripe. It was the right time of the year after all. Chris-jan, Pieter and Louisa were watching her. If she swallowed she was dead.

AHMED ESSOP
GERTY'S BROTHER

AHMED ESSOP (b. 1931 and lives in Lenasia). 'Gerty's Brother' first appeared in *The Purple Renoster*, No. 9 of Spring 1969, and was included in his first collection, *The Hajji and Other Stories* in 1978, which won him the Olive Schreiner Prize. He has since published a further collection called *Noorjehan*.

I first saw Gerty in a shop in Vrededorp. Vrededorp, as everyone knows, is cleft in two by Delarey Street: on the one side it is colonised by us non-whites and on the other side by whites. The whites come over to our side when they want to do their shopping, and return with a spurious bargain or two. I saw her in a shop in the garishly decorated Indian shopping lane called Fourteenth Street. I had gone there with my friend Hussein who wanted to see a shopkeeper friend of his. I think the shop was called Dior Fashions, but of that I am not quite sure because shop follows shop there and this shop didn't strike me as being in any way fashionable. Anyway, that is where I saw her. My friend spoke to the shopkeeper – a fat dark man with a darker moustache – and I just looked around and smoked a cigarette as I didn't see anything interesting.

I sat down on a chair and smoked another cigarette and then I noticed two figures darken the doorway and enter the shop, a girl and a boy. The shopkeeper spoke to the girl and then suddenly laughed. She laughed too, I think. I wouldn't have taken any further notice of the group as I was seated at the back of the shop. But then the shopkeeper switched to Gujarati and spoke to my friend. I heard him say that she was easy and would not give much trouble in removing her undergarments to anyone, but one had to be careful as there was the usual risk involved. Hussein replied that he was keen and that he wouldn't like to waste much time about the matter. I think the shopkeeper introduced him to her at this stage, but I am not quite sure for he went on speaking in Gujarati. He said that he was going to organise a dance at his place on the following Saturday evening, he was in the mood for jollification, and that he was going to invite Gerty and if Hussein was interested he could take her away from his place. All this he said in Gujarati, rather coarsely I thought. I wasn't very interested and thought of smoking another cigarette and going out to buy the afternoon newspaper. Girls were girls and one was as good as another, and if Hussein wanted to sleep with her he could have her and it would make no difference to me.

Later, when Hussein and I had climbed into his Volkswagen and were on our way to Fordsburg, he informed me that to soften her before the party on Saturday he had bought the girl a frock. He asked me how I liked her and I said she was all right as far as I was concerned, though, of course, I had not been near enough to see her properly and size her up. But I said she was all right and he felt very satisfied at having bumped into a white girl. He told me that she lived in Vrededorp, 'on the other side', and that she seemed to be very easy. He said that when he had done with her he would throw her over to me and I could have her as well. I answered with a vague 'Let the time come'. He then said something about 'pillar to post', and laughed as the car tore its way through the traffic into Fordsburg.

Saturday night I was at my landlady's, stripped to the waist because of the heat, reading an old issue of *The New Statesman*. There was a knock on the door and somebody asked for me and entered. It was Hussein all dressed up and titivated with bow tie and cuff-links and shoes that were out of place in my disorderly room.

'Where to, my dandy friend?' I asked admiringly.

'To the dance party. I thought you would be ready. You promised to come with me.'

I said I had forgotten, but that I would be ready in a minute. I dressed quickly, but didn't care to put on a white shirt or a tie. I wasn't very particular about what I wore, and I think it pleased my friend because my appearance was something of a foil to his, and set off to advantage his carefully put-together looks.

We set off in his Volkswagen for Vrededorp and in a few minutes the car braked sharply in Eleventh Street in front of the house of Hussein's shopkeeper friend. There were other cars near the house, but we managed to squeeze our car between two.

We were quite early and there were not many people present. Hussein's friend was happy to see us and he introduced us to those who were there. There were some lovely-looking girls in shimmering coral and amber and amethyst-coloured saris and others in more sober evening dresses and I looked forward to a swinging evening.

Then Hussein wanted to see the shopkeeper privately, and I think they went out to the front veranda of the house. When they returned I saw that Hussein was not too pleased about something or other, but as it was not my business I didn't bother to ask. Other girls arrived, all gaily dressed and very chic and charming and I was beginning to feel at ease. The girls offered me tea and cake and other tasty things to eat and I didn't refuse as my boarding-house wasn't quite a liberal establishment. All this time my friend Hussein was walking in and out of the room, and was on the look-out whenever someone knocked on the door and entered the house. The party got going and we danced, ate the refreshments provided and talked some euphonious nonsense. I was just getting interested in a girl, when my friend interrupted me and said that he wanted to see me urgently. I followed him and we went to the veranda. Some-one had switched off the lights and I saw two figures standing there, a girl and a small boy. He introduced her to me as Gerty and he asked me if I remembered her. I thought a bit and then told him. He said that I had a good memory or something of the sort. He then took me aside and asked me if I could drive the two of them to the Johannesburg Lake immediately and leave them in the park for a while, and if I could keep her brother company while he saw to Gerty's needs. As it was a risky business he didn't want the others in the party to know. He would like to get done with it before joining the party.

I said I didn't mind and the four of us got into the car. I drove to the Lake. It was a lovely night in December and we breathed in the luminous wind of the city streets as the car sped along. Hussein and Gerty sat in the back seat. They didn't say much to each other, but I guessed that they were holding hands and fondling. Gerty's brother sat beside me. He must have been seven or eight, but I didn't take much notice of him. He was eating some cakes and chocolates that Hussein had taken from the house.

I dropped the pair in a park near the Lake. Hussein asked me to return again in about an hour's time. The park was a darkness of trees and lawns and flowers, and it occurred to me that it made no difference if one slept with a white or a black girl there.

Gerty told her brother that he mustn't worry and that she was all right and that he should go with me for a while.

Before I drove off Gerty's brother asked me what they were going to do and I said they must be a bit tired and wanted to rest, but that did not sound convincing. Then I said that they had something to discuss in private and the best place was in the park. He agreed with me and I started the car.

I didn't feel like driving aimlessly about for an hour so I drove towards the lake. I asked the boy what his name was and he said Riekie.

I parked the car under some pine trees near a brightly-lit restaurant. There were people dining on the terrace amid blaring music, others were strolling on the lawns or resting on the benches. I asked Riekie if he would like an ice cream and took him to the restaurant and bought him one. We went down to the water's edge. The lake is small with an islet in the middle; a fountain spouted water into shifting rays of variegated light. Riekie was fascinated by it all and asked me several questions.

I asked him if he had ever sat in a boat. He said he hadn't. I took him to the boat-house and hired one. The white attendant looked at me for a moment and then at Riekie. I knew what he was thinking about but I said nothing. He went towards the landing stage and pointed to a boat. I told Riekie to jump in, but he hesitated. So I lifted him and put him into the boat. He was light in weight and I felt the ribs under his arms. A sensation of tenderness for the boy went through me. You must understand that this was the first time I had ever picked up a white child.

I rowed out towards the middle of the lake, and went around the fountain of kaleidoscopic lights. Riekie was gripped by wonder. He trailed his hands in the cool water smelling of rotted weeds, and tried to grab the overhanging branches of the willows along the banks.

It was time to pick up Hussein and Gerty. Riekie looked disappointed, but I said I would bring him there again. At this he seemed satisfied and I rowed towards the landing stage.

Hussein and Gerty were waiting for us. They got into the car and we returned to the party in Eleventh Street.

The party was now in full swing. There were many girls and I didn't waste much time. My friend stuck to Gerty, and if he was not dancing with her he was talking to her. And by the time the party ended at midnight Riekie had fallen asleep on a sofa and had to be doused with water to wake him.

We dropped Gerty and her brother at a street corner on our way to Fordsburg. Hussein had rooms of his own in Park Road, situated in a small yard at the end of a passage. A tall iron gate barred the entrance to the passage. There were only three rooms in the yard. Hussein occupied two and the other was occupied by a decrepit pensioner who lived in his room like some caged animal, except that no one ever came to see him.

At first Hussein was afraid to tell Gerty where he lived. There was the usual risk involved. But I think eventually he came to the conclusion that in life certain risks had to be taken if one was to live at all. And so Gerty and her brother came to his rooms and she took on the role of mistress and domestic servant and Riekie became the pageboy.

Gerty and Riekie were very fond of each other. The harsh realities of life – they were orphans and lived in poverty with an alcoholic elder brother – had entwined them. Hussein didn't mind Riekie's presence. In fact the boy attached himself to him. My friend was generous, and besides providing Gerty with frocks for summer, he bought the boy clothing and several pairs of shoes. Riekie was obedient and always ready to run to the shops for Hussein, to polish his shoes or wash the car. In time his cheeks began to take on colour and he began to look quite handsome. I noticed that he wasn't interested in boys of his own age; his attachment to his sister seemed to satisfy him.

Riekie would often come to my landlady's in the company of Hussein, or my friend would leave him there when he had some business with Gerty. If I was in the mood to go to the movies I would take him with me.

And then things took a different turn. Hussein came to understand that the police had an eye on him, that somehow they had come to know of Gerty and were waiting for an opportunity to arrest him in incriminating circumstances. Someone had seen a car parked for several nights near his rooms and noticed the movements of suspicious-looking persons. And he was convinced the police were after him when one night, returning home late, he saw a man examining the lock of the gate. As there was no point in carrying on with Gerty – he was not in the mood for a spell in prison – he told her that she should keep away from him for some time, and that he would see her again as soon as things were clear. But I think both of them realised that there wasn't much chance of that.

There wasn't much that one could tell Riekie about the end of the affair. My friend left it to Gerty, and went to Durban to attend to his late father's affairs.

One Sunday morning I was on my way to post some letters and when I turned the corner in Park Road there was Riekie, standing beside the iron gate that led to my friend's rooms. He was clutching two bars with his hands, and shouting for Hussein. I stood and watched as he shouted. His voice was bewildered.

The ugly animal living in the yard lurched out of his room and croaked: 'Goh way boy, goh way white boy. No Hussein here. Goh way.'

Riekie shook the barred gate and called for Hussein over and over again, and his voice was smothered by the croaks of the old man.

I stood at the corner of the street, in my hand the two letters I intended to post, and I felt again the child's body as I lifted him and put him onto the boat many nights ago, a child's body in my arms embraced by the beauty of the night on the lake, and I returned to my landlady's with the hackles of revolt rising within me.

NADINE GORDIMER
YOU NAME IT

NADINE GORDIMER (b. 1923 in Springs, resident in Johannesburg). 'You Name It' first appeared in *The London Magazine* in the June-July number of 1974 and was included in her subsequent collection, *A Soldier's Embrace* of 1980. In 1991 she was awarded the Nobel Prize for Literature.

She has never questioned who her father was. Why should she? Why should I tell her?

And yet there are times – times when we are getting on each other's nerves as only women and their daughters can – I have such a flash of irritable impulse: You are not ... I had –

I think I am stopped only by not knowing how to put it most sensationally. How to make her stand in her tracks as she's walking out the door with her boy for a 'drive' (= to make love in the car, that old synonym). To see her face, when she's been keeping it turned away from me half-listening while I talk to her, suddenly wrenched round. Or when I feel it's time to leave the room because I've been monopolising the conversation among her friends and they are boring, anyway. How to break in: with a name, a statement.

I took a piece of cane waste from the flotsam and wrote on the wet sand:

Arno   Arno Arkanius.

The cane was hollow, blackened by fire, and the sharp broken end was a bold quill; it incised letters cleanly.

She couldn't read. There were hundreds of tiny flies feeding on the rotting seaweed among the cane and she sat turning her hands from the wrist in their swarm. She enjoyed the weightless feel of the insects or admired their gratifying response to her presence, I don't know which, she was still too young to speak. While the other children were at kindergarten we walked every morning on that beach which could not be called deserted because there never had been anyone there to be counted absent, except the island women who came to dig for bait. Their black legs in the water and their hunched backsides in old sacks had the profile of wading birds. They did not look up and I never learnt so much as a greeting in their language. We made the staggering progress of a woman with a small child who cannot speak, has no sense of time, and to whom the dirt rim of the sea's bathtub is something to grasp while the blown-glass swells of the Indian Ocean, the porpoises jack-knifing in and out of the water, the spice off the spray and the cliffs and hollows of Strelitzia palms in flower are outside awareness. Yes – it was a kind of paradise, I suppose, the kind open to people who drill for oil or man air bases or negotiate the world's purchase of sugar or coconut oil. I was born on one and married onto another and met the man who made her with me when transferred to this one. Our names were no guide to our place of habitation. They were the names of different origins all over Europe, cross-pollinated in the sports and games and parties in colonies and islands to which none were native. I don't know exactly what he was; Swedes sometimes have Latin names, but he came from a cotton pasha family that had had to leave Egypt, went to school in Lausanne, and was in the trade section of the consulate of one of the European countries who were losing their colonies but still setting the price for what they bought from them. He stayed two years before he was posted somewhere else – it was the usual tour of duty.

When the baby was born it looked, the first time, exactly like him but it was all right: never again. When I saw it I was filled with love – not for the infant but for him. It was six months since he had made love to me in the stripped bed with suitcase standing by ready for the airport. Once again I yearned wildly. The emotion brought milk to my breasts. A few warm drops welled from the nipples, like tears. The nurses were pleased. My husband, delighted to have a girl child after two boys, tender and jocular in his happiness: *Now I'm prepared to let her off any more. Duty nobly done, dynasty assured. Unfortunately my daughter's as ugly as her brothers but give her time, we'll marry her yet.*

It was true that she became like her brothers as babies; a baby like all other babies, drooling saliva down the back of my dress when I held her the way she yelled to be held with her face over my shoulder, going slowly red in the face with silent concentration when she sat relieving herself, clutching my skirt when she wanted to pull herself up from the floor, holding her breath to the point of suffocation, in temper; looking so beautiful in her nightly drunken stupor with her bottle slack in her hand that my husband would take guests into the bedroom to gaze at her.

Her father never saw her. We wrote to each other all through the months before she was born; he had tried to persuade an island doctor whom he knew to give me an abortion, but there was his position at the consulate to consider, and my husband's position in the company. We were afraid the story would leak out. Whereas there was nothing exceptionable about my having a third child. He dared not keep a photograph of her in case his wife came upon it. By the time the child was nearly a year old he was on home leave – apparently Europe was selected as home – and we wrote more seldom but I could take advantage of Christmas to send a card showing a colour photograph of the family with the baby smiling in the middle. He wrote that she seemed to have a very large mouth? – was that just the photograph? His wife had remarked on it, too. I remember that I walked around the house carrying the letter and stared – nothing but sea, out there, nothing to be got from it but the sound of its endlessly long yawn and the tough glitter of its midday skin, and I went into the bedroom and lay down on the floor in the darkened room with my legs open, spread-eagled on my own cross, waiting for him. I cried to relieve myself, rolled onto my face and let the saliva run out of my open mouth upon the dust and lint of the carpet, like the baby. After a long time I began to hear the sea again, and saw, under the bed in which I slept with my husband, a coin and his lost espadrilles with the backs flattened to the soles by the way he always pushed his feet into them. When the island girl who helped with the children brought them up from the beach I met the baby with resentment for not being prettier, but she did not notice; like everything and everyone around me, she was living a life where this did not matter; and there was no other. There was no other, for me.

I had boasted to him of men who pursued me, including an ambassador, very distinguished and old enough to be my father. But now I wrote that I wanted a tidal wave to engulf the whole stupid life of the island; I did not tell him that I was flirting, and getting drunk at parties, and quarrelling with my husband because he said I neglected the children; to tell the truth these things didn't seem to me to be real – they were what I did to pass the time. Sometimes I wrote and said I was going to get divorced and take the baby and live alone. He replied that he was terrified 'something would happen to me'. We wrote as if these two sets of circumstances – his fearing for me, and my deciding to get divorced – had come about independently of each other, and of us. He instructed me not to write again until he could send a suitable new address – the two years were up once more, he was being reposted once more, and we didn't want my letters lying round the consulate for prying hands to forward. At this time my husband had taken it upon himself to send for his mother to supervise the children and the atmosphere in the house was one of blinding, deafening, obsessive antagonism: the tidal wave that I had wished on myself – I did not even realise that a month had passed without any new address coming. Now I did leave my husband, I went without the baby, without any child. The old reason for leaving was submerged under the fierce rows and recriminations that swept through the house so that the servants went about subdued, eyes lowered, before all that was laid waste while furniture and flower vases stood as usual and the outside man went on skimming the swimming pool with a net scoop. Once my husband had suddenly shouted that I ought to have been taken to a doctor, that's what he should have done – it was only since the last baby was born that I'd behaved like this, I'd changed with the birth of that baby, he wished the bloody baby had never been born!

He, who was so besotted with her that she has been the over-indulged darling of the family, all her life. And I, not having the impulse then, at all, to fling back at him a name, a statement to stand out on his face harder than the print of any hand.

It was true that pretty terrible things could happen to me. I took a job as an air hostess on the inter-island service. I had no training for any occupation. The ceiling of the old DC3's flight was in the blanket of humidity and turbulence that rose from lonely mountains covered in tropical forest and lowland plantations of silky green cane. The cabins were not pressurised and I went up and down the aisles collecting paper bags of vomit. He must have heard about it, I'm sure, in his new posting to another set of island paradises, in Malaysia. Because of course, carrying my burdens along the isles, I met the astonished eyes of passengers who knew me as the wife of the such-and-such company's man. The ambassador who had once brought me a box of real lilies-of-the-valley from Europe (orchids were nothing, they grew wild on the island) stared at me from his seat, unsure whether or not to recognise me, although, like most women who have good taste in clothes and who for some reason have to put on a vulgarly provocative outfit, a waitress's dirndl or an air hostess's Courrèges, I know my looks had been made more sexual by the uniform. Another passenger and his wife, to whom I made myself known as a face from the sailing club and diplomatic parties, were on their way to a new posting and she remarked that it was to be Malaysia, this time, where, of course, the —s were now; it would be good to have someone they already knew, when they got there, and the —s had always been such fun, the island hadn't been the same since they left, had it? She would give them my best wishes, they would be glad to have news of their friends.

No letter. I did not expect one; I thought of him passionately as someone just as I was, ejected from the mould of myself, unrecognisable even to myself, spending nights in towns that while familiar (all the islands had the same palms, nightclubs, fruit-bats, the same creaking air conditioners and the long yawn of the sea) were not home. Being the distinguished man he was, the ambassador had been particularly friendly and amusing, once I had shown I was to be recognised in my new circumstances, but now that I was, theoretically, available, he did not try to see me again. The pilots were bored with their wives and pestered me. I slept in Curepipe one night with a Canadian businessman who felt it fated because twice, three months apart, he had come to the islands and found me serving his whisky on the plane. I got what I wanted out of the encounter; a climax of sobbing and self-pity gave me back my yearning for my lover.

Long after, many months later, when I was home and my husband and I were having the house altered and the garden landscaped, there was a letter. *Are you mad? A mixture between a skivvy and a chorus-girl on one of those terrible old crates? What will happen to you?* How he must have struggled with himself, telling himself, as I did every day, there was no use to write. I would see my face in the mirror as if he were looking at it: only twenty-nine, thinner in the jaw since the drudgery and irregular hours of the airlines, longer hair, now, and the haughty look that unhappiness and dissatisfaction give when you are still young. My husband had gone into the shipping business, on his own initiative; the island was about to run up the new flag as an independent state and he had ingratiated himself with the ruling coterie. I still couldn't speak a word of the language but I was one of the first white women to appear at official banquets wearing the long, graceful island dress. My husband became confidential financial adviser to the new president; any-one from the foreign trade consulates who wanted privileges in the regime had to come to him, now.

There were riots down in the native town or the upcountry dis-tricts but we really only were aware of them from the newspapers. The regime survived and my husband made a lot of money. His triumph in my return had opened a source of energy in him that nothing could check. Not that we had ever been poor; once you had a house in the bluff district, a swimming pool and some sort of craft in the yacht club harbour, there wasn't much else money could add to life on the island. Anybody could have the sea, sun, the flowers for the picking and the oysters off the rocks. He wanted to send pictures of the children taken with his super cameras as Christmas cards but I flew out against it and he liked confidently to give in to my whims. He had to travel often to Europe and enjoyed taking me with him. I did a lot of shopping for myself; his greatest pleasure was to buy presents for the children, in particular pretty dresses for the girl. In those days my lady ran about the beach like a little bedraggled princess, wearing hand-tucked Liberty lawn as a bathing wrap – a wild and spoilt child. We used to have to visit his mother who had retired to a hill village in the South of France and on one of these visits I drove into Nice to shop. Sitting in a café open to and noisy as the street I found I had lost the car key; and it was there, in the telephone booth that smelt (I remember it perfectly) of sweaty feet and sour wine, while I was waiting distaste-fully for my call to the village, that I saw out of the scribblings on the dirty wall, a name.

Arno   Arno   Arno Arkanius.

Someone had stood waiting for a connection in that telephone booth in that café and written, again and again, as you might pick up a stick and write on the sand where no one will read, that name. There were many others jotted down, with numbers that belonged along with them; Pierre, Jan, Delphine, Marc, Maria, Horst, Robert. I read them all carefully. They were names common to thousands of men and women, but this name, this combination of first and surname – could it come about to signify another identity? I knew, as if my own hand had held that dark-leaded pencil (it was not a ball-point; a ball-point would never have written so clearly on that greasy wall), that this was he, this statement was about him and no other. Impossible to say who made it, or when; only why. The telephone ring leapt counter to the dulled noise from without pressing upon the glass door and I spoke what I had to say, not taking my eyes off the wall. Arno Arno Arno Arkanius. I hung up. I collected from the dirty floor my bag and parcels and went to the bar to pay for the call. So I had forgotten. Somebody else wept and indulged erotic fantasies, somebody else pronounced the name as a devout Jew might secretly speak the forbidden name of Jehovah. While this had been happening I had forgotten, the baby with the big mouth had become my husband's child – it was true, I was deceived and not he, about her identity – because I had forgotten, for days, months on end. I had thought I was permanently unhappy but how could that be? – I had forgotten. There must be many children such as she, happy to be who they are, whose real identity could be resuscitated only if their mother's youth could be brought back to life again.

BESSIE HEAD
THE PRISONER WHO WORE GLASSES

BESSIE HEAD (b. 1937, d. in Serowe, Botswana, 1986). 'The Prisoner who Wore Glasses' first appeared in the October-November number of *The London Magazine* in 1973 and has been reproduced in several anthologies since then. In 1989 it was included in the posthumous collection of her stories called *Tales of Tenderness and Power*.

Scarcely a breath of wind disturbed the stillness of the day and the long rows of cabbages were bright green in the sunlight. Large white clouds drifted slowly across the deep blue sky. Now and then they obscured the sun and caused a chill on the backs of the prisoners who had to work all day long in the cabbage field. This trick the clouds were playing with the sun eventually caused one of the prisoners who wore glasses to stop work, straighten up and peer shortsightedly at them. He was a thin little fellow with a hollowed-out chest and comic knobbly knees. He also had a lot of fanciful ideas because he smiled at the clouds.

'Perhaps they want me to send a message to the children,' he thought, tenderly, noting that the clouds were drifting in the direction of his home some hundred miles away. But before he could frame the message, the warder in charge of his work span shouted: 'Hey, what you think you're doing, Brille?'

The prisoner swung round, blinking rapidly, yet at the same time sizing up the enemy. He was a new warder, named Jacobus Stephanus Hannetjie. His eyes were the colour of the sky but they were frightening. A simple, primitive, brutal soul gazed out of them. The prisoner bent down quickly and a message was quietly passed down the line: 'We're in for trouble this time, comrades.'

'Why?' rippled back up the line.

'Because he's not human,' the reply rippled down and yet only the crunching of the spades as they turned over the earth disturbed the stillness.

This particular work span was known as Span One. It was composed of ten men and they were all political prisoners. They were grouped together for convenience as it was one of the prison regulations that no black warder should be in charge of a political prisoner lest this prisoner convert him to his views. It never seemed to occur to the authorities that this very reasoning was the strength of Span One and a clue to the strange terror they aroused in the warders. As political prisoners they were unlike the other prisoners in the sense that they felt no guilt nor were they outcasts of society. All guilty men instinctively cower, which was why it was the kind of prison where men got knocked out cold with a blow at the back of the head from an iron bar. Up until the arrival of Warder Hannetjie, no warder had dared beat any member of Span One and no warder had lasted more than a week with them. The battle was entirely psychological. Span One was assertive and it was beyond the scope of white warders to handle assertive black men. Thus, Span One had got out of control. They were the best thieves and liars in the camp. They lived all day on raw cabbages. They chatted and smoked tobacco. And since they moved, thought and acted as one, they had perfected every technique of group concealment.

Trouble began that very day between Span One and Warder Hannetjie. It was because of the shortsightedness of Brille. That was the nickname he was given in prison and is the Afrikaans word for someone who wears glasses. Brille could never judge the approach of the prison gates and on several previous occasions he had munched on cabbages and dropped them almost at the feet of the warder and all previous warders had overlooked this. Not so Warder Hannetjie.

'Who dropped that cabbage?' he thundered.

Brille stepped out of line.

'I did,' he said meekly.

'All right,' said Hannetjie. 'The whole Span goes three meals off.'

'But I told you I did it,' Brille protested.

The blood rushed to Warder Hannetjie's face.

'Look 'ere,' he said. 'I don't take orders from a kaffir. I don't know what kind of kaffir you tink you are. Why don't you say Baas. I'm your Baas. Why don't you say Baas, hey?'

Brille blinked his eyes rapidly but by contrast his voice was strangely calm.

'I'm twenty years older than you,' he said. It was the first thing that came to mind but the comrades seemed to think it a huge joke. A titter swept up the line. The next thing Warder Hannetjie whipped out a knobkerrie and gave Brille several blows about the head.

What surprised his comrades was the speed with which Brille had removed his glasses or else they would have been smashed to pieces on the ground.

That evening in the cell Brille was very apologetic.

'I'm sorry, comrades,' he said. 'I've put you into a hell of a mess.'

'Never mind, brother,' they said. 'What happens to one of us, happens to all.'

'I'll try to make up for it, comrades,' he said. 'I'll steal something so that you don't go hungry.'

Privately, Brille was very philosophical about his head wounds. It was the first time an act of violence had been perpetrated against him but he had long been a witness of extreme, almost unbelievable human brutality. He had twelve children and his mind travelled back that evening through the sixteen years of bedlam in which he had lived. It had all happened in a small drab little three-bedroomed house in a small drab little street in the Eastern Cape and the children kept coming year after year because neither he nor Martha ever managed the contraceptives the right way and a teacher's salary never allowed moving to a bigger house and he was always taking exams to improve his salary only to have it all eaten up by hungry mouths. Everything was pretty horrible, especially the way the children fought. They'd get hold of each other's heads and give them a good bashing against the wall. Martha gave up somewhere along the line so they worked out a thing between them. The bashing, biting and blood were to operate in full swing until he came home. He was to be the bogeyman and when it worked he never failed to have a sense of godhead at the way in which his presence could change savages into fairly reasonable human beings.

Yet somehow it was this chaos and mismanagement at the centre of his life that drove him into politics. It was really an ordered beautiful world with just a few basic slogans to learn along with the rights of mankind. At one stage, before things became very bad, there were conferences to attend, all very far away from home.

'Let's face it,' he thought ruefully. 'I'm only learning right now what it means to be a politician. All this while I've been running away from Martha and the kids.'

And the pain in his head brought a hard lump to his throat. That was what the children did to each other daily and Martha wasn't managing and if Warder Hannetjie had not interrupted him that morning he would have sent the following message: 'Be good comrades, my children. Co-operate, then life will run smoothly.'

The next day Warder Hannetjie caught this old man of twelve children stealing grapes from the farm shed. They were an enormous quantity of grapes in a ten-gallon tin and for this misdeed the old man spent a week in the isolation cell. In fact, Span One as a whole was in constant trouble. Warder Hannetjie seemed to have eyes at the back of his head. He uncovered the trick about the cabbages, how they were split in two with the spade and immediately covered with earth and then unearthed again and eaten with split-second timing. He found out how tobacco smoke was beaten into the ground and he found out how conversations were whispered down the wind.

For about two weeks Span One lived in acute misery. The cabbages, tobacco and conversations had been the pivot of jail life to them. Then one evening they noticed that their good old comrade who wore the glasses was looking rather pleased with himself. He pulled out a four ounce packet of tobacco by way of explanation and the comrades fell upon it with great greed. Brille merely smiled. After all, he was the father of many children. But when the last shred had disappeared, it occurred to the comrades that they ought to be puzzled. Someone said: 'I say, brother. We're watched like hawks these days. Where did you get the tobacco?'

'Hannetjie gave it to me,' said Brille.

There was a long silence. Into it dropped a quiet bombshell.

'I saw Hannetjie in the shed today,' and the failing eyesight blinked rapidly. 'I caught him in the act of stealing five bags of fertiliser and he bribed me to keep my mouth shut.'

There was another long silence.

'Prison is an evil life,' Brille continued, apparently discussing some irrelevant matter. 'It makes a man contemplate all kinds of evil deeds.'

He held out his hand and closed it.

'You know, comrades,' he said. 'I've got Hannetjie. I'll betray him tomorrow.'

Everyone began talking at once.

'Forget it, brother. You'll get shot.'

Brille laughed.

'I won't,' he said. 'That is what I mean about evil. I am a father of children and I saw today that Hannetjie is just a child and stupidly truthful. I'm going to punish him severely because we need a good warder.'

The following day, with Brille as witness, Hannetjie confessed to the theft of the fertiliser and was fined a large sum of money. From then on Span One did very much as they pleased while Warder Hannetjie stood by and said nothing. But it was Brille who carried this to extremes. One day, at the close of work Warder Hannetjie said: 'Brille, pick up my jacket and carry it back to the camp.'

'But nothing in the regulations says I'm your servant, Hannetjie,' Brille replied coolly.

'I've told you not to call me Hannetjie. You must say Baas,' but Warder Hannetjie's voice lacked conviction. In turn, Brille squinted up at him.

'I'll tell you something about this Baas business, Hannetjie,' he said. 'One of these days we are going to run the country. You are going to clean my car. Now, I have a fifteen-year-old son and I'd die of shame if you had to tell him that I ever called you Baas.'

Warder Hannetjie went red in the face and picked up his coat.

On another occasion Brille was seen to be walking about the prison yard, openly smoking tobacco. On being taken before the prison commander he claimed to have received the tobacco from Warder Hannetjie. All throughout the tirade from his chief, Warder Hannetjie failed to defend himself but his nerve broke completely. He called Brille to one side.

'Brille,' he said. 'This thing between you and me must end. You may not know it but I have a wife and children and you're driving me to suicide.'

'Why, don't you like your own medicine, Hannetjie?' Brille asked quietly.

'I can give you anything you want,' Warder Hannetjie said in desperation.

'It's not only me but the whole of Span One,' said Brille, cunningly. 'The whole of Span One wants something from you.'

Warder Hannetjie brightened with relief.

'I think I can manage if it's tobacco you want,' he said.

Brille looked at him, for the first time struck with pity, and guilt. He wondered if he had carried the whole business too far. The man was really a child.

'It's not tobacco we want, but you,' he said. 'We want you on our side. We want a good warder because without a good warder we won't be able to manage the long stretch ahead.'

Warder Hannetjie interpreted this request in his own fashion and his interpretation of what was good and human often left the prisoners of Span One speechless with surprise. He had a way of slipping off his revolver and picking up a spade and digging alongside Span One. He had a way of producing unheard-of luxuries like boiled eggs from his farm nearby and things like cigarettes, and Span One responded nobly and got the reputation of being the best work span in the camp. And it wasn't only take from their side. They were awfully good at stealing certain commodities like fertiliser which were needed on the farm of Warder Hannetjie.

SIPHO SEPAMLA
MAPULENG

SIPHO SEPAMLA (b. 1932 in Krugersdorp, lives on the East Rand). 'MaPuleng' was first published in *On the Edge of the World* when he was preparing his first volume of poetry, *Hurry Up to It!* (1975). He went on to revive *The Classic* as *New Classic* in 1975, where he published several later stories.

For days on end it rained. Listless, interminable rain. People began to wonder. They began to fear. There was something ominous about that rain. Falling as it did after an event which had shaken the whole world, they feared for the world. Might it be coming to an end? And right at their doorstep, they feared for the only big shop within their easy reach. For the level of the dam behind the shop was rising. The banks were hardly visible. If the dam itself looked submerged, then the likelihood of the water streaming over the doorstep of the shop was real. The whole township was in a panic.

It was on one of those rainy days that a child was born to MaMokwena: one of the blessings of the rain. And to celebrate the event, the child, being a girl, was named Puleng. Thereafter MaMokwena became MaPuleng.

Very few people could claim to know the girl's father. One or two possibilities were always mentioned. Even so, many people admired MaPuleng for the courage of trying to face up to life without the permanent anchor of a husband.

Perhaps it was more to lift herself out of loneliness, rather than to seek more hands to make ends meet, that she would take in a man for a spell. And because it was her room, the men's sojourn was dependent upon her very fancy moods. The men never spoke about their ejectment – for manly reasons. Instead MaPuleng would grumble: 'I didn't come to town for charity!'

MaPuleng's finger always pinched a bit of snuff from a little box tucked away somewhere around her hip. The same finger would then be thrust out to point at some house-chores Puleng had to do. Thus the little girl grew up with her nostrils sniffing the air as if looking for something.

To make ends meet at all, MaPuleng took in a lot of washing

from Indian families. The earnings from four of them combined to make up her monthly pay. More money came from her temporary sojourners.

Puleng never got to know her father. By association every adult male became Papa So-and-So. She never asked the big question largely because she had so much to do in the room. Then too there was the washing to carry away on her head. And of course the ten cent trips to the shop. The very few occasions when mother and child found themselves together got eaten up by MaPuleng grumbling about the inadequacies of her current man.

All in all, Puleng was in a way as useful to her mother as the snuff-box. Also she was kept under the mother's roving finger like the snuff-box. Because she was soft of character and charming, she didn't seem to resent all that.

There was common talk among the neighbours that MaPuleng treated her child like a slave. This always made MaPuleng curse within the four walls. Fuming, she would walk out to the washing-line, peg up a garment or two and then continue to swear at the four winds. The scene always ended up with her thrusting a ten cent piece into Puleng's hand, saying: 'Take! Bring me a packet of sugar ...! And you must hurry up ...! Rubbish!' It was never clear to whom 'rubbish' referred. For her part Puleng would run the forward journey. On her way back she lingered with friends and the sights on her way. She got home to find her mother swearing. This time the daughter would be the butt of her condemnation. And the neighbours who happened to be within earshot.

One day the prohibition on liquor sales to all people was revoked. From then on everyone was free to buy and guzzle whatever suited his taste. The number of men who got drunk rose rapidly. No one could say where everyone drank because many homes became shebeens. MaPuleng saw the potential. Besides, everybody knew she had no husband. And she had begun to complain about the ill effects of handling too much water.

In her little room she began a liquor business. She would buy K. B. from the municipal depot and resell it at a profit. Soon her market became greater than she could get supplies for. For one thing the depot closed at night, the very time when demand was at its peak. And it wasn't as if her room was next door to the depot. No, as a result of these inconveniences she found she had to augment the supply from the depot. It so happened that her specially flavoured brand of K. B. had the sort of taste and kick which met the requirements of customers. Her room became popular. And its size decreased. What with the number of four-gallon tins growing daily, she couldn't cope.

She changed into the bottled beer business. Profits climbed. She dropped the snuff-box and clipped a cigarette between the fingers. Puleng had to float about to meet the demands of the customers and the moment.

Perhaps her neighbours were jealous or she grew airs, it wasn't clear. All the same she fell out with them. Sometimes she complained that the females around her provoked a quarrel with her. Other times they said she belittled them. It all stemmed from the husbands of these females. They drank to be drunk and forgot themselves. Never knew who they were nor where they came from. So as Puleng swept the stubs of cigarettes off the floor, her mother had to usher these men into the street. That way the admiration MaPuleng once enjoyed trickled into the gutter the neighbourhood used for dirty water and pee.

Mother and daughter looked happy. Puleng was growing rapidly. In time she had adjusted her sights to those of her mother. How much she accepted unbegrudgingly, it could not be said. She went about the room and work confidently. She was able to joke or tease a customer, slapping her own vaselined thigh into the bargain. Her smiles helped to slay a hesitant customer. Under her spell a man would spend more than he had fixed when he first walked into the room. MaPuleng was happy with the efficiency of her daughter, happier to place more cash in her bosom, her favourite hiding place.

Came a day, MaPuleng was bowled over by Bomvana Radebe, one of her customers. He was one of those men who succeeded in giving the impression they are unimpeachable bachelors. In fact he had a family in the Transkei. In a sense then he was a free man.

MaPuleng moved into Bomvana's four-roomed house. She was a great acquisition to Bomvana. For deep down there he was a won't-work. All day long he pottered around the house looking for nails to knock into place. Or he could offer to help a customer quaff his drink in company. It was MaPuleng who paid the rent and bought food. It was her daughter who cleaned the floors whilst she, MaPuleng, for the benefit of curious neighbours and passers-by, tended to the needs of the yard.

Something Bomvana enjoyed doing was to kill time with Puleng. Once he told her of his own daughter, Faith. She was somewhere in the Transkei. Unlike Puleng, she had been to school and had had an excellent school career. At an early age she had been turned into a lady teacher. He told Puleng he had heard that school children called his daughter 'Mam'. This tickled him. He had never thought his Faith could end up a 'Mam'.

Puleng was left envious, her mind drifting wishfully. She longed for the kind of independence Faith enjoyed. Her problem was how to achieve that. The thing lived in her like an undercurrent.

While Bomvana and Puleng grew to like each other so that she was ready to call herself his daughter, MaPuleng anchored herself in the new neighbourhood. She and Bomvana were soon accepted, at least on the surface, as man and wife.

Presently one of MaPuleng's relatives from the homelands arrived. He was Kgoropedi Manthata, a young man of about twenty-two. His mother and MaPuleng were blood sisters. Knowing nobody around except his aunt, long lost to the homelands, he moved in with her. MaPuleng saw in him more cash flowing into her bosom.

Kgoropedi was made to feel at home by his aunt, his Malume Bomvana and Ntsala Puleng. They were all concerned that he found a job, the reason for coming at all.

But there was a problem in his finding work. He had no pass-book. That meant he was unknown in the area and as such didn't qualify to be a work-seeker in the area. It was left to MaPuleng's resourcefulness to find a solution. Luckily the clerks from the local office were all her customers. Receiving their cheques at the end of a month, they were always at her mercy in the middle of it. Their contribution toward the solution was a fargone thing.

The first step required the Superintendent at the local office to sign some documents. That way Kgoropedi's face would acquire some appearance.

When MaPuleng and Kgoropedi presented themselves before the Super, he showed great interest in the story she recited. Largely it had to do with why he hadn't taken out a pass-book until that late age. She laid it on fine: how he had been born under great odds; how his father (whereabouts unknown) had deserted her and made the child an illegitimate. Neither the Super nor MaPuleng smiled or grinned throughout the narration. As for Kgoropedi, he sat there masked by fear and innocence.

At the end of it all the Super grumbled something about not liking 'this cock and bull story'. Nonetheless he signed the necessary documents. And so paved the way for Kgoropedi to obtain a pass and find work.

The name entered in the pass was Kgoropedi Mokwena. Thanks to the clerks.

Thereafter finding work was no problem. The warmth of his aunt grew greater. Meanwhile the affection between the cousins strengthened. Every time Puleng teased a customer, her cousin would be at hand to share the laughter. Even the iniquities of drunken men they turned into mirth together.

MaPuleng wasn't indifferent to this example of brotherhood, being unenthusiastic about it. Not wanting to upset anyone, she said quietly to her daughter one day: 'Be careful of men.' Puleng passed on the warning to her cousin. It stung him. Coming as it did when he was beginning to flex his muscles with all the money he received on Fridays, it really upset him. For some time he had been feeling an uneasiness in the midst of his aunt and his cousin. The one sucked his manhood's rewards, the other confounded this manhood.

Kgoropedi moved into a hired room of his own. This made MaPuleng to grouse: 'Today's children are very ungrateful!' All the same she offered him the evening meal and the washing of his shirts and so on. Because this would give him the excuse to continue seeing his cousin, he accepted the arrangement.

By this time Kgoropedi and Puleng had come to value the company of each other very much. For her his company was uplifting. She felt a hot happiness. It was for this reason she often slipped away to his room.

It became a matter of time before the neighbours said it loud that the cousins were after all in love. In answer the young ones would reply, albeit as a joke: 'The cows are returning to their kraal.' The expression meant the marriage of cousins was a wise proposition. The cattle for lobola would circulate within the family.

MaPuleng heard the rumour. She was terribly hurt and upset. She was concerned about being the butt of ridicule. For what goes in the homelands is often taboo in town.

She confronted her daughter. 'What are you up to?' she said.

'I don't understand,' Puleng replied, displaying innocence.

'Hey! Don't think I'm blind!' her voice had an edge to it.

'What's mother talking about?'

'You and Kgoropedi!' she blurted, arms akimbo.

'There's nothing we have done.'

'Standing in shadows sucking a finger, there's nothing you've done?'

'Mother says strange things!'

'Hey! Don't think I don't see you! Every time he's around you are as restless as a hen in a storm!'

Puleng felt a whirlwind build up in her bosom. But she held her tongue. She feared she would shout. That would lose her the game. She had to tell her gently that her happiness could be found only with his company. Her silence was loud.

'Your silence shows up the snake in your heart!' MaPuleng hurled her judgement.

Again Puleng battled to suppress the heaving of her breast. But a thought she must have nurtured in her heart for a time strained at her lips. She flung it out like phlegm. Only her humbleness turned it into a stinging: 'Why do you hate me, mother?'

MaPuleng was thrown into disarray. She never thought her child was growing all ways. More than that, she never suspected her mind could harbour such a thought. 'I hate you? Are you mad?' she yelled.

'You hate me.' Puleng shouted in turn. 'You hate me!' she repeated and left the room in a huff.

The days that followed were silent and distant. Mother and daughter went about their share of work without a word to each other. MaPuleng smoked more cigarettes. She exhibited the fact of being mistress of the house more often. Puleng shelled herself within a song. This made MaPuleng furious and she would try to rattle her with jibes such as: 'Better get on with your work. The municipality has built a hall for singers!' A heavy atmosphere would then descend upon the house. If Bomvana noticed anything, he didn't say it loud. He feared to lose the women.

MaPuleng was still simmering when Kgoropedi called on them. And to assert her stand, she turned him out of the house. That day her wrath stood bristling in her eye: 'Out! Out you go!' she said, her forefinger pointing to one end of the world. 'I'm not going to have anyone make a fool of me!'

Caught unawares, Kgoropedi stood at the door hesitating.

MaPuleng continued: 'Blood or no blood, I don't care! I don't want you here anymore, finish and *klaar!*'

Puleng looked away in disgust. Kgoropedi hunched his shoulders and dragged himself away.

Bomvana kept mumbling: 'M'm ya! M'm ya!' until the first customer came to rescue his spirits.

The event marked the final spiritual break between mother and daughter. Many a time Puleng felt tempted to walk out of her home. She wrestled with the idea for days. She couldn't say what made her stick within her ma's place beyond the consideration that it was her home. Perhaps she still hoped for the kind of success she thought was possible as Bomvana's daughter.

As so often happens, the run of events gave answer to her dilemma. Her anger sacrificed her virginity. She found her way to Kgoropedi's room in rapid succession. Entered the physical act with ravenous fury. It was as if each motion was a slapping on her mother's face. Not long after, she became pregnant.

Again it was the neighbours who began to talk about Puleng's condition. MaPuleng seemed blind to it. But when at last she caught up with it she turned grey-black. She gazed at her daughter as if to cry. Then she threw up her hand, palm facing upward, and said bitterly: 'What are you going to get from a thing that hardly has a name? It shows you don't care whether people laugh at me or not …! He doesn't care, after all I'm not his mother!'

At first Puleng managed to hold her tongue. Perhaps the child's motherly condition made her keep silent. But it was this very sharp silence which drove MaPuleng mad. She taunted her daughter: 'What made you feel so excited about that country boy that you spread yourself before him so? … *Hayi! Mense!* This world is *mos snaaks!*'

With that she left her daughter staring. She glared at her mother until she disappeared into another room for one reason or another.

Next time MaPuleng said to her daughter: 'My mother can bear witness in her grave, I never did funny things under her nose! I was miles away when I got you. I was working in town and she was way back in the homelands … And you want to know something, my man had money … What has that country boy? M'm, tell me, what has he? Nothing! He hardly knows which direction the door of a bank faces!'

Perhaps Puleng would have borne all these jibes from her mother if only to save her own face in the public eye. But then her mother said: 'I shall never forgive you … You have shamed me in the eyes of the devil himself!'

This Puleng couldn't stomach. She despised her mother for being such a liar. She told herself: 'I've grown up enough not to be treated like a baby. Mother has no right to speak to me as if I have sinned. After all, what example is she? How much harder have I grown up without a picture of my father …! I've had to bear the tag of illegitimate child without question. And for all that I am accused like a sinner … It is true mother hates me. Silence is pointless.' Aloud she said to her mother: 'I love Kgoropedi!'

'Love him? What cheek! Go to him then!' MaPuleng said this, arm stretched out, forefinger pointed at Kgoropedi's room some two miles away: 'Gwan, go!'

It was meant as a challenge and nothing more. Puleng was her daughter. She would take this as she had taken all beatings from her in the past. Besides the hour was late for Puleng to take as much as a step outside the gate.

Puleng stiffened for a second or two. She drew in a huge breath as if she wanted to cheat her mother of all air that still circulated in the house despite the sour smell of beers mingled with the stale stench of cigarettes. Then she stormed into her room. Picked up a blanket, threw it over her shoulder and slammed the outside door behind her. Bomvana's feeble pleas rang in her ears in vain.

'Let her go! Let her go! Who begs her? Not me!' cried MaPuleng.

Bomvana settled his conscience by walking into the bedroom. After the house had acquired a heavy silence, Bomvana came out of the bedroom. He muttered: 'I don't understand town children.'

That evening MaPuleng swore by her dead mother she would fix up Puleng. As if that were not enough, she repeated the oath saying: 'I swear by my grandmother lying in her grave, I'll show Puleng who her mother is! She doesn't know me!'

Not to be considered indifferent, Bomvana said: 'You know, I have never liked children growing up in town. That's why I sent Faith to a country school.'

'School?' sneered MaPuleng, 'what wouldn't she do if I sent her to school? No doubt she would have said I am not her mother! That's what happens when they begin to speak English through their nostrils. Suddenly they become welfare cases, picked up in forsaken cardboard boxes. Yoo! I'm not mad!'

A few days later mother and daughter stood before the Super-intendent. MaPuleng opened the case: 'Morena,' she said, 'I don't want to stand in her way if she wants to get married. All I ask is that she returns home and things be settled properly.'

In answer to which the Super asked for the ages of the two women. Perhaps he was influenced by the pregnancy of the younger one.

MaPuleng suddenly melted into a smile and said: 'I never went to school, Morena.'

Asked to identify an event near her birthday and that of Puleng, she said she was a young girl when the miners were said to have gone mad in Johannesburg. The Super interjected: 'Mad?'

'I don't know, Morena,' she said, shrugging her shoulders. 'That is what I heard.'

'That must be the 1922 Miners' Strike, I suppose.'

'Yes, yes, Morena is right!'

'And the girl?'

'After Hitler's war there was rain, Morena. It fell for days and nights. It fell as if it would never stop. That is when she was born.'

'M'm, I see.'

There was a silence in which the Super seemed to be engaged in thought. When he opened his mouth it was to remind the women about their traditional ways. He said according to custom 'you people' should not be in this sort of meeting taking place then. MaPuleng was about forty-nine and the daughter nineteen. The matter was so domestic they ought to be ashamed to have brought it out in public.

Turning to Puleng, he said in a stern but calm voice: 'Young girl, go back to your mother before ...'

The man had hardly finished when Puleng, shifting her feet as if to stamp the floor, said: 'She's not my mother!'

The Super was taken aback. MaPuleng was stunned.

'What do you mean she's not your mother?' asked the Super.

'She's not!' repeated Puleng, eyes burning, face tensed. She went on: 'My mother died a long time ago!'

'She lies! She lies! I'm her mother!'

'You are not!'

'I am! Ask –'

'It's not true!'

'Shut up! Shut up!' said the Super, banging his desk as if with a mallet. Things were getting out of hand. 'Kyk hiersô, you people have forgotten yourselves! This is my office, not a shebeen!' The father of the people thought to assert his authority which had been somewhat battered by the women in conflict. So he said: 'Both of you must keep quiet now. You will open your mouths only when I tell you to do so, do you hear me?'

Only MaPuleng said she understood. Puleng was too furious to care about the meaning of standing before the Super.

At once he gave precedence to MaPuleng: 'Is there something you can show me which will prove this girl is your daughter?'

It was as if MaPuleng had been hit with another blow. For a moment words escaped her.

Then she said in a very emotional voice: 'S-someth-thing t-to show you? H-how do you mean er-M-morena?'

'Birth certificate ... baptismal certificate, even if it's a duplicate?'

'No, I've neither of them.'

'Nothing! ... You mean, you mean yours is another of these cases ...' The Super threw up his hand to conclude the thought.

'I never went to school!'

'That's got nothing to do with it. These things are not issued by the Department of Education.'

Again there was a silence. The Super looked at MaPuleng. And then at Puleng. He saw the fact of her pregnancy once more. It disturbed him no end.

'Let me see your house permit?' he asked MaPuleng. Then when the thing lay before him he kept nodding his head, his teeth digging into his lower lip as if to extract some blood to witness this grave situation.

At last he said to MaPuleng: 'What are you to Bomvana Radebe?'

Again MaPuleng had to search for words. The question was awkward under the circumstances: 'He's my boyfriend.' She blurted out the words so that they remained in the air. Then she added: 'I live with him!'

Meanwhile the Super had touched an ear as if the words had hurt. It was as if that kind of thing was new in his experience. Yet he knew it well in that world. He turned to Puleng. 'And what are you?'

'He's my father!' she didn't hesitate.

'Puleng Radebe, yes?'

'Yes!'

'And Perfidia Mokwena, you?' addressing MaPuleng.

'Yes!' Then she added: 'But I'm her mother!'

'That's not true!'

The Super eyed Puleng and turned to MaPuleng: 'Where's her father?'

'I don't know!' she said sadly.

'You don't know?'

The Super touched his furrowed brow.

'That is strange.' That is all he could say. Common as the thing was in his work, he couldn't get used to it, like death.

'He was here with building contractors. I've never heard from him ever since they left.'

'Shame!' said the Super spontaneously. Then: 'Who is this Kgoropedi Mokwena?' asked the Super, reading a name from the permit.

The two women hurried to answer that one, speaking almost simultaneously.

'He's my son!' said MaPuleng.

'My boyfriend!' said Puleng.

This time the Superintendent stood up. The oppression of the matter before him was unbearable. He craved for relief. A pipe or a glass of very cold beer would have come in handy then. He did the least. He lit a pipe that had been slanting in an ashtray.

'Look here, only Christ could perform miracles. And I'm not Him ...'

Silence.

He turned to Puleng: 'Who did that to you?'

'Kgoropedi!'

'Your brother?'

'Cousin!'

'But she said just now he is her son.'

'That's not true!'

'Oh! *Here!*' exclaimed the Super, 'you people don't know your-selves!' And in an effort to draw this whole thing to some conclu-sion, he said: 'Come on, come on, don't waste my time!'

'I'm telling the truth!' said Puleng.

'I'm telling the truth!' said MaPuleng. Just then MaPuleng wiped off something that had been glistening in her eye.

Her heart became heavier when the Super said: 'I wash my hands!' For with that he sat down again. He looked at MaPuleng whose eyes were wet with the pains of childbirth. She was now drying them in readiness to see the regrets which would live in her heart for a long time. He looked at Puleng. It wasn't for long. Her condition dazzled the eye. There was a shame facing the girl, pregnant at that young age, yet brave enough to deny the womb which must have carried the resemblance of their facial features. So the Super said finally: 'You may go! You'll see me when you have made up your minds!'

There was little he could do. MaPuleng lacked the proof. Puleng was of age, and she had gone far already.

Perfidia Mokwena went to the house of Bomvana Radebe, muttering inaudible curses. Puleng Radebe went to the room of Kgoropedi Mokwena, clicking her tongue and wrapping a blanket round her waist now and again.

That day the sun went down as usual for everybody else.

MONGANE SEROTE
LET'S WANDER TOGETHER

MONGANE SEROTE (b. 1944 in Sophiatown). 'Let's Wander Together' is one of three sketches first published in Johannesburg's *The Classic*, Vol. 3, No. 4, of 1971. His latest work is *Hyenas* (2001), a meditation on the African Renaissance.

There is this young man. Handsome. He has this smile that cuts doubt and restriction like teeth do the peels of fruit. That is how I recall him; those days when I was young and he was too and there was hope.

Now I recall that night when he came and slipped next to me in the blankets. I was angry with him. It was close to two in the morning. He knocked, I opened; he came in smiling that smile of his. Hell. I told him to stop his nocturnal knocks; people want to rest, you know. I remember clearly by people I meant me.

He said nothing. He started to undress; I slipped into the blankets murmuring things intended to hurt him. He seemed indifferent and that angered me. Every time I caught this silly stinking smell of liquor when he coughed. The smell was real dirty. He seemed to be doing something. I don't know what, and his head was next to mine. I was silent with biting anger.

I told him to go to his bed. With his strange positiveness, that always made him have his way even when people he had wronged were on the verge of murdering him, he slipped into the blankets. I felt his cold thighs touch mine. And those thighs were so thin! Good God, I thought, what cheek! He has urinated his thighs wet and he just comes into the blankets like that? I felt his hand move between his and my thigh. I lifted my head to have a clear picture of this beast: I was numb, I could hardly say a word. He looked at me with such sad and painful eyes.

'Brother, I'm in pain,' he said. Strange, I realised this immediately. Immediately I was out of bed. He followed suit, slowly. His nude body turned to the candlelight. And there, like a eye, a strangely opened and bleeding wound looked at me. I looked at him questioningly.

'The night watchman stabbed me with his assegai,' he answered. We did things to that wound that night.

The following day, after I had dug out all my persuasive powers, he refused to go to the clinic. And the following day's night he came back drunk again. Weeks passed.

Many things happened. He still came and went. The right time being the night time, to come back. He still knocked at night, I opened; he still slipped next to me, having divorced his bed. We used to talk. Things: 'Sexing' as he used to say, and 'Religion like' and 'them the white people thing'; he used to talk! It is very possible that we saw eye to eye, but he had this 'you inducated too much' idea about me. He would say it, with his index finger shaking warningly at me, he would frown, meaning that spells trouble, 'mmmmmmmm', I'm saying that.

He was born in Benoni Location but lived most of his young days, years, in Alexandra with my father. He persevered through school up to Standard Six. He gave up school to become a caddie. That meant buying anything he wanted. Foodwise, he was good at it; clothes excellent. I loved him. He went, back to Benoni.

When we met again, I was a little man with big thoughts of high school. I think it was at a relative's funeral. He was talking strangely with those wires holding his jaws. He held a small boy's head, jesting about how impossible it was to 'support them, with that girl there' – he pointed at the thin-legged girl who stood staring at the many people.

The next time I saw him, it was the year that includes among its days the night of the wounded thigh. I came home late at night. He was there in my room with my brother.

He was not wearing his clothes; they were hanging from his shoulders and hips. His eyes were blood-shot. His huge hair, beard and the gold earring made him look like he was about to say 'Ha!' You would have really run with fright if he had. He said he wanted a job.

He got a job and lost it. Pass problems. The Benoni Alexandra 'place of abode' thing pointed and picked him out as undesirable to be employed in the 'above-mentioned area'. He got another job and lost it. He refused to say 'baas' and nearly used a hammer in defence of his principle. He went jobless for many, many months. Hot at home, 'you won't work'. Hot outside 'Section 29', as the knowledgeable people say.

He came home late at night, with the dirty smell of his breath and he left in the morning, eyes red.

He stopped talking to me: I had fisted him because he had smoked my cigarettes, a whole packet. I do not think he was ever sorry for that; when there is no hope, things nearest are yours.

I left home. When I came back, maybe prodigally, he had left a day after me. These township boys know what I am talking about here, you want to go but you come back.

Weeks passed and no one knew where this young man was. Months. I met him. It was early morning, about five. He was playing soccer, using a tennis ball, with these grey-bellied kids in the street. He invited me to tea, 'You don't take hot stuff,' he said. As we walked to this house I realised that he had a piece of plastic bandage above the right eye. What's up? I asked. His hand caressed the bandage; I saw that the whole white of his eye was red – black-red.

'I'm one-eyed, brother,' he said sadly. God!

Something else caught up with my mind. We were on this dusty stoep, he was ahead of me. I could hear people shouting, a man and a woman. He went into the house and welcomed me loudly so his voice could be heard above the shouting. He gave me a chair. I was unsure of sitting down because this man and woman were about to pounce at each other. He seemed not to care, he was telling me how glad he was to see me. And that he was sorry to bring me to a house of people who fight. At that stage the man who had been defending himself for sleeping out came and shook my hand and immediately he answered a new accusation thrown at him by his wife.

I was sipping this real hot and very sweet black tea when this man came and told me we should stay out of the way of unthinking women. We sat on the stoep. He and the young man shared beer and I had tea. I was introduced to this man as 'my beautiful brother', and he shook my hand again and for a very long time. And now and then the shouts slipped out of the door from the woman.

Then we left. No doubt his eye was blind and the wound above the eyes was rotting. I suggested the clinic to him. He refused; I hijacked him there. Established blind eye; more treatments; which he did not go for.

Hymns. People gathered at night. It is a Friday, vigil day in most townships. Venue: home.

I was very angry, perhaps frightened, as I threw soil into that grave. Burying the young man's hopes, and the stab wound, this time, sorry, not a stab wound, but a gash. That killed him. It was so sudden, yet expected.

PETER WILHELM

LION

PETER WILHELM (b. 1943, living in Cape Town). His 'Lion' first appeared in *Contrast* in August 1974 and was included in his collection of 1979, *LM and Other Stories*, and more recently in his selected stories, *The Bayonet Field* (2001). His journalism is collected as *The State We're In*.

Towards the end of summer, everything poised for decay, the final bold shapes tottering under parabolas of hot straining insects, a lion was observed wandering across the rich farmlands to the north-west of Johannesburg: only miles from the city, a golden shape barred by trees fringing mapped-out regions of cultivation and order, crossing the thrusting highways in vast lopes that evaded destruction by the thundering, astonished traffic.

There was no formal record of the lion, so he sprang into the city's awareness fully extant, fused out of the shining air; and the first premonitory twitches of fear manifested themselves in the dreams of the inhabitants of Sandown, Bryanston, Houghton, all the green suburbs with women beside blue swimming pools with drinks at 11 a.m. The pounce, the yellow teeth, the cavernous dark jaws, the feral rush through the flowering shrubbery – it was all there, a night-time code.

Posses of police and farmers – guns out and oiled, trusty – walked through the high grass and weeds, stung by immature maize stalks, looking. They had dogs with them who cringed and whimpered, showing their own calcium-charged fangs, white and somehow delectable like the tips of asparagus. They and the children who ran after them shrieking with terror and breathlessness, black and white tumbled together in the mordant adventure, were all on a hampered search; the skills of tracking were forgotten, they could only go by the obvious. Members of the press went along too, with flushed faces and cameras.

At an early stage it was decided that, given the high price of lions on the international zoo market, the animal would not, when found, be killed: anaesthetic darts would be used to stun it first, then it would be lifted into a cage and transported to a convenient central point for the disposition of lions.

They followed a trail of kills, day after day, puffing and lagging. Here they found a dog contemptuously munched and discarded; there a mournful heifer, brown licked eyes startled by death, a haunch ripped open – purple and blue ravines, Grade A waste spoiled for the abattoir and the hungry steakhouses.

The heavy, overripe rains had given a lush feel to the fields, spreading green paint over growth, and wild flowers and weeds hammered into the air from uncultivated edges. Fruit fell into mud with sodden plops; irrigation ditches and small streams throbbed, the water corded and waxy. It had been a superb year, a harvest of a year, and the granaries and exchequer were loaded. So the lion penetrated a structure of assent and gratitude with a dark trajectory: his streaming mane, a Tarzan image, cast gaunt shadows on the end of the commercial year.

The boots of the hunters stuck in the mud; they were like soldiers going over the top in 1916, sent into barbed wire and indeterminate sludge by drunken generals; they floundered; the brims of their hats filled with rain; their pants soaked through like those of terrified schoolboys. They made no headway.

Inexorably, champing at the livestock, the lion ate his way towards the northern suburbs of the city, past roadhouses and drive-in cinemas showing documentaries of wild-life and the adventures of Captain Caprivi.

The frequency of dreams involving lions and lion-like beings increased significantly among the inhabitants of the green park-like suburbs of the city. The thud of tennis balls against the netting of racquets lost its precision: the shadow was there, in the tennis court, in the cool waves of the swimming pool, in the last bitter juices of the evening cocktail, tasting of aniseed.

The lion came down.

The farmers – who grew plump chickens for the frozen food ranges of the great supermarkets, and poppies for certain anniversaries – were furious at the terroristic incursion. It blighted their reality, shaming them. They woke to fences offensively broken, to minor household animals sardonically slaughtered, not even used for a snack on the road.

The lion behaved precisely like a lion; each animal was decisively killed; there was never any maiming, inadvertent or intentional; his great jaws crunched down on bone and splintered through domesticity.

He took a roving way toward the city: first directly south through well-manured farmlands, then tracing a stream westwards away from the sprawl of concrete and glass – sniffing at it, perhaps, and choosing to skirt.

He seemed to vanish, back into the diminishing lights of early autumn, back into the air, his lithe yellowish body no longer even glimpsed at a distance by the frenzied posses, watched from behind earth walls by large-eyed farmhands, and howled at by dogs with their black testicles in the dust.

The pressure abruptly diminished like that in a garden hose when the tap is turned commandingly to the left.

Something like silence descended, mote-like and uneasy. The lion had gone away; there had never been a lion; the lion had been a hypnagogic hallucination.

Then he killed a man, most savagely tearing out his guts next to a road, and pinpointed on a map the kill showed that the westward drift had been temporary and that the lion had in reality resumed coming back on the opposite bank: all he had done was seek out a place to cross.

Until the occurrence of the first human death, the press and other communications media had adopted an editorial stance towards the lion in which a certain light-heartedness had been mandatory. There had been jibes at authority's inability to find the beast, or even trace its origins. Now, as telephones began to ring incessantly with queries from troubled householders as to the lion's progress, and a sermon was preached in which the light of Christianity was set favourably against the unplumbed blackness of the wilderness and its denizens, the newspapers realised that public opinion was turning against the lion, and they adopted a harder line: the lion must be shot, or at least swiftly captured, before there were more deaths.

The dead man was reported to be a Bantu male called Samuel Buthelezi, a distant relation of the Zulu royal family.

It emerged that the followers had in fact passed the lion, going west when he was coming east; he had been asleep on a rock, or in a warm bowl of sand, sunning himself invisibly. And so the feeling arose that the search had to be made by professionals; a former professional game hunter was accordingly brought out of retirement to put the affair on a more scientific or knowing footing. However, it was impossible to search by night, which was too

preponderantly black to make for ease of vision, silence of movement, or comfort of heart; and so the lion continued to get away.
His getting away became the present tense of the searchers and
they began to feel it was invincible, that he took devious routes
with prior awareness of topography and demography; and when
a day or so passed without reports of a kill they indulged in
grotesque fantasies – remarking that the lion must be dead in a
ditch, or whimpering in a cave with a thorn in his foot. Any of a
dozen possibilities, and impossibilities, presented themselves
according to the number of searchers involved.

The former professional game hunter was an alcoholic; he drank
himself into a stupor and issued contradictory orders.

Small units of the army and air force were summoned to help
in the search: it was reasoned that the experience would aid them
in tracing terrorists in hostile terrain. Platoons of young men in
green and khaki camouflage uniform – bayonets ready at the tips
of their rifles – moved lumpily over hills and through lower
muddy regions looking for the lion, their boots mired indescrib-
ably. In the air fighter and reconnaissance jets flashed from one
edge of the horizon to the other, ceaselessly photographing. A
helicopter, normally used for the control of traffic and the detec-
tion of illegally cultivated marijuana, also chopped its way through
the search pattern.

The first white person to be killed by the lion was Dr Margaret
Brierwood. A graduate in palaeontology, Dr Brierwood had taken
her two children to school and was settling down beside the swimming pool of her and her husband's three-acre holding in a wooded
area only ten miles from the city centre. In the course of the pre-
ceding night the lion had doubled the distance between him and
his pursuers, racing along the fringes of a dual highway connecting
the cities of Pretoria and Johannesburg. He had failed to make a kill
at dawn and was correspondingly nettled at his own inadequacies –
a horse had whinnied to freedom because of a misjudged leap – and
driven by hunger.

The Brierwoods' estate was surrounded by a low wooden fence,
easily hurdled, and the lion sat for some time within the grounds,
panting softly, his tail rapidly frisking dust and grass, before
moving. He observed the morning activity narrowly, tempted at
one point to carry off a black man who swept the floor of the
swimming pool with a long vacuum brush. He was deterred by

innumerable activities in his immediate environment: a large fly that bit his haunch and made him snap irritably at the air, two birds that made trilling love in overhead leaves, a subtle alteration in the quality of the morning light which stirred inchoate levels of unease in the beast.

The strangeness of the pool – its non-drinking-place aspects – had a dazzling effect on the mind of the lion. It made him indecisive about striking.

Eventually, however, he made his charge – out of the wooded garden, up a grass slope to the pool's verge, then a leap across a tea table – glass shattering, sugar cubes ascending white in the clear air – and a last controlled embrace with Dr Brierwood, his vast paws over her breasts, the talons holding firm, his jaws clamping down on her neck to draw up spouts of blood.

Dr Brierwood had been mid-way through a paragraph in an article pointing out certain anomalies in a palaeontologist's analysis of recent finds at unexpected levels of the Olduvai Gorge in Kenya. When the intimidating, blood-freezing, total horror of the lion's roar swept over her like a wave of pure death from an opened crypt, she looked up and screamed. The lion dropped down out of the sky to seize her; one finger convulsively jabbed at the place where she had stopped reading; and she felt her bones being crushed with more force than she had ever conceived.

Terrified servants ran for help. Within an hour a cordon of men and weaponry had been set in a ring around the Brierwood estate. For miles in all directions traffic began to slow, to stop, to impact into jarring hooting masses. Thousands of sightseers came from all directions, hampering operations.

At the centre of command was the former professional game hunter, who was half mad from anxiety and gracelessly attempted to defer to anyone in uniform; but orders had been given that he alone was in charge, and as the crisis gained dimension, moving towards a critical moment when something would after all have to be done, he realised that a decision – on something, anything – would have to be taken. He pushed his way through people who shouted into each others' faces and went into a house which instantly transformed into a headquarters. Maps were pinned on walls, markers were moved on boards, grids were established: the military apparatus became dominant, and he realised that a military decision might be inevitable.

To think more clearly the game hunter locked himself in a lavatory and drank.

The lion left the remains of his kill beside the swimming pool and made his way into the woods to sleep. It was a fine autumn morning, holding the last of the summer heat in the bright dappled areas of light under the trees, and soothing and cool in the shade. Drowsiness overcame him and he stretched at his full length to digest Dr Brierwood.

The small, frightened, trigger-happy group which – under the dilatory leadership of the former professional game hunter – finally made its way to the swimming pool and found the dead woman, was incapacitated by the sight. Each registered an atrocity; each felt an impulse to shout, or rescript the terms of the find; inevitably there was a sickly anticipation of retribution and subsequent guilt.

In the judicial inquiry which was later held into the circumstances of the killing, it was considered extraordinary that the grounds of the Brierwood estate were not fully, immediately searched. No search was made; once Mrs Brierwood had been removed the servants were questioned on the movements of the lion, and when two agreed that he had been seen wandering along a stretch of country road north of the estate there was a surge in that direction. The testimony of the servants was instantly accepted: it had a satisfactory emotional content, and the searchers were in any case dazed at the fury that had broken out at the edge of the swimming pool.

On the bed of brown fallen leaves at the outer boundary of the Brierwood estate the lion slept peacefully all day; he moaned softly in his sleep like a dreaming cat, his immense male head on his paws.

By midnight the curious had moved away, and the searchers were bunched together indecisively in a small army camp. A violent electric storm had disrupted communications, and the various groups who were out on the roads and in the fields with torches and guns blundered through wet darkness, seeing nothing, knowing nothing, dead at heart. Damage to an underground telephone cable at 2 a.m. put several thousand receivers out of order in the area; and this contributed to an impression of profound devastation. There was a universal sense of depression, and sleepers were driven down into grey underworlds where faceless statues intoned meaningless arguments.

Shortly after dawn the lion left the woods, through which horizontal light splintered prismatically. He sniffed the wind and plodded south again, through landscaped terraces and sprawling ranch-style homesteads. Down pine-needle matted lanes and across dew-spotted lawns he padded with no more noise than soft rustlings and the snap of small twigs.

Soon the terrain changed, and taking the easiest way he was beguiled towards the exact heart of Johannesburg along the concrete swaths of the M1 motorway. It was a bright, crisp morning, the sky was enormous, blue to violet at the zenith, streaked with high tufts of cirrus, almost invisible. Ahead, the dark autumnal cone of ash and smoke remained to be burned off the city, dense, dirty, but giving a solid emphasis to the tower blocks: an appropriate frame.

He went on through the awakening suburbs, stinging smells of coffee and morning toast, the first cars coughing into life. And then the first cars began to pass him, early motorists staring with incredulity, astonishment, in tumults of weirdness at the apparition. They accelerated around the lion, so that there was an aspect of untampered serenity about his passage.

He walked into Johannesburg, quite alone after a time, since once word had reached the authorities of his route the motorway was closed and for the second time in twenty-four hours traffic choked to a standstill. The lion could hear distant clangour and uproar, meaningless. Soon he began to sniff irritably at acrid fumes and the like, but his entry remained inflexible, he took no off-ramps, and remained on the left of the road within the speed limit.

By mid-morning he was weary, and stopped, and looked around. This was the city; geometrical mountains advanced into themselves, making no horizon, netting together like stone fronds into an impassivity of yellow, grey, gold, black. He had no sense of distance or perspective and could not see into the new environment.

He roared at it.

His roar echoed back.

He stood at the edge of the motorway, where it swept over old buildings and streets and looked down past John Vorster Square to the Magistrates' Courts and the Stock Exchange, and beyond that to the Trust Bank and the Carlton Centre: the shapes impacted up against his sight.

Below him, when he looked again, men and women seethed, their clothing briskly making fresh patterns as they moved around, then settling or resettling into something else.

North and south the motorway spread dully; nothing whatsoever moved; a small wind beat miserably at pieces of brown newspaper gusted over the tar.

He roared at everything. And, tinnily, a kind of echo came back: but buzzing, inconsequential, intermittent. Far above a small black dot came down at him.

The helicopter, the former professional game hunter.

Suddenly the lion was deafened and shaken by fear: a metal thing jabbered at him only yards away, black grit tossed up by mad winds into his nose. Men with strained white faces spilled out into the motorway, pincered him.

And then, of course, the military solution.

PIETER-DIRK UYS
GOD WILL SEE YOU NOW

PIETER-DIRK UYS (b. 1945 in Cape Town), satirist and entertainer. 'God will See You Now' was first written as a sketch to fill his weekly column in *The Sunday Express*, Johannesburg, and was included in the augmented *Modern South African Stories* in 1980.

The television newsreader didn't dare allow his eternal poise to drop when he announced the end of the world. 'Our nuclear missile is on its way to the northern hemisphere, a spokesman for the Department of Defence said a few minutes ago. We have twenty-five minutes left. Massive international retaliation against South Africa has already taken place. Good night.'

His eyes stared out at me for a moment, professional in their glassiness. His purple tie and orange shirt harmonised loudly like an Arab and an Israeli round a braaivleis. But then, unfortunately, his face crumbled and he covered his damaged façade with shaking hands. His image was tactfully faded from the expensive screen.

Good night? The ghost image of the horror hopped around the empty media arena and played games with my eyes. The moment of terrified screen tension passed and a series of confused and easily recognisable pictures paraded gently across my vision: the SABC-TV logo, an overweight but pretending continuity lady in tears, the dramatic start of a Dogmor advert, labrador in full song, and then, like a cherry on the boil, the pre-recorded Weather Report filled the room with its cheerful news of tomorrow's sunshine and mild afternoon showers. Tomorrow? What tomorrow?

But then, as suddenly, this 'latest rumour' vanished and a running brooklet gurgled across the screen to the tinkles of a Schumann piano piece. Graceful, happy, the alternative to 'Do not adjust your sets.' That too dissolved, this time into a still unreal technicolour picture of Mary Magdalene washing the feet of Jesus, while sombre gravelly religious music whined in solitude, in collaboration, in vain. Why this picture, I thought, still wondering if the newscast hadn't been the end of a recent disaster movie.

Twenty-five minutes? I looked down at my watch. Twenty-two minutes! What had happened to the other precious three?

A scream of pure terror came filtering through the windows from somewhere down the street, followed by a woman sobbing and a car hooter blowing and a baby coughing. It was the first time I'd heard a baby cough. Was it sick? Did it matter? Twenty-two minutes to care and wonder and live.

Twenty-one and a half. But to do what in?

I looked around me and became aware that everything was there for tomorrow and the day after, for a future and a life. Twenty-one minutes.

My friends! My family! I rushed to the phone and started dialling Cape Town desperately to talk to my father. What would I say to him? 'Hello Pa, the world's ending in twenty minutes goodbye ...'

But then what if he hadn't heard the news? It had all happened so quickly. Yesterday we'd signed the Accord and the United Nations troops had walked around with vygies in their guns and eating kudu-biltong with a smile, and yet now hell was on the way. How can you explain the end of the world calmly and still say: 'Goodbye, I love you' in nineteen minutes?

Eighteen minutes. Suddenly I wanted to cry. I ran out of the little house into the front garden and stared into the street, hoping to find anyone to talk to, to argue with, with whom to die. The darkness hung over me like dirt.

Seventeen minutes. I slammed the door loudly, needing the sound, and walked up and down the small passage of my home, wringing my hands as if I had flu, feeling pain in every joint while staring pointlessly at all the little bits of expendable rubbish that made up my life. Photographs with empty smiles and never-blinking eyes, unaware of the terrible urgency around them. Books filled with enough words to hold together a civilisation but no answer to the inevitable demand: why?

Sixteen minutes. I sat at the typewriter and started banging out a necklace of letters that might help, but all that came out in fault-less spelling was: O God, if only we had time ...

There seemed to be no breath left in the room. I took deep gasps of the night air, trying not to imagine what terrors lay in store through death by fire. Roasting, singed, bubbling flesh, popping eyeballs, splintered bones.

The ordinary daily sound of the piercing laughter of a black domestic servant across the road sounded like the final air-raid siren. Laughter at a time like this? Maybe for once we were all in the same boat, both haughty madam and humble maid. Death was not for whites only and heaven only a homeland for those who were good and prayed and fed the poor, and few of 'us' were qualified.

I looked up with repentance and prayer in mind. A jetliner slowly flew across the faces of the angels on its way to safety. Where – Australia maybe? Would the captain greet his passengers like a cheerful door-to-door salesman and point out the silver missiles as they passed and watch the mushroom cloud smudge the horizon fifteen minutes away?

I closed the door to the world as the television changed gear. Mary Magdalene and the mournful Bach vanished and last night's Epilogue tinkled its way into the ending of my life. The good shepherd of a panicked flock smiled and tried to remember his lines. His message to the next fourteen minutes would be 'For God so loved the world ...' but I switched off in mid-sentence and refused to believe in his canned comfort.

I had put on the kettle somewhere between minutes thirteen and twelve so that I could still have a coffee in my Blue Train Souvenir mug. Out of habit, decaffeinated coffee. Better for the health. No sugar. No cookies. More habit. I had to smile and, with ten minutes left to pick up weight, I stirred in six spoons to make up for all the bitter discipline of the past year. But it was too hot to drink.

There were ants in the cookies. Nine minutes and then the horrible realisation that the ants would probably survive the holocaust while I wouldn't crossed my line of thoughts. Over my dead body, I snarled and gleefully murdered billions before I realised I only had eight-times-sixty left.

I became aware of the prettiest fig-tree in the backyard, standing proudly and bandy-legged in the shaft of light. I never remembered ever having seen it before.

The telephone screamed. I picked it up, not knowing whom to expect. A strangely calm voice asked for Mevrou Van Staden. I had to say: sorry, wrong number and then there were only six minutes left.

My last ever phonecall. Five minutes and I thought of a million terribly important things and couldn't remember one. I lay down and closed my eyes, but got up immediately, instinctively not wanting to be caught waiting for the end.

I pulled a record out of the shelf at random and put it on at full volume. It was Judy Garland singing: 'Somewhere over the rainbow ...' I had to laugh at her optimism.

Two minutes. I silenced Judy and sat listening for the sounds as the angels of death beat their wings on their way to me. But there was nothing that made this evening any different from any other. One minute.

'Oh no,' I shouted at no one in particular, 'it's not fair!' And as I thought 'Who'd feed the kitty?', I did hear the noise and everything went white and very hot.

ELLEKE BOEHMER
27 APRIL 1994

ELLEKE BOEHMER (b. 1961 in Durban, lives in the United Kingdom). Her '27 April 1994' first appeared in *Kunapipi*, Vol. 17, No. 2 of 1995, published in Aarhus, Denmark, and has since been reprinted in both *The Journal of Commonwealth Literature* and *The Journal of Southern African Studies*. Her third novel is *Bloodlines* (2000). She has also contributed to *The Penguin Book of Contemporary South African Short Stories* (1993).

Freeze-dried drama. About a week after it all happened I see the Benetton ad on the London Underground. A black hand takes a baton from a white hand. Both are fuzzed by motion. Across the bottom right-hand corner is the date, 27 April 1994. Green numbers on yellow, red, black, blue, enough colours to rival the new flag. The United Colours flag. A man leans up against the edge of the ad frowning. There are no trains and the air is smoky. I am very far away from where I was last week. I don't know how commuters read this image. This is not how it was at all.

On their plinths stand the stern worthies of another time, Victoria, Grey, Brown. Their eyes are without eyeballs. They are in another world. The sun shines, it is dry and clear, a perfect day. All along the pavement, and the marigold beds, and the public toilets, stand people evenly spaced. We face the City Hall, last used for symphony concerts. A man on a park bench plays 'Hark the Herald Angels Sing' on a mouth organ. It is a thin tune, not out of place. Could anything be out of place, now, on this day, in this recharged, turned-about country? We face forwards, waiting patiently as statues for history to happen. As it will. As it must. We trust this. We can trust this now. Now we can use this plural – we.

The camera crews make much of the statues, the Royal Hotel across the street, the buildings marked Colonial and the queue. They are in quest of stories, quaint oppositions. Tomorrow in the paper there will be the anecdote about the elderly man in Cape Town who came out to support Jan Smuts.

Someone from *The Los Angeles Sentinel* plucks me out of the queue for five minutes. They want a testimony, the tale of a conversion. Like, I am white, but have come this distance to vote. Or, my father supported apartheid, and here I stand, unarmed. What I say is, this is a dream come true. My friend says, it is all I ever wanted. Desmond Tutu is saying, it is like falling in love.

And truly it is all of these things, but it is also none of them. Because, just looking at the scene, the sunshine, the line of people, their bright T-shirts, the sunglasses brilliant with light, the ice-cream man going up and down with a white and blue cooler box calling 'ice-cream', outdoing the man going up and down inaudibly murmuring the name of a party: just looking at this scene there is in fact nothing to it, nothing much to it. There is no visible drama here. That was yesterday, the toyi-toying crowds, Cry Freedom. Not today. It has been a long road but the fact is – today we are simply voting. Making our x's in South Africa.

A man says, we are standing here like skittles, someone like Barend Strydom could easily come and pick us off, we are sitting ducks. This is of course true. However here is another strange plain truth. We make a queue more orderly and evenly spaced than at a bus stop in England. Somewhere, somehow, people have learned this patience.

Just in front are a mother and a son and her mother. The younger woman wears crisp new green cotton in honour of the day. The older woman keeps her arms folded. She tells me her grandchild is six months short of his eighteenth birthday, he cannot vote. I can, she says, without expression, without doubt.

As his mother turns away to buy cold Coke the boy slyly slips her ID out of her pocket. Then he asks, with consternation, where is your ID?

She spends minutes looking, patting herself, crying Ai, Ai. But when he hands it back to her, she simply hugs him. She doesn't laugh. The older woman looks on, silent and baleful.

The breeze brings a faint smell of the sea and the toilets. My friend has wandered off to read Henry Miller in the shade of the frangipani trees. I keep her place in the line. This is okay. People keep peeling off to go on short strolls, to stretch their legs, buy hot dogs. Two portly men in shiny shirts come up to talk. They have heard there is better voting up at the High School on the Bluff. You'll have less of a wait. No one takes much notice. We have been here for hours, for decades.

I have heard talk in the past of the banality of evil. In this place we have seen enough of what that might mean. You can swim here, but *you* cannot swim here: we may not swim together. That well-known grammar of illogicality.

Today another banality must be put on record, a banality that is beautiful, that is benign. There is this ordinariness of queueing, of passing the time, of dodging a neighbour's toppling ice-cream, and her apologising to the woman whose shoes are now stained.

Finally there is the little electric fan, a blue plastic propeller in a frail metal cage, that looks as if it might not last the day but is still working. This is to dry the invisible ink on our hands, the ink to prevent fraud. And there are whispered reports here at the end of the queue, before we file in, of voting chaos and ballot boxes gone missing. Someone has heard it on her transistor radio. But at the comical blue fan talk stops. The woman guarding the silver metal box says 'push', as in child-birth, because the wide slot is over-stuffed.

Above these ramshackle plywood booths, I try to get a glimpse of the stuccoed City Hall ceiling, which I remember as grand, imperial, but there is no time. My ice-cream stained hands stick to the pencil. The stickiness I think will transmit to the next person.

'Push,' the woman says again.

There are voters behind, voters ahead. It is so ordinary, it is so miraculous. A warm breeze blows in from the sea through the open door.

My friend steps out into the sun. Beer? she says. Down at the beach or up on the Bluff? We have a few hours before the creche closes for the day. I say, The beach.

The queue is garishly sun-lit, sedate and still very long. This is the beauty of the banal.

RUSTUM KOZAIN
THE TONGUE

RUSTUM KOZAIN (born in Paarl in 1966). 'The Tongue' first appeared in *New Contrast*, No. 101 of March 1998. He has also contributed to *The Southern African Review of Books*.

The orderly is patient. Shreds of nerves and fibre dangle from the wound at the foot of the tongue. So as not to chafe this wound unnecessarily, the orderly proceeds gently, wrapping into a sheet the long, pink body that lies stretched on the table.

With the reports about the tongue, there is much confusion in distinguishing witness from storyteller and, also, fact from memory, memory from delirium. Its wound was either self-inflicted or an accident – someone slashing about drunkenly with his sabre, mistaking the tongue for his own demon. It was either found, half-drowned on the banks of the river or bleeding in the cellars, or it found its own way to the command post, slapping the earth like a giant barbel as it made its way along the eastern trail. It was either from hereabouts – had moved among them unnoticed, as fellow – or it was a foreign citizen.

The slightest tautening of the sheet, so carefully wound, causes the tongue immense pain. In the struggle to lift the tongue into the waggon, the six soldiers assigned to the task unknowingly hurt it as their grip pulls the sheet tight. Or knowingly. It is so perhaps because their tenderness is commanded, not in their nature, the mask of compassion inadequate, not hiding the frank power that comes with such men.

The tongue cannot cry out. Or it does, but, wound in linen, its agony is muffled, like that of a cow moaning through a clamped mouth. As the men lift the thing into their arms, it squirms as the first pangs shoot through its length. Then, wildly, the tongue curls upright in the men's arms, the power intended for screams transmuted now into spasms. The men struggle to keep the thrashing muscle steady, for if it were to throw itself to the ground, the pain would surely kill it.

A few women, some children and a dog stop their business and playing and drift towards the perimeter formed by more soldiers standing firmly around the commotion in front of the dispensary that serves the post. The women and children gawk at the giant white cocoon curling and uncurling in the arms of soldiers. Already blood has started to seep through the linen, forming stains that will grow and dry, large and fixed as maps.

The women bend close to the guards and whisper, asking questions. The guards have no answers. Perhaps a child giggles into a palm. The dog wavers, drawn to the spectacular movements, the groans of the soldiers, their shuffling feet, yet turning frequently as if to run off. The low moans of the tongue hold its attention while some force simultaneously compels its head in another direction.

And then the tongue disappears under the canopy. Were the circumstances different, it would have felt itself ensconced in voluptuous bedding. Instead, it welcomes unfeeling, which washes over its public disgrace. The pain dulls a little, the moans fall to whimpers.

The dog leaves the moment the tongue slips from sight and the soldiers dust their hands and light their pipes. The crowd lingers, hoping answers will sprout from the rumour-bound murmurs among them.

Soon, a nerve-bitten officer hails his men. They mount. The waggoner sweeps his whip through the air and snaps it back, like a fisherman who casts a net only to jerk it back, deciding at the last moment to recast into the next spot of water. But the waggoner coaxes a loud crack from his whip with every jerk of the arm.

The ox-herd hies the oxen and, its cargo loaded, the team begins the three week journey to the capital. Long before the cacophony of creaking yoke and harness, the whip's crack, the clang of swinging utensils and the loud voices urging self and team on disappears westwards, the crowd drifts off, victim to apprehension.

RACHELLE GREEFF
TELL HIM IT IS NEVER TOO LATE

RACHELLE GREEFF (b. 1957 in Cape Town). Her 'Tell Him It is Never Too Late' is the first short story written by her in English. It was included in *The Torn Veil: Women's Short Stories from the Continent of Africa* (1998) and from there won her the Sanlam Literary Award for Short Fiction in 1999. She continues to publish stories in Afrikaans.

Maria dos Ramos lived with the absence like one would with a disability. She suppressed her sadness. Buried her rebelliousness. Accepted it only in moments of spiritual clarity and arranged her life around the vacuum.

When she and Mario, her husband, retired to the home for the aged, Maria did not have to unpack and sort the fragments of a child's life. There were no boxes labelled in dusty, old-fashioned letters. No gloomy oak wardrobe reeking of mothballs. No outdated posters on the walls. Not one memory of a child who had already exchanged this musty bedroom for the world outside.

Still, the contents of their house crowded their new home, even though there were only two of them. It was a small semi-detached in a row of similar little houses. 'It doesn't even have a back door,' complained Mario, who insisted on referring to it as a flat. Maria preferred the word 'cottage'.

When Maria opened the fridge in the tiny kitchen she could move neither in nor out of the room. The rubbish bin was squeezed under the sink. And the first time she baked her Christmas cake it rose right up against the top of the dinky oven.

From the first day of their marriage fifty-seven years ago Maria and Mario did the dishes together at night. He washed, she dried. (A man, he declared, had a firmer grip for cleaner dishes. And why would she challenge him? He was a difficult man, he didn't like queries or criticism. Besides, she owed him so much.)

And when they washed the dishes they talked, but the new kitchen was too tight.

They were shattered, and their disappointment was as palpable as a guest in their new home, crowding in even more. Mario said nothing. Maria groped for words. They did not know how to talk about matters of importance or intimacy other than with his hands in foam and water and hers under the willing softness of the dishcloth.

That night, as always, Mario held her tight. His arm around her as if he owned her. Often Maria had difficulty falling asleep like this; even in love Mario was impossible.

In the dark Mario shrivelled up. He was so small in his dream, he recalled sadly to Maria as they lay in bed next morning, that she had had to carry him about in her thimble.

Her nocturnal fantasy was different and she gladly relived it: their new little roof had slipped open. They rustled their feathers, flew out on easy wings, circled into the limitless, breathtaking expanse, higher and even higher, until the people on the ground were merely black dots. In the flame-blue firmament they were weightless.

'Like the pigeons,' Mario sighed, reminding her how they watched, always charmed, as their homing-pigeons dissolved, floating upward.

'They didn't disappear,' Maria reminded him. 'They merely went where we could not see. And they always returned.'

Shortly afterwards, Mario left her.

As she walked into the bedroom with his coffee one morning, which she did every morning before they lay down again together, he looked at her in surprise. Something was terribly wrong, he said. He tried to prop himself up on one elbow and grumbled: 'Christ Almighty, I still have to do the lawn edges which the boy didn't do, what ruddy bad timing.'

With a small sigh he fell back on the pillow as she stood, stupidly, with his black, bitter coffee in her hand. The perfect death, like switching off a light – but this she only thought later as her mind replayed the moment like a stuck record.

Somehow she was expecting more, something more impressive. But there was nothing. Only Mario who stared right past her and a stillness, a quietness which seemed to listen to her.

So that was that.

It was as if Mario slipped away through the back door of his own eyes. She closed his eyelids, not registering that a blind had been drawn within her. He looked as if he was only sleeping. He might wake up any second.

She sat down beside him, quietly taking leave of him, her husband, lover, friend, object of her anger, her love, her life. She lingered, but compared to the exploration of a lifetime, it was fleeting. She paused at every mole and freckle. At the slight white growth in his ears. The lobes. With age his ears had grown into the tender framework of wings. His stomach was flat even now, only at the sides it prolapsed gently. The calloused soles of his feet. He had walked many miles in the veld with these feet. With these toes ever neatly kept. This strong bridge.

Only when she slipped her wedding-band from his left hand, realising that the warmth of the ring was now fading fast and forever, did she collapse onto her knees beside the bed. Her tears were loud.

Eventually, at tea-time, she lifted the telephone to call the nursing sister in frail-care. Strange, she thought as she waited for her to pick up the ringing phone, the absence of protestation from Mario.

Hereafter Maria thought differently about death. It was not such an extraordinary event after all. It was merely another exit.

Now that she was one, rather than two, she had to leave the semi. The houses were only for married couples and she had to move to a room on the first floor of the main building.

The room was long enough for one single bed and armchair, wide enough for a wardrobe and a wastepaper-basket. From the window she saw the home's washing-line with floral dresses and large flesh-coloured knickers flapping shapelessly in the southeaster like spectres struggling to quit. Behind this was another wing, and even further away she knew, though she could not see, were the bottle green slopes of Kirstenbosch. This view she loved more than the front face of Table Mountain, the one on the postcards.

After only eighteen months of living in her space like a hamster, she was ordered to move downstairs into the room with Miss Watson. She was now considered not fit enough to be on her own, too far from the watchful eyes of the nursing staff. Miss Watson's room-mate, Miss Ivy, had died. Management paired people of similar religion, and the same sex of course, once they got to the double-room stage. This was the first obvious move onto the conveyor belt which ended abruptly at the double wooden door. This unadorned door at the back of the frail-care section was not a trademan's entrance nor a soiled linen exit.

Within the first hour Maria understood why Miss Ivy had to move on.

Miss Watson, formerly headmistress of a well-known girls' school in the city, was an insufferable, raucous old crow. She scolded everyone who crossed the threshold: nurses, matron, doctor, the woman who did their feet, even Father Thomas. She ranted about everybody's 'bad, bad manners just walking into my privacy'.

The verbal abuse Maria could tolerate. More unbearable was the flatulence slipping from Miss Watson in successions of timid, but rancid emissions. Internally, thought Maria (a handkerchief sprinkled with wintergreen oil held to her nose), Miss Watson was already rotting. Mario would not have put up with this. He would have summoned the matron, or the manager, or both. He would have demanded something be done at once about Miss Watson's slack anal sphincter.

She and Mario met in the autumn of 1938, when they used to stroll at dusk from the boarding house to the dappled clump of bluegums where he taught her magic. He could blow an angelic melody on a gum leaf.

At first they were accompanied by a mutual friend, Harvey Thomas, who is now her priest. Back then he was a student in theology. Though they remained friends Harvey withdrew from those intimate outings. When he realised Maria had chosen Mario, he took up the cloth. He projected his feelings to where he would never be rejected. Later he thanked Maria. She had married him off to love eternal.

But spiritually Maria and Harvey remained close. Maria was always fascinated by the angle, invisible to others, from which Harvey observed the world. In her prayers she acknowledged how blessed she was to have a companion of profound but simple divinity. One who was funny too. Their cups of tea were regularly followed by uproarious laughter. Maria never laughed that way with Mario.

But, strangely, Mario never seemed in the least jealous of this friendship.

Because he was the one she grew to love more than herself. She often wondered if love could be greater than this. People said maternal feeling was stronger than conjugal love. Later, after a few years of marriage, Maria began one of the first pre-schools in the Boland village where they lived at the time, and she often gazed intently at the mothers and their children. She endeavoured to weigh mother love, to compare it to her marital love.

For many years she hoped she would know one day when she had her own child. She visited doctor after doctor. Answering the same questions, in the same position under the flimsy blanket on the examination bed. Could they not please dim the terrible light? Was there not a nurse who could do this?

However, no reason could be found as to why she should not be impregnated. Her husband should come for a consultation.

But her husband refused. Bluntly replied it would be too humiliating.

Maria understood, and she did not blame him for not wanting to go. For him it would be just too much.

As a girl, later as Mario's young bride, she dreamt of hearing the pitter-patter of toddler feet, of a little flock chirping sweetly about her. She had such a long and weighty name, it had to be balanced by a large family. She wanted enough offspring for all eight chairs around her heirloom table – one which had dwarfed her parents and her, an only child – and always another little one would be on the way, pushing her belly against the side of the table with its happy dinner-time pandemonium.

But it never happened.

Only much later, already in the single room upstairs, her stomach swelled. It continued, very slowly, under Miss Watson's gassing. How much Mario had wanted to see her like this, she thought self-consciously; her thoughts were so utterly inappropriate. She was decades beyond child-bearing age. Maybe she'd never even been fertile.

She did not want to draw attention to her rounded stomach and insisted on still washing herself.

Eventually the pain, not the swelling, compelled her to talk to the nursing sister. Three days later she lay under a nil-per-mouth sign and half a day after that she spat bile into a small kidney-shaped bowl. Harvey, ah, it's him, she recognised through the haze. He is holding my hand.

After seven more days and nights, Maria knew the tumour had been removed and that chemotherapy and radiation could help. They could try. The prognosis could be positive. She could have a few years more.

But, politely, thank you, she refused the offer.

Well, in that case nine months. At the most.

And Maria was satisfied. Because the longer Mario was away,

the larger her loss grew. This was a growth which could not be cut out, and it hurt.

As long as the Almighty provided a large enough place for doing the dishes this time so that she and Mario could talk as in days gone by over two plates and two side-plates and two everything.

She had news for him too, a most wondrous announcement.

The surgeon who performed her operation was a young lad with a crown in the middle of his hair falling straight down his forehead. When he visited her the morning after the surgical procedure he had with him a small glass jar.

The neoplasm was hardly news to her, she'd been suspecting it for a long time. 'And I do not care to see it,' she thanked him as she motioned dismissively towards the jar still in his hand.

'No, no, Mrs dos Ramos,' suddenly the young physician's clear countenance glowed. He looked excited. 'It's not what you think.'

He held the jar high, like a schoolboy showing his trophy. 'Look what we found in your abdomen!'

Behind the glass floated something which at first looked like slime, then, maybe, like a snippet of cartilage. It was creamy, the colour of bone. It was minuscule. It was a calcified foetus.

Maria listened intently to the medical explanation. Not once did she interrupt him.

'At some stage you were impregnated extra-uterinely, Mrs dos Ramos. And what then happens is that the embryo attaches itself to the membranes outside the uterus, where it literally stays. Lithopedion, that's what we call it. It's a rare phenomenon, one usually only reads about it.'

When he left he wanted to take the jar with him to show his medical students.

Only then did Maria speak. 'No, it stays, it's mine.'

In the remaining months of her life in the frail-care section of the home for the aged, the glass jar with the tiny baby of stone stood next to her bed. The nurses and the cleaners busied themselves round it. They knew, primordially or practically, but they knew, all of them, about children. The life, the loss, the yearning.

Often Maria picked it up, nursing the jar against her bedjacket. She also lifted it from the formaldehyde. Closed her hand around the perfectly and minutely formed fingers, the ribs transparent like little fish bones, the large, amorphous head.

We do have a baby child, Mario, one which I carried inside me for all these years, hugged between you and me.

Then, one day, Maria asked the nurse to phone Father Thomas, who had not been to visit her that week. He must come for the last sacrament. And ask him, please, to also bring the water and the oil of the catechumen. Tell him it's never too late.

They pulled the curtain around her bed. Inside the cubicle of cream fabric there were only the two of them. She called him Harvey, as she always did when they were alone.

And he prepared his soulmate, Maria Teresa Jacquina dos Ramos, for her final death on earth. 'The rites, Maria, will now carry you as they carried me all these years. As they will when you are not here.'

For the second sacrament he lifted the small calcified child from the fluid and, cradling it in his hand, performed the rite of baptism. His voice faded to a whisper, 'Give this child new life in abundance.'

He kissed Maria on the lips, she closed her eyes.

She felt his tears on her eyelids, trickling down her temples, becoming one with her own. Far away she heard the rattling of food trolleys, the clanging of dishes. It must be twelve, time for lunch. Most were already seated. The others trailed behind, stiff, bent, shuffling. Tottering into the blessing like a phrase out of place.

Harvey took Maria's hand, his other hand still cupped her baby.

In her palm was delicate life. It was a dying bird faintly stirring, one last time, in remembered flight.

PETER RULE
ECLIPSE

PETER RULE'S work first appeared in *Forces' Favourites* (1987) while he was a student. A selection of his stories is included in *Unity in Flight*, the anthology from Botsotso Publishing, 2001. 'Eclipse' has not been published previously. He lives in Pietermaritzburg. He was born in Johannesburg in 1936.

It was late afternoon on Good Friday when he went to the mountains, the time between death and rising, as Father Hattingh would say, the dark time in the tomb. He had been nursing his wife for close on a week, often staying up through the night, snatching a few hours of sleep during the day when she was quiet. He seemed to have lost the darkness, the solace of night, the embrace of dreams. There was always the sun outside clattering off surfaces, or the hum of neon, the imprint of tungsten on his eyeballs. Noise and light. He had lost the season of sleep like a bird left behind by the migrations, just as his wife had lost her sanity with the small boy's disappearance.

He called it a disappearance. He had not seen the small boy since they had phoned her that afternoon while he was out at the bank. Unlike his wife, he regarded the small boy as simply absent, somewhat delayed, but bound to turn up. He would not hear of anything else. The boy had not come home from school to them as he usually did on Tuesdays. 'It's "granny Tuesday",' his wife had said the night before, as she always did. 'I'd better straighten out his bedroom.' But the boy was not there when he returned from the bank. There were no dirty socks on the bedroom floor or plastic Space Invaders on the garden path or ring of grime in the bath, and the boy's own plate and small set of cutlery lay untouched as they ate later. Of course there were phone calls, heels clicking in the passage, doors banging, a general uproar, the beginning of her insanity. But there was no sign of him. The marks that the boy left on him – the cursory kiss on the forehead, the tight grips of their evening wrestle on the rug, the slackening of his fingers as he fell asleep – the weekly infusions from the small boy's body and spirit that he relied on to keep him alive, were fading. The boy was absent; he had not come home, whatever else they said.

They talked about a funeral on Easter Saturday, but he said that he was going to the mountains. 'You have a turn with your mother,' he told his son and daughter-in-law, who both seemed to have shrunk in the small boy's absence, whose bodies had lost themselves in all the winter paraphernalia of coats and scarves and boots with the sudden cold front that blew in from the berg, whitening their knuckles and stretching their skin tightly over their bones. Their eyes were oddly withdrawn, their voices smaller to him. Neither of them seemed to know what to do with their hands and so they fussed over mother, drew up lists, arranged flowers, dialled numbers, held onto each other like rock climbers about to fall. He said the light was hurting his eyes. His head was beginning to tighten at the temples. He needed some air.

'Dad, we have to have you here. We must be together at the funeral, all of us, and especially you. You were closer to him than anyone else. He would want us to be together.'

They looked at him with their withdrawn gaze, old photographs taken into the winter sun, their words whining like insects around his ears as he packed. His wife's breathing was ragged. Her eyes had left home and roamed wildly about her face, not able to rest on anything for a moment.

'You handle her for a while. I'll be back,' he said, snapping his suitcase shut and pushing past them to the car. Reversing down the drive, he heard his daughter-in-law keening, a sound he had once heard at an African wake when one of his clerks was shot in a hijacking. Did none of them know how to be quiet?

He arrived at the camp at dusk. The sun set red through the trees, behind the little berg, the flagrant red of death. Exhausted, he dozed in his hut for an hour, his fitful dreams punctuated by the song of birds bedding in the trees and on the thatched roofs of the camp. When he awoke and stepped outside to stretch it was dark, not the attenuated peripheral darkness of the city but a dense mass of night. He looked up and halted; the great sky struck him still. A torrent, a funnel of stars whirling across from the east to the west. Standing there, he on this single tiny planet dwarfed by raging suns and the stupendous passages of time. His feet crunched remotely on the track as he walked into the veld, away from the camp lights. He understood then, unable to see his own hands and feet, how darkness and light had shaped him. How in all this darkness he was utterly dark, his thoughts of no consequence, too small to measure; he was only a pulse in an opaque body, a hidden muscle squeezing air.

It was not his bicycle. It could not be.

Front wheel buckled, bent back on itself, spokes snapped, pedal twisted, chain dangling.

He laid it down carefully at the back of the garage. The manufacturers mass produced them, selling thousands at the big chain stores. It was a popular colour. Even in Pietermaritzburg, there must have been hundreds of kids with the same bike.

Handles turned in one direction, the wheel in another, a deep scratch down along the paintwork of the cross bar. A kind of thin black rind between the gear lever and the brake cable that powdered beneath the fingertips. Scraping it with his fingernail, he realises it is dry blood.

Kids pranged their bicycles every day. A few bruises, at most a broken wrist. He had broken both arms as a kid in high school, his class mates tattooing his plaster of paris with arrowed hearts and initials and, on the underside, a cross-eyed Hitler with his abbreviated moustache and small vitriolic mouth. That was in the late thirties when war was in the air, the global warming of fascism. No, there was no relation between this mangled piece of scrap and the small boy's bike, and he holding the small boy on his bike when he first climbed on, and the boy's shoulder blades pressing into his chest, the left shoulder blade and then the right as he began to pedal, moving out of his arms and away.

He walked through the night. At last, it was dark and he felt the burden of the days lifting from his shoulders, the unloading of the packhorse, as he stretched his legs and began to breathe. The mountains were somewhere above him, beyond the foothills, silent and darker than the night itself. He had left his wife behind, her hand wringing, her constant weeping, her inclination to go into the small boy's bedroom and tidy up. 'For God's sake, Julienne, it can't get any tidier. The boy couldn't ask for more when he next comes.' Her maddening tendency to cling to him then and half strangle him with her arms around his neck and all sorts of nonsense about how he should release his grief. He had never seen anything like it in all their years of marriage. The lack of control annoyed him – it was unbecoming – but he had retained his equanimity. He had kept perfectly calm and attended to her. It was just that his head hurt. The lights were always on, and she seemed luminous with her wandering eyes and fiery cheeks, almost translucent, as if she were burning up some enormous reserve of energy within her that would leave her completely withered. He had to hold things together, in the absence of the boy who was their usual focus of attention and occupation, for the sake of them all.

Christ our light, Father Hattingh sang at the Easter service – five, six years before? – striking the orange flame in the mauve of morning. And the congregation: *Thanks be to God.* The small boy was there among the trousers and skirts, pressing back against him with the stillness of a child enchanted by fire. The small boy who dropped his candle when the wax burnt his fingers and cried inconsolably until they relit it. And the procession through the garden into the church, the smell of the waking earth and the rumbling of the sidesman's stomach. Then the sudden jubilant crashing and leaping of the marimbas as, at long last, after the abstinence of Lent, they could sing: *Glory to God in the highest.*

But not in these dark mountains. There was no God and no glory here, just the ache of unpractised muscles, the sour and inescapable smell of himself and the unrelenting earth pushing back at him, dragging at his ascent, mutely offering itself to him: *Sooner or later, you all fall down, and the mountain still stands.*

'Two o'clock, Michael. Time for you to fetch Anthony from school.'

'It's about time he got here under his own steam, don't you think? After all, he's nearly ten. And the school just down the road.'

'A bicycle? Do you think it's safe?'

'Don't mollycoddle him, Julienne. He has to learn to fend for himself in this world. He won't always have four adults attending to his every bowel movement.'

'Michael Cartwright!' She always used his full name when he annoyed her. 'The boy is only nine years old! You make it sound as if he's nineteen.'

'When I was nine I was already riding a bike. I used to hang onto the back of the trams in Joburg, on the side where the conductor couldn't see me. Hell, we used to have fun. These days kids get driven everywhere and have to make an appointment to visit their friends.'

'And I suppose it built your character to risk your neck.'

They bought him a red mountain bike with twelve gears. He fell off it twice and was soon skidding round the back of the house like Schumacher, and he the timekeeper with peaked cap and stop watch in hand on the back stoep. They also bought him a helmet and elbow pads, at Julienne's insistence. The boy rode to them every Tuesday from Bisley Park Primary, along King Edward Road, past the university entrance, across Durban Road, to the house in Scottsville. He would sit in the lounge and wait for him, timing him. *Now he's on that long flat stretch just before the shops,* he would think. *Here in five-and-a-half minutes if the lights are green.*

'But what if a car goes through a stop street or jumps a robot? It happens all the time, Michael.'

She had a habit of revisiting decisions that they had taken, seeking assurance.

'Your son agrees with me on this one, Julienne. We can't keep the boy in a bubble. I can get shot by robbers at the bank or hijacked at a stop street any day. Does that mean we should stop living?'

He remembered the endless monotony of the desert war and the sudden terror of whistling shells, the seething of the sand around them, the bursting of metal and flesh. Yes you were afraid. Everyone was afraid. You never get accustomed to fear, but you learn to manage it. You hold it back with a wisecrack, a shared cigarette. You face it down. All the things they taught you at school, on the playing fields, in the barracks, at the family hearth. Control yourself. You learn to put on a show, a brave face, the appearance of bravado. The small boy had disappeared. He had not made an appearance. And now his own appearance was falling under cover of darkness as he climbed slowly, stubbornly, without a face in the night.

Yes, we all fall down. A damn good thing too. How else is one supposed to escape from the mediocrity of days, the numbing decline. But not at ten years old. Not when the blood is still rising. Not when the mind is about to catch alight and shame all the darkness of the ages. Yes, we all fall down, but the small boy gets up taller each time he falls, harder each time he knocks his head. His scars are badges of burgeoning strength. Not the small boy because the small boy is immortal. He is always disappearing, getting dressed up in this or that outfit, my walking stick and mother's scarf and a pair of gumboots and the old school tie around his waist and he is a pirate, posing on the kitchen stool, about to raid the wide world, about to set upon life.

Of course it is foolish to try to climb a mountain in the dark. One might commit the route to memory but not every nuance, every toehold, every crevice and ledge. Or perhaps if one were younger with the elasticity of muscles that allows for a quick adjustment, a nimble revision of grip or tread when the foot slips, the rock slides, perhaps then one might climb the dark mountain until it is nothing but a footrest, the end of a path, and it is he who stands in the sky as the young do. Of course it is foolish to climb in the dark when one is old, but the refuge that darkness brings is a hiding place for an old fool. And when one falls it is in the dark where no one sees and there is no shame, just the sudden turning of the mountain to the sky, the shift of the deep earth and the pouring of the stars on an old fool's eyes where one lies among the stones. And then the sudden pain that comes like an afterthought, that seems to rise out of the ground and split the rock and strike, parting skin and bone, the force that stirs graves before dawn so that one might see the sky blurring in the dark and feel the raining of the stars on a pair of old eyes right through to the back of the skull.

He rises from where he has fallen in the aisle of the church and shrugs them off. He is not sure whether he cried out when he entered and saw it all, his stubborn old legs giving way beneath him. Surely such a strange sound could not have come from him, usually so gruff and reticent, and turned their heads? But he heard it echoing against the walls, the altar, the large wooden cross in the sanctuary. An odd blending of parade ground command and mullah's call to prayer and plain fright. Could the voice of one's childhood come calling back at such moments, the shock of the lungs' first strange breaths, the sight of body parts in the desert sands, long buried in silence?

They look at him, but he shrugs off their curiosity, their alarm, their commiseration. An old fool has the right to fall down when he outlives his only grandchild and sees the small box before the altar. An old fool has the right to stand up and walk slowly to the front and take the space they have left for him beside his wife and son and daughter-in-law. Coming from darkness, an old fool may wear his shame and nothing else, no matter what anyone thinks, when time has come to an end.

ROSE MOSS
A GEM SQUASH

ROSE MOSS (born in Johannesburg in 1937, emigrated to the United States in 1964, where she lives in Cambridge, Mass.). The winner of numerous awards for her short stories. 'A Gem Squash' was first published recently in *Agni*, Boston, and was included in *Ravan: Twenty-five Years* in 1997 in South Africa.

Thin as a weed, Derek brings his own food in a cooler and re-packs it into Ruth's refrigerator, taking note of what she eats with disapproval. Ruth disapproves too. Food should be shared and bring people together, not say that hers is not good enough for him.

He puts a bottle of Poland Springs on the section of counter she uses for chopping. No need to say anything now. She'll move it tomorrow if she needs the space.

'I notice you aren't changing filters as often as you should.'

'I've been told Cambridge water's clean.'

'You don't deny that it contains chlorine, and chlorine's carcinogenic.'

If it's not the Special Branch, it's cancer. Ruth feels tempted to say, 'This obsession is so American.'

Nothing would insult him more. He has been damning Americans for thirty years, and does it now, impatient to expose the iniquity, 'Did you hear the radio? About the police torturing that Haitian prisoner?'

Of course she heard. It rang through her whole body and is ringing still. As though this is the only story, crying out to heaven with a voice of blood.

Her parents talked about such stories, awed by the evil and the terror. 'Just like the Nazis.'

Of course Derek also hears the story ringing with others like it. The police committing torture. Shooting a black child. Or – this is, after all, America – a Mexican child. For the same wanton desire to kick and injure and be the beast on top they grew up with, 'Damn Americans.' Just like South Africa, the just object of his tireless fury.

One of these days, she fears, she'll lose it and tell him to grow up. For now she offers wine.

'Water. I've brought my own … My nutritionist says I must drink a gallon a day.'

One of these days, she'll say, how do you think Moses or Jesus would see this obsession with food?

She hands him one of her blue glasses and a bowl of nuts, gestures to the white chair by the window and pours wine for herself.

'Are you going for tests this visit?'

'No. They say I'm all clear.' But not clear of trouble. 'I've got to see the tax people about going bankrupt.' He sounds calm. Living on faith? For thirty years, running the Fund for Justice, he lived on little more and sent as much as he could to political prisoners.

'So you've decided to do it.' Last spring he was investing in a pyramid scheme he hoped would bring in enough to pay off his debts. He's a babe in the woods. Ruth wonders how, being so naïve, he ever managed to funnel all surreptitious money to its destinations. 'Can you keep your cabin?'

'I think so … I brought you some ashes. You must tell me where to put them.'

'Thanks for remembering my garden.'

'Well, when you heat with wood …'

'What time d'you see the tax people?'

'I've got to phone for an appointment.' Procrastinating? Maybe not. In need's tight grip he must count things like the cost of a long distance call. She used to.

He is leafing through her *Times*, stroking his beard and looking for iniquities.

'Another pillow?' Ruth asks, 'Okay. See you tomorrow. Take a shower if you like. You won't disturb me. Sleep late. It's your vacation you said.'

Throughout the night she hears his door swinging open and his steps to the bathroom. She sinks back into the dark water. A child is sick. No. She pulls to the surface. Her sons are grown and gone. She can sleep. Derek's in the bathroom and leaves without flushing. Fearing, perhaps, to wake her.

How does he survive the dark months in Maine, alone, sick?

Under the surface, water moving into an ocean. Blood, darkness, furling over each other. Time flowing away. Medium of this short life.

He is going to the bathroom again. Like an old, incontinent man. Her father in his last days. No one by his side. Still a stranger in the country he came to. Also a babe in the woods. His immigrant incompetence used to infuriate her. She hurt him with scorn. A man of suffering. Why are some born to pain? Why is a Jew a Jew? A black, black? Can anyone change it?

Shipwrecks where schools of fish with dark faces open and close their mouths. Shuffling, streaming. Something monstrous there, beyond the crusted submarine, two men twisting another, his head down to his toes, yes baas. She cannot help.

Harsh crows announce dawn. A jay gives its fierce call. They are not angry. Soon finches will come to her feeder.

Near Maseru, in a morning light, hoopoes courted on the yellow grass and frost flowed like threads of gold in the cream mountains. Heavy with the rocks someone hung on her back, she met the eyes of other people. Also heavy laden. They knew each other.

Ruth moves his Poland Springs bottle to make coffee. Last visit, he spread his stuff everywhere. Curbing irritation, she takes her cup to the patio where red geraniums parade like toy soldiers and begins to read. The Haitian prisoner is in critical condition, his intestines torn. The policemen were raping him with a toilet plunger. Her parents' lament, Just like … in Bosnia … She puts down the paper. Enough. Looks at the red geraniums. Okay. Okay.

She reads again. A real estate deal. A manoeuvre against the special prosecutor. Recipes using tomatoes. Okay.

Walking to her office she sees the bathroom door closed and through the open door of the guest room that Derek, messy as ever, has spread pills and packages on the table, papers on the floor.

Something is missing. His short-wave radio. Where is the grey box he used to bring like a child, excusing himself every few hours to go off and attend to it, urgent for every detail? Last night, he did not even listen to the news.

She stares at her neighbour's maples. As long as she's known Derek, he has listened to the news. Even after the Fund for Justice dissolved in a spate of quarrels. Even after The Election, he clung to the news as to the voice of the Lord. He must know, know now, know who. Something is happening to him.

Ruth's heart rises in hope. Now that apartheid's over and there's nothing he can do for South Africa, something more gentle could happen.

She sees signs. The gift of woodash. Resignation about going bankrupt. Calling this visit a vacation. A shred of joy here and there.

She opens her e-mail.

'Môre miesies.' Derek pokes his head in her office door, smiling.

He's always enjoyed a few words of Afrikaans with her. In the small office the minister at Harvard set aside for anti-apartheid work, where students met to plan a Sharpeville commemoration and denounce American imperialism in Vietnam, he said 'Voetsek' to her, smiling, the taste of home in his mouth. They were so homesick.

'I'll have coffee with you.'

'My nutritionist says, no coffee. But join me.' Becoming her host.

Ruth brews a fresh cup while he goes to the bathroom again, it's those eight glasses a day, sets a place, and decides not to wait for him.

She is not accustomed to this co-ordinating any more. He has never been married, though a few years ago he talked about it. An American active in anti-apartheid work and of independent means. Then he stopped talking about marriage.

The paragraph about goals calls for a change in the paragraph about design, and ...

Back in the kitchen, she finds him with the *Times* spread over the table, eating alternately from a large bowl of beige slurry and a black banana in his left hand.

'Americans don't know how to eat bananas. They should let them get black. That's when the starch breaks down into sugar and they get sweet.' He points to her bowl of fruit. 'You should never buy those yellow bananas. They're not ripe.'

Too much. To be preached at! About bananas! It may seem late to give up their friendship, though there was a long stretch of years when she despaired of South Africa and they hardly talked to each other, but if he carries on like this ... not that she'll close her house to him. He's too poor. But she won't open her heart as you do with a friend.

He stops eating to fold some of the paper away and she sits at the cleared space near his colony of bottles surrounding her salt and pepper. Camomile. Garlic. Willow bark. With sovereign properties she used to read about when she was writing her dissertation, '*Pearl*, a fourteenth century mystical jewel.'

He picks up the banana again, takes a small bite, a spoonful from the bowl, and chews. While he chews, she talks. 'Your garden giving enough for winter?'

'I couldn't plant much. With this fatigue ... But my neighbours said I must eat from their garden this year. People in Maine are so kind. When I had my operation, Mike looked at my woodpile and said, You can't carry those big logs. He brought his sons and they split my wood into small pieces I could carry. Can you imagine? And Anne brought over such a pie ... but with very little sugar.'

Perhaps through neighbours like these he will see what she started to see when she gave up *Pearl* and recognised that people around her in factories and offices were also doing what they must, working to support their children.

'They sound like good people.'

'Not like most damn Americans ...'

Ruth wants to defend Americans. Not ideological, they build their world bit by bit. They do not seem to need a story that makes sense of everything. They take explanations handy enough for making soap and packaging and improving market share. They wonder how to pollute less. All caught in the web of capitalism.

Derek sees nothing in capitalism but mine owners in houses with brilliant flower gardens and lawns green during a time of drought, while at the hostels for migrant workers men shovel mealiepap onto enamel plates and push them at humiliated slaves. Capitalism is a miner who sleeps on a concrete bunk, in a cell with five others, owning little more than one set of clothes. Capitalism makes migrant labourers everywhere, cuts husband from wife, mother from child.

Now, capitalism seems a neutral force to her. There is no other more merciful. There is need, work, capital, greed. Railing does not affect them. If anyone is ever to fly free, it will be by understanding what cannot be avoided, by something ingenious and not discovered yet, something you can't think of until you almost do it, like how to make steel fly lighter than air.

Derek has never worked for money. He's been a colonial Englishman all along, supercilious about the natives. In this case, Americans.

'Is Mike the man who arranged for you to get some preaching?'

His smile dims. 'He's got connections. Knows everybody.' Wistful. His own network gone. What does he do all day in Maine? Collect iniquities?

If he's going to rant on about Americans, they'd better not talk too much. 'I'm working today, but if there's something you want … You can use this phone to call the tax people.'

'Have you got a telephone book?'

'In my office.'

He follows her, she hands him the directory and he lingers, looking at her books. Not only about the moral universe where apartheid is the key pattern of evil, repeating in her own life what happened to her grandparents. And happens still. To the Haitian prisoner.

She will never lay down this weight, but now the books in her office are about computers and genetics. When she learned technical writing, she started to see the world a new way, not only as the moral universe of suffering and courage. She saw an alphabet of utmost simplicity expressing utmost subtlety, and another code, an alphabet for writing the words that make life.

The great work of her time is a human endeavour to master these alphabets. She began to be glad she was in America, near the heart of this work.

When she read about what was driving technology, she glimpsed yet another power to master. Communism and capitalism changed under her eyes from a choice of the poor against the rich, the suffering against the callous, into a choice of techniques. Both try to map and navigate oceans of desire and need. The code of that turbulence is still hidden, not yet like the digital code and the genetic code. She thinks, if I had another lifetime, that's what I'd like to learn.

For this lifetime, she believes, the moral choice remains, but wise choice must acknowledge the nature of things.

'Can I borrow this?' He holds out a memoir by someone from Kroonstad.

'Take it. I don't know when I'm ever going to read it.' He's stuck. Wilfully blind. Pitiful.

No. No! She is blind. His choice has also been the great work of their time. Justice is the great work of every time.

She hears him going to the bathroom again, probably reading and unaware of anyone else.

In the middle of the morning, she wanders back to the kitchen for a last cup of coffee.

'Do you want this article?' About sweatshops. 'I want to cut it out.'

'Go ahead,' ashamed of the rancid gesture that makes her rich, him poor.

The end of apartheid has stranded him here in America, where an encompassing ideology seems strange to the temper of people. Two sermons a week. Two hundred dollars. For thirty years he gave every day to the cause, hundreds of prisoners depended on his work, and now it is gone.

At the Election, he went back. No longer a political refugee, he gloated, 'I've got a passport for the first time in my life!' It must have been a complex visit for Derek, fulfilling a lifetime of longing and showing him, however that happened, that he could not go back. He did not talk of that decision. The main story he told her was about a man he sat next to on the plane from Cape Town to Durban.

'Aren't you Derek Wardell?'

'How d'you know?'

'I know you, man. I got your dossier. I'm with the political cops since 1965. I know you better than you know your own hand. No hard feelings, hey.'

'You still with them?'

'Retired. Just in time. Jirre! I never thought we'd meet this way.'

Ruth also wondered at the enigmatic coincidence.

'What a meeting, Derek! What did you do when he told you?'

'There we were, sitting next to each other. We had a beer. He talked about how the times are upside down, and kept saying, "It's like the Bible says." He wanted me to tell him, as a minister, if it was the end of the world.'

'The end of his world, for sure. "I will cast the mighty aside in the conceit of their hearts and will fill the hungry with good things." Isn't that how it goes? You think he meant that? The prisoner would be president?'

'Those guys knew what was going on. They knew.'

'What was it like, talking to him?'

'Like meeting the Angel of Death and seeing liver spots on his hands. Twisted, but still human. Bald, a tremor in his right hand. He was my Angel of Death. He had my whole life in his records.'

'Did you hate him?'

'Not there in the plane.'

For Derek too, the Election must have been the end of his world, turning everything in his future upside down.

If God exists at all, it is as One Who Is invisible, present, everywhere hidden.

He has been leafing through the magazines by the white chair, making heaps of pieces he wants to tear out.

She faces him as she eases her shoulders, rolling them forward and back, 'I need a break. Let's go to the farmstand and get fresh corn. It's almost a sin not to eat it in August. Butter-and-sugar.'

'American corn is so sweet.'

Is that good or damned? 'As a kid, I used to long for mealie season,' she confides. 'Mealies, and the first rain.'

'God, yes, the first rain.'

Her mother believed the children must wait for the first rain before it was safe to go swimming. After that blissful downpour streaming from hair to face they could go to the municipal swimming pool. Then, endless under the sky, blue and receding and near and blue, blue, the water, the sky, distant, pure, forever, as she floated and stared, the sun dazzling, the water tender, silent and happy, time without history, without smirch, without fear, simply being, being alive.

She has never seen such blue outside South Africa.

The fanatic for what should be, he exclaims, 'Children long with such passion. Can you imagine what the world would be like if we longed like that for justice?'

After longing for swimming, the children longed for mealies. The taste of butter and kernels connected them to Sunday afternoon drives to Hartebeespoort Dam and Parys and huge skies where cumulus clouds with heavy bellies pressed on the lower layer of air.

In dry Johannesburg their mother sighed for misty fields by a river, mushrooms in the woods, northern berries, cucumbers, the white nights of summer and fresh snow where she would beat herself with birch branches after bathing in steam.

At weddings, there'd be a table where *landsleit* gathered. The children went off to find others impatient with their parents' conversation.

He is willing to risk one ear of corn. She pulls the husks, leaving one layer over the seeds for flavour.

'Remember loquats?'

'We're like my parents with their *landsleit.*'

'What's *landsleit*?'

When she was growing up, at the dinner table in Yeoville, stories thickened around words like Hitler. At Purim her mother baked poppyseed *hammantaschen*, and said Haman also wanted to exterminate the Jews. When Ambrose, the gardener, asked for a note with permission to come home after the curfew, her father told her Jews used to need permission to travel. Cossacks would tear up Jews' papers for spite and spit on parents in front of their children. The pogroms of 1905.

With Derek here today, she is living in the pattern of her parents, half in Vilna, half in Johannesburg; half in South Africa, half in New England. She and Derek are creatures of the same species, amphibians under water with their nostrils in the air. Even if he becomes too impossible for friendship, they are closer than *landsleit*, relatives who last with each other when much else falls away.

Living in the North, she sees why people from the South feel misunderstood. She finds her friends among Americans who live now out of the places they were born to, gay men from Texas, journalists who have had their minds turned on Indian reservations. Her other friends are foreigners, Czechs who could not go home after 68, Chinese born in Hong Kong. She finds herself among people who have been colonised, who have travelled labyrinths, who know daily that they must live in a world where they will be misunderstood.

It seems more difficult to make friends among blacks here than under apartheid. Segregation happens here without the guns and laws of South Africa, or Eichmann's trains. Something makes American apartheid stronger. Capitalism?

Perhaps America really does reproduce apartheid, as Derek says, and she is blind here, like so many whites in South Africa. Wilfully blind. Perhaps she is too comfortable now. She has heard about the Haitian prisoner and read about him, but her day is full of pleasure. If she can live with such suffering and be calm after all, isn't she damned?

How can anyone live in this world where there is so much suffering and where you can still go out on a sunny day to buy butter-and-sugar corn and take it home to eat with ... a friend?

She has disappointed Derek. When they drove out for corn, he wanted a detour to buy a German beer he cannot find in Maine. Like the ascetic missionaries she knew near Maseru, he allows himself one daily indulgence, a beer, and gives the choosing and enjoying of it the attention of a gourmet. Of course it is not American and he drinks it warm. She feels this sensuality important and human. He is not a cold disapprover of other people's pleasures, not part of the bitter Christianity they used to see every Sabbath when every city fell silent before a frowning God. 'There's a liquor store round the corner.'

They find his favourite pilsener, but he wants to repeat an hour of companionable shopping in a discount store they visited last spring.

'Not today, Derek. I've got to work.'

'Isn't it only five minutes?'

'It is five miles. Twenty minutes at least.' Closing a gate that keeps him outside her work and place in this world. The day's abundance shrinks behind the gate. She is shut in a garden with brilliant flowers and a high wall hides the open world.

'Did you see the editorial about immigrants?'

'I did.'

'Damn Americans.'

'Derek, there's something funny about the way you see things. Millions of people wish they could be Americans. They risk their lives to come.'

'Don't you remember how they used the same argument against us in South Africa?'

'But here it's not like Africa, from greater misery.' Made by capitalists and colonial powers. She knows his script. 'People come from Europe and Asia, with talent and education. So many want to come to America. How can you think you know better than everyone else?' Deepening the personal edge.

'Because I do know better.'

'Oh then, well, of course, I have to agree.'

He leaves the room, his back straight, catching her eye. An Englishman does not bow to injury.

Dammit, why couldn't I hold my tongue? How could I talk to him like that? Such an old friend. Going through such a hard time?

When he comes back to the room, proud and smiling, he says, 'It's good we could make a joke.'

'Ag, man.' But she's drawn blood, she fears. What a mess. No one else shares all these years. They were together when Verwoerd was assassinated, when the Portuguese gave up, when Biko was killed. During the treason trials they called each other. He was the prophet who told her, 'De Klerk is a man of faith and knows what he is called to do.'

She is still repenting when he says, 'I'm off to the Divinity School to buy books and meet Clive.'

'Old haunts and old friends, hey? See you later, then.' Wanting to sound warm, not crotchety like before.

He bears his straight body with ease now and could stroll out to a game of cricket wearing that cotton shirt and the quiet decorum of men who know themselves masters.

No wonder America remains shocking to him. People must take as privileged what he takes as normal. Few can see the privation that is working in him like a yeast, making him tolerant and forgiving.

Sometimes, she thinks, God, if there is a God, will do anything to get a person straight, even if it means breaking every limb in his body.

Whatever God is up to, if there is a God, it remains inscrutable and she sets to finishing the proposal. The work engrosses her like pleasure and she stops only when the screen blurs. She stands and looks out at her neighbour's red maples, the flux of thought still moving muscles under her mind, until objects regain clear outlines.

When Derek comes in, she is still working, 'I'll just be a minute,' and hurries to finish.

After the save command, she finds him reading the weekend magazine. 'Are you finished with this?' The piece on deaf Mexicans lured to New York and enslaved to sell trinkets on subway stations. Another iniquity.

'Have it.' After his life of sacrifice, this stinting poverty. South Africa and her parents' stories have taught her not to believe that wealth equals merit. Americans say, 'You deserve ...' this house, the chocolate. Not seeing that if all should get their just deserts, none would escape whipping. Derek believes that his world does not judge as God judges. She believes that, if God exists, the One Who Is is working quietly through a code more simple and abundant than anything Americans know. Or anyone knows. The one probable sign to the mind is paradoxes. And to the heart, love.

'Clive gave me a wonderful thing.' He has put it on the kitchen counter for her to admire. 'A gem squash.' A green ball no bigger than the globe an infant Jesus holds in one hand.

'Where on earth did he find a gem squash in America?'

'In his own garden. He smuggled in seeds.'

Her mother also loved gem squash, and did not hanker to be in another place when she had it on her plate. 'What a treasure for you. He's lucky they don't train dogs to sniff the seeds in airports.'

'It's not cocaine.'

'If it was, you'd be able to buy it here.' Capitalism at work.

'He gave me two. I'm saving one, but we should share one.'

She resists the urge to refuse, to say that gem squash means nothing to her and so much to him he should enjoy it all himself. It is important to share, to give companionship as she takes the holy food. Especially today, when she has cut him and he is forgiving her. Choosing reconciliation, like a South African.

She contemplates the orb enclosing the world he longs for. His pearl. A dark sphere without lustre.

'How should we cook it?'

As they eat it, steamed, with butter and salt and pepper, the way her mother loved it, Derek tells her about his first year in the ministry.

'I was much younger than most ministers, you know. There was a good priest in Kingwilliamstown, and he told me to go to university first, but I was so determined ... Then there was a crisis, and they needed someone in the circuit near Thaba 'Nchu, so they asked if I'd go. They gave me a collar and permission to distribute the Eucharist. It wasn't really allowed for someone who wasn't ordained yet, but they did it.

'That was the first time I went into a township. There were two churches of course. A big stone one, almost empty. Six people came to the Eucharist. And another church in the township. So I went there. What a shock!'

He must have seen something like the crowded shacks of corrugated iron she used to see. Smoke. A chicken scavenging. Children with their fists in their mouths. Skeletons with swollen bellies.

Still in primary school, she watched two piccanins searching rubbish bins in the street outside, taking out half-eaten mealie cobs. Outside the Coliseum with its starry sky and artificial scraps of cloud, she saw piccanins dancing for money. One played a penny whistle. They wore men's jackets gaping over bodies as bony as prisoners' in the newsreels of concentration camps she had just seen.

She never got used to it, and then there was more. More. Always more suffering. At a settlement of tents on the banks of a dried out river, a child playing in a puddle next to the dirt road, the smell of urine, someone saying, 'They have to drink that, you know.' The next day at the mission hospital, her first corpse, a child dead of gastro-enteritis.

Derek continues, indignant as though he is still in that circuit, 'And the church itself! Just a room of corrugated iron. The roof was rusting away. The rain was coming through. The floor was mud. People kneeled on that floor to pray. Their faith, their faith ...' His voice full of awe. Tender as a man in love.

That's what keeps him going. All the lonely years, this gold has been shining in him like a river of God. That's why he hates America. So much outward piety, so little of what he has seen as faith, hope, compassion.

'That wasn't all. After the service, a Coloured parishioner came to me. He said, "I know how little money they give you young ministers. I've been giving five pounds a month to the one who was here before you, and I want you to take five pounds from me now." So there I was, a white man, taking charity from a Coloured. That was a shock, too.'

He relishes it, sweet as the gem squash luscious with butter. Nourishing him with something better than justice.

'The third thing ... It's not everyone who has the chance to know when they open a dossier on you, but that's what happened to me. I preached about the township, and one of my six white parishioners came to me, worried. He was my age, working for the police and expecting to join the Special Branch. It was his circuit too. He wanted to warn me. If I went on preaching like that, I'd get into trouble.

'I had the whole country there. Everything clear in that one circuit.'

That country she knows as hers. Where she saw people at prayer and felt awed at their dignity. In a church in Ladysmith where her nanny had gone to die, women wearing blankets kneeled on bare mud, concentrating and still. Children of God. Their posture alone affirmed trust. Not railing about justice, they set aside the judgment of this world where victory goes to the bullies. They held such peace in their bodies that, looking at them, she saw why artists invented haloes to suggest that luminous quality. They could not know why they must live as the wretched of the earth, as Jews do not know why they are chosen and persecuted. Not for what they have done, the German notion, and not because they deserved it, the simple American idea, but by an inscrutable choice or by accident. If there is no God, working in the world in a subtle code, if it is all an accident and does not mean anything, there is no justice and no hope. But, even with no God, nothing can take from her mind's eye the dignity of those women praying. Her faith in their faith.

Derek's story brings back that morning when the veld was white with frost on the brittle grass and wind knifed through the church. Her hands burned with cold, her feet were heavy with pain. She did not know how long she would be able to sit on the chair one of the women had brought for her because she was white and must not kneel on the mud.

She and Derek came from the same place, grew from the same womb, were formed in the same code, like brother and sister.

In all these years far from her first home, he has been there, but she did not know why.

'Thanks for sharing the gem squash with me. It was great.' The American word irks her like a lie, uneasy in the company of her gratitude that Derek has shown her where she is rooted and what she believes.

She wishes she had led his life. Dedicated to serving these poor. With this ending?

She has been like an American looking at his life and seeing that he is poor. But the God of the poor who calls him is, after all, the one who fed Elijah, renewing the meal at the bottom of the widow's barrel one handful at a time, and the oil drop by drop, until the end of the drought. Derek has enough.

Does his preaching reach to the heart like this in Maine? Another country where people live one handful at a time, and understand that money does not reveal merit.

'Tell me about your congregations.'

'I'm afraid I may lose one of them.'

'How come?'

'I went to see the Berrigans and talked with them about their protest at the nuclear submarine. I preached about the millions, billions of dollars spent on military projects like that without need, when there are so many people who do need. It offended people in the congregation. Not the comfortable, but the working class. I had to preach. It was just like my sermon about the township.'

She cannot hold her tongue. She wants to protect him. She wants to scold him. She wants to save him from the faith at the core of his life, the faith she has just felt she shares.

'Oh Derek, why do you have to be a prophet? You're a Jeremiah. They'll stone you.'

She wants to stone him herself.

SHAUN LEVIN
THE GOOD OUTSIDE

SHAUN LEVIN (born in Port Elizabeth in 1963, has lived in Israel, is currently settled in the United Kingdom, where he teaches creative writing). There he has published several pieces in *Stand* and *The Gay Times Book of Short Stories*, in Canada in *Queer View Mirror* and also in anthologies in the United States. 'The Good Outside' marks his debut publication in South Africa and has not previously appeared.

Now that all the others have said their goodbyes and gone home for the night, Peter and Davide sit alone in the garden. Eventually they'll begin to talk about Jonathan. Davide will start, Peter will be reluctant. He'd rather sit quietly for a while and then head off to bed. To the sofa, in fact. He hasn't had much sleep since leaving Italy and it's been a densely hot day in the garden. But now with everyone gone until tomorrow, the air seems fresher. Twilight takes the edge off the lingering heat.

Cushions and mattresses are scattered across the lawn and there's a low coffee table under the apple tree. Someone brought it out for those sitting in the shade by the fish pond. This was Jonathan's garden. He had tomatoes and zucchini growing along one wall, gooseberries along the back, and honeysuckle up the other side and around the small patio where Davide and Peter are sitting. Their table is covered with the mugs, glasses and plates used during the day. Everything needs to be cleared away and tidied before people come back in the morning.

The second day of the shiva has been long and drawn-out. Peter spent most of the day, like the day before, gathering up as much news as he could. He's been in Italy for ten years. He left South Africa as soon as he thought of himself as a painter, and being an abstract artist he believed he carried his inspiration inside him. He left South Africa to get away. And from what? From death and from politics. At first he'd had a lover, Gianni, and then it was just himself in the small house he'd bought with his mother's money.

Davide is dead Jonathan's boyfriend. Peter, the painter, watched Davide from the moment he arrived at their house, hoping to catch memories of Jonathan in his gestures. He watched him greet people with a pained, grateful smile, like in-laws accepting gifts for the bride and groom. He watched Davide cry, and saw him being comforted by friends and by Jonathan's mother. It was only when Davide was quiet, alone, physically present but his mind elsewhere. It was when he was sitting like that on a cast iron chair, legs folded, elbows on the arm-rests, that Peter saw Jonathan in him.

Davide had caught Peter staring at him during the day. He could tell Peter knew he was keeping something from him. He felt pity for Peter, and saw how he longed to be told that he meant so much to Jonathan. But Davide couldn't lie to him. He didn't have to; Peter wasn't his friend. He watched Peter trying to get people to talk to him. He noticed how he listened. Jonathan had told him that, if anything, Peter was a good listener. But then someone would come up to Davide and embrace him, sit by his side for a while, talk, and then go off to join one of the groups in the garden.

The larger group, mainly friends of Jonathan's, had spent the day at the edge of the garden under the apple tree. Peter sat with them most of the time. They'd all been to school together. Every so often a shriek of muffled giggle would come from the group, and if Davide turned to look, someone would point into the apple tree by way of an explanation and an apology. Another group had stayed nearer the round table on the patio, near Davide, close to the food.

Peter and Davide are sitting at that table in silence, each slowly moving away from being part of a gardenful of people to being alone together, something that hasn't happened very often over the past, what's it, twelve years? As far as Peter remembers he's never been alone with Davide, Jonathan's boyfriend. He wants to say: You two built a lovely home here. But Davide speaks first.

'Our Jonathan,' he says.

Peter imagines Davide is about to tell him that Jonathan left him something of great significance.

'What a fucking slut,' Davide says, throwing his head back and laughing out loud.

'Slut?' Peter says, telling himself not to smile.

'All day I've felt secrets raising their heads. Like rats.'

'What secrets?' Peter says.

'Was it just me?' Davide says. 'Or did he keep secrets from everyone?'

'Not from me he didn't,' Peter says. 'He never kept secrets from me.'

Peter has known Jonathan since nursery school. Since they were little boys at the Summerstrand Hebrew Nursery School. Since they were two bricks and a piss-pot high. They'd go snake-hunting in the veld behind the Greek grocers and comb the dunes near Peter's house for bits of broken clay. They went to the same junior school, and in high school Peter was head boy and Jonathan deputy head. They were a good team. They could be kids again, playing sheriff. They told each other everything.

'So you knew all about this, did you?' Davide says.

'About what?' Peter says.

'All these strange little affairs he was having.'

There was that period of five years when they went off to university: Jonathan to become a doctor; Peter to study art. They'd written lively, graphic letters to each other and spent three of the five summers together in PE. The other two summers they'd travelled abroad: Jonathan to Europe; Peter to his mother's family in Israel.

'It must have been during those trips that the secrets began,' Davide says.

'What kind of secrets?' Peter says. 'He told me everything. He always told me everything when he got back.'

'So you did know, then,' Davide says.

Peter could have given examples, and he was tempted to. But Jonathan had made him swear never to tell anyone. Not about the sex he'd had with two eighty-year-old men in Paris. In a café near the Eiffel Tower he'd got chatting to a beautiful Moroccan who sold sex to men in old-age homes. They were so old, he told Peter, they smelt like his grandfather. Their arseholes were as loose as saloon doors. And not about the arrest on the other trip, this time to London, where he'd been caught in the toilets on Leicester Square.

Dead Jonathan had told Peter all this and more in elaborate detail. They'd be lying on his bed, his bags still unpacked, the duty-free bottle of whisky almost empty, screeching and waggling their legs in the air like upturned cockroaches. Jonathan went to fetch more ice from the kitchen and on his way back stood over the bed and said: Don't you dare tell anyone about this. Ever. And Peter said: I swear. Cross my heart. And when, some years later they'd laughed again about these incidents, just before Peter went off to Italy, Davide already in the picture, Jonathan made Peter swear never to tell a soul.

'I don't know anything you don't know,' Peter says.

'Then why are you so silent?' Davide says.

'Am I?'

That wasn't all Peter knew about Jonathan. He knew about the bad patch. Jonathan had found out about Davide's affair and had played on his Catholic guilt. Davide believed adultery was a sin and that hell was a real place. And in all their years together, Jonathan had never told Davide about his own infidelities. He used Davide's one slip to keep the accusing finger pointed away from him. Jonathan wrote to Peter in Italy about cruising on Donkin Hill and landing up in strangers' beds. Just two years ago there'd been that black guy, the ANC guy, who'd taken Jonathan to his room in the Orthodox church where his mother worked. Jonathan said they were thinking of coming to Europe after the elections.

'I hate not knowing,' Davide says. 'I hate that he's dead and left me with all these stories to find out.'

'Shouldn't we go inside?' Peter says. 'Let's take this stuff into the kitchen.'

In all the twelve years Davide had been Jonathan's boyfriend, he hadn't heard him say one good word about Peter. Davide had been dreading this evening. He hadn't expected Peter to come to the funeral. Then he'd hoped Peter would be delayed in Italy, or have an exhibition he couldn't get away from. He'd met Peter a few times before he left South Africa. But he'd heard Jonathan's stories. Peter would take Jonathan drinking and Jonathan would drink more than he'd intended to. He'd land up sharing things with Peter he'd meant to keep to himself. But no one knew him like Peter did and there was no one else to confide in. He told Davide, proudly at first, and then as if he was burdened by it, that his relationship with Peter had no room for small talk.

'It's all so heavy,' Jonathan had said. 'Heavy and abstract. Even with all the alcohol.'

Davide and Jonathan were relieved when Peter finally left for Italy. Jonathan would write to him occasionally, always in response to one of Peter's long, ruminative letters, and Davide looked forward to Jonathan confiding in him. He was, after all, a writer, and writers knew how to listen, too.

'There couldn't have been any big secrets, could there?' Davide says. 'I mean, how many secrets can a man have? You'd think that after twelve years I'd know all of them.'

'The in-between secrets are the tricky ones,' says Peter. 'The little indiscretions people think they've already shared with lovers, but somehow forget to mention. The tiny things that slip peoples' minds because they're there all the time. It's like you don't tell your lover about the mole on your back. He knows it's there.'

'He loved telling me secrets,' Davide says.

'He did love telling secrets,' Peter says.

They are discussing him in the past tense. So soon. Too soon. Fighting over him like vultures. Tearing him apart as if that could keep him alive. Like Bacchus.

'What a day,' Davide says.

'And there's more tomorrow,' Peter says.

Davide had insisted the shiva be held at their house. And because it was summer, almost Christmas, and they had no air-conditioning, they'd had the shiva in the small, clean, well-kept garden. Jonathan's garden. Things hadn't gone smoothly. Jonathan's father had walked out that morning.

'Solly wasn't happy,' Peter says.

'"I will not have this turned into a garden party,"' Davide says, sitting upright in his chair, hands on hips. '"This place looks like something out of Alice in fucking Wonderland."'

'Jonathan would have loved that,' says Peter.

Solly's wife, Mina, had tried to persuade him to stay, but he wouldn't listen. She'd followed him through the house to the front door. She'd stopped there and watched him march down the road to get the car. She'd have stayed if he hadn't driven up to the front door and said: Are you coming? She'd turned to Davide who was standing behind her in the kitchen, embarrassed, putting cheese and crackers onto a tray.

'I hope they come back tomorrow,' Davide says.

'Maybe you should give them a ring,' Peter says. 'I still remember their number off by heart.'

'All the numbers have changed since you left,' Davide says.

The sky is strips of purple and navy blue and dark pink clouds. Peter notices how deep the colours are in the garden. Oranges and purples and whites, bold against the chrysanthemum leaves. The sweet-pea blossoms are beginning to brown, and the tomatoes are too ripe, the zucchini too heavy. Jonathan was going to pick and cook them the weekend they took him to hospital to die.

'Everything's changed since I left,' Peter says. 'Nothing's the same.'

'We've got democracy now,' Davide says. 'We're the happy rainbow nation.'

Peter's hungry and he wants Davide to offer him food. The mourners had all brought their offerings, as was customary, and there were, as far as Peter could remember, at least two untouched dishes in the kitchen. One of them was Jonathan's Aunt Gertie's famous cheese sticks.

'Part of you does get taken away when they die,' Davide says. 'No matter how much you expect it.'

Peter is not going to share anything with Davide. He cannot say to him: You two were so close. I cannot imagine how you'll survive. I've been thinking about Gianni for five years. He has never gone away.

'I think I'll give his clothes to charity,' Davide says.

'What?'

'I don't want to see people I know wearing his clothes.'

Again, Davide is sitting in his chair like Jonathan. He looks like a writer, surveying the garden, detached, just like Jonathan did when he was in doctor mode. No matter how drunk he was. Peter, too, has adopted a way of being, a way of sitting that suits the reclusive artist he has become. Three posers, he thinks, which brings to mind the photograph of him and Jonathan and the other gay man in their class at school. The one they'd taken in PE during a term break.

'Simon hasn't been here yet,' Peter says.

Simon is a fashion designer with a chain of stores across the country.

'I wish he'd come,' Davide says. 'He'd know what to do with the clothes.'

'He did call earlier,' Peter says. 'He'll be around tomorrow.'

'No one told me he called,' Davide says.

Peter is starving and can't take his mind off the large silver plate of cheese sticks neatly arranged around a bowl of avocado dip. He'd dip the sticks into the lemony spread and eat them with the bread-and-butter pickles Mina had brought. It was when she'd turned up with the preserving jar that morning that her husband,

Solly, had said: I will not have this thing turned into a garden party.

Hunger pangs lasted for twenty minutes. In less than twenty minutes he'd be fine. He'll have lost his appetite. From where he's sitting that seems unlikely. Peter knows exactly what those cheese things with the avocado dip are going to taste like and feel like in his mouth. And those pickles. He remembers them from when they were kids. Just two bricks and a piss-pot high, as Mina used to say.

'His shirts,' Peter hears Davide say. 'I'll give his shirts to Simon. He did make most of them after all.'

Peter hasn't seen Simon since moving to Italy. He never knew Jonathan had kept in touch. Maybe there were secrets. About five years ago, when Jonathan came to visit him in Italy soon after Gianni moved out, he told Peter about the Saturday mornings he and Barry Sher used to go oyster-hunting in the rock pools in Summerstrand and sell them for twenty cents a dozen to the Marine Hotel. Peter couldn't remember. And even though thirty years had passed, he still felt left out and jealous that he hadn't known about something he could've been part of.

'What kinds of secrets?' Peter asks Davide.

'Oh, I don't know,' Davide says. 'Nothing comes to mind. But just sitting here in the garden, hearing people talk about him, I know there are things I didn't know.'

'Maybe they're just that,' Peter says. 'Things you don't know. Not secrets.'

'Maybe,' Davide says.

How awkward Jonathan would have felt seeing Peter and Davide together in his small garden, chatting away. The three of them had hardly ever been alone together. Except when Peter had had boyfriends before he left for Italy, and then he, and the boyfriend, would be invited for dinner at Davide and Jonathan's.

'Remember Steve?' Peter says. 'He called from Joburg.'

'You should have let me speak to him.'

'Why him?'

'He's your ex,' Davide says. 'That makes him part of the family.'

'Hardly,' Peter says.

'I liked Steve,' Davide says. 'He was nice.'

'He was a shit,' Peter says. 'He went back to that wife of his.'

'But he left her again,' Davide says. 'Maybe he'll come tomorrow.'

The garden will be filled with people tomorrow. Peter will have old friends to gather more news from. There'll be Simon to fill him in and Mina to remind him of when he was a boy. He needs all this to take with him back to Italy.

'Do you want something to eat?' says Peter.

'Maybe just a little something,' Davide says. 'I'm not that hungry.'

'What would you like?' Peter says.

'Maybe some of those cheese things,' Davide says.

'I've been thinking about them,' Peter says.

'I tasted one when she brought them,' Davide says. 'They're perfect.'

'Still?' Peter says. 'I'll bring out the whole tray.'

Peter is glad to be alone in the house. The lights are still off, so he makes his way through the house from memory. He leans against the kitchen doorway. He'd helped Jonathan take the door down when he moved in. He could still see where the hinges had been screwed off, the holes covered up with Polyfilla, and painted. Even after Davide had moved in, and was asleep upstairs, they'd come back to Jonathan's kitchen at the end of a night out. Now Peter walks in and bumps his hip against the butcher's block that hadn't been there when Jonathan moved in.

'They're over there,' Davide says, switching on the kitchen light.

'What's that?'

'I hid them,' Davide says. 'The cheese sticks. I hid them behind the microwave.'

Peter takes the plate of cheese sticks and dip, and gets serviettes from the drawer by the sink.

'Still in the same drawer,' he says.

'You know what's frustrating?' Davide says, opening the fridge and taking out a bottle of wine. 'I can hate him all I fucking well like and it won't make a difference.'

'Yes,' Peter says.

'Solly won't talk to me about Jonathan,' Davide says. 'He won't tell me a thing. Mina does. But I want the stories from him. He's punishing me. He's keeping the stories to himself. You tell me about Jonathan.'

'I haven't heard from Jonathan in ages. You must know that,' Peter says. 'I've had one letter from him in the past two years. All he did was write to let me know he had the virus. He never answered any of my letters after that. Why did he stop writing?'

'This is horrible. This is not the way it should be,' says Davide. 'We're like two building blocks in his game. He pulls away and look what happens.'

'Why did he stop writing?' Peter says.

'I don't know, Peter,' Davide says, holding the wine bottle in both hands. 'I really don't know. I just don't want to feel so empty.'

Peter puts down the plate and serviettes and opens his arms for Davide. Davide frowns at him.

'Please don't make me cry,' he says.

Peter takes the wine bottle from Davide and puts it on the counter. He holds him and Davide cries into his shoulder. Peter's body turns to stone and, eyes wide open, he looks over Davide's shoulder. He stares blankly through to the garden where the man who will love him is standing. He is waiting for Peter to come to him, having seen how bravely he holds this man's grief. And then Peter will be comforted.

Davide smells of sweat and two-day-old aftershave. He isn't going to wash or shave during the shiva. Yesterday morning, with Jonathan's mother, they'd covered the mirrors with scarves and pillow-cases. She'd taught him how the Jews mourn for their dead. Davide's body trembles and Peter becomes a life-time's worth of goodbyes to him. Davide feels so empty he wants to scream.

At Rome airport, when Peter had driven Jonathan there five years ago to catch the plane back to South Africa, Jonathan had hugged him in the waiting lounge. Peter, this time, had cried like a little boy being abandoned in the world. Jonathan had held Peter's cheeks in his palms and for the first time ever kissed him on his lips. Then he got on the plane and Peter went back to his little house, back to speaking Italian to everyone, back to finding ways to translate his demons into shapes and colours. That's all he had to rely on. Now he is grateful for Davide's fingers pressing into his back.

Davide is a stranger in a foreign country. He feels himself getting smaller and smaller. This isn't his home anymore. From the moment Peter walked in it stopped being home. Was this how he used to feel when Peter spent the night after drunken binges? Is this why he always made sure he was asleep before they got back? As if knowing Jonathan longer made the house more Peter's than his. Peter carries images of Jonathan from a time Davide didn't know him, so he digs his fists into Peter's back and opens him like stage curtains.

'What am I supposed to do?' Davide says.

Davide loosens his grip on Peter's back, and Peter is left alone again.

'Let's eat,' Peter says, stepping back and offering Davide a cheese stick.

'And drink,' Davide says, taking the bottle of wine.

Back in the garden Davide makes room on the table for the wine and the glasses and the plate of cheese sticks. Then he pours wine into the glasses, and they wish each other a long life, as is custom.

SHAUN DE WAAL

EXPOSURE

SHAUN DE WAAL (b. 1965 in Johannesburg). He is the book editor of the *Mail & Guardian* in Johannesburg. His first collection of a dozen short stories, *These Things Happen*, was published by Ad. Donker in 1996. His 'Exposure' dates from since then.

'His name is Alex Chambers and he'll be coming to take your picture. How's Monday?'

'Fine. I'll be home all day.'

'Good. I'll tell him to phone before he comes. And I've given him a copy of your book to read.'

'Great,' I said, though I wondered if that would be help or hindrance.

'By the way,' she said, 'I *loved* it. It was so ... so *honest*.'

'Thanks.'

'And beautifully written, of course.'

'Thanks.'

'Okay, so, Monday?'

'Right. Thanks.'

It was late morning on Monday when the bell rang. 'Alex Chambers,' said the voice.

I let him in and stood on the stoep to watch a young man coming up the driveway with energetic strides, his body tilted to balance the huge shining case slung over one shoulder.

They've sent the junior, I thought. Ag well, I'm only a writer. Doubtless a rather low priority for a big Sunday paper with a taste for the sensational. 'Hi,' I said as he approached.

'Hi,' he replied, coming up the steps on to the stoep. 'Keith?'

'Yes,' I said. 'Pleased to meet you.'

He set down his case and extended a hand. I shook it. His grip was alarmingly firm. He, in fact, was alarmingly firm. Or so I presumed, but on good evidence judged by an eye trained by years of man-evaluating habit. Short and stocky, he had thick tanned arms sticking from a T-shirt that could only have enclosed a tough little torso. He wore slightly ragged, faded jeans and big, scuffed brown boots. Around his waist was a money pouch. His hair was spiked short, his face broad but shaped by Slavic-style cheekbones. Mmmm, I thought; I'm rather glad they sent the junior.

'Well,' I said, with a small, slightly self-conscious laugh, 'where do you want me?'

'Uh ...' he knelt and opened his metal case, revealing cameras and lenses lodged in grey nippled foam. Taking out a camera, he examined it closely, then rummaged in his money pouch for a spool of film. He stood and loaded it into the camera, then looked around him. 'Maybe ... okay, just sit there, let me get a couple ...'

I sat down in the wire chair he had indicated. It had its back to the garden, or what I called the garden, a walled yard really, a metre or so lower than the stoep. I suppose that's a good idea, I thought: the magenta bougainvillaea tumbling behind me would make a good backdrop. I crossed my legs and waited for him. He crouched down and turned the camera on me. I realised I was holding my breath, waiting for the click.

'Just relax,' he said.

I tried. The camera clicked, though 'clicked' is hardly the word for that complex sound, a set of tiny overlapping impulses, a gate opening and closing via a complex miniature mechanism, the noise perhaps that of something closing in on something else, seizing it.

I looked away from him, gazing toward the pool lodged neatly in the courtyard, its water slowly turning with the artificial tide of the pump. That camera noise again: in a comic book, say, one might represent it orthographically with a hard K sound at beginning and end, a nearly elided SH in between, almost vowelless. *Kssh'k.*

'Uh ...' He stood up, casting his eyes vaguely around him. 'Can I have a look around? See if ...' He seemed unwilling to finish his sentences.

'Sure,' I said. 'Come inside.'

I led him into the house. 'Would you like something to drink?' I asked. 'Tea? Coffee? Beer? Coke?'

'Coke's fine.'

I went into the kitchen. He followed me, camera in hand, his head moving from side to side as he took in the environment, the possible backdrops. I took a Coke from the fridge and handed it to him. I watched his bicep bunch as he ripped its hatch open and lifted the can to his mouth.

He swallowed and said, 'I read your book.'

'Oh,' I said, as if surprised. 'And?'

'Not all of it. Just some. But my girlfriend read it all.' He was looking away from me down toward the low cupboards: no backdrop there, surely? 'She said it was quite good. What d'you call it, post - ?'

'Post-modern?'

'Mmm. She's got a degree. English.'

'Well, please tell her I appreciate the compliment very much,' I said, smiling at him.

'I don't read a lot,' he said.

'So few people do.'

Of course, I thought, the girlfriend had to be mentioned, sooner or later. Sooner, no doubt, because the novel in question, the book that's getting reviewed this coming Sunday, is all gay characters and their diverse sex lives. And here is this girlfriend-attached straight boy (how old could he be? twenty-five?), junior photographer, having to take a picture of the author of this book, whom he must presume to be a moffie himself. Did that scare him at all? Did it, perhaps, explain his bluntly mumbling demeanour?

'How about my study?' I suggested.

I led him there.

'It's always a mess,' I apologised, waving at the heaps of books and papers that almost engulfed the PC. 'But maybe I could stand against a bookshelf. Get some books in the background ...' I was thinking of Karsh's famous photo of Graham Greene, in a pale mackintosh as though he'd just been out in the rain, but resting his left shoulder against a bookcase. I remembered looking carefully at the few titles visible, in the way one immediately scans the shelves in homes one visits – *The Art of the Conquistadors, Looking at Pictures, The Voice of Silence, The Letters of W. B. Yeats, The Thousand Nights and One Night.*

'Uh ...' Alex paused. This time the sound seemed to indicate uncertainty. 'Bit of a cliché,' he muttered. 'Writer, books ...'

I shrugged. 'I'm sure you're right. The lounge?'

Again, I led him through the house.

'There isn't really anywhere else.' In the lounge I said, 'If I sat in that chair over there, you could get that painting in the background. It would make quite a nice backdrop, wouldn't it?' I went over and sat in the armchair before the big Jenny Stadler, all dragged ridges of pigment clashing in complementary colours.

'Interiors ...' he mused.

He looked around the room. I looked at him, feeling the flare of lust: the T-shirt had no signs or logos on its washed-out yellow surface, leaving it merely to outline bulbous pectorals centred on the tiny jut of his nipples.

Suddenly he said, 'Not inside. Too many portraits inside. And the light ...'

'The light?' I prompted.

'Don't have any lights,' he said, giving me a slightly sullen glance. 'An ordinary flash ...'

'Flashes are too harsh,' I said. 'Aren't they? They flatten things and ...'

'Shadows,' he said, and turned and walked out of the room.

Now I was following him, back to the stoep. He knelt and fumbled in his silvery case again, changing lenses.

'By the pool?' I asked.

Without looking at me he grunted. It seemed to signify assent, so I went down into the walled courtyard (no room for a garden as such, just the four large pots containing pointed yuccas, and a small strip of bed along the driveway with some colour – irises, gladioli). Two chaises longues stood on the paving. I sat down on the edge of one. It was scorchingly hot, the sun grilling the bricks and lending the pool's blue bottom a moving, spangled lattice-work of refracted light.

'Okay ...'

He stood on the pool's edge and looked around with eyes slitted in the glare. His frowning gaze seemed to show he was matching external vision with inner idea. The concentrating gaze of the image-seeker.

'Okay.' Suddenly he was next to me, pulling at the chaise. 'Put this like this ...' I stood and he yanked the chaise away so that it stood right on the rim of the pool, facing toward the driveway. 'Now, if you lie down ...'

Obediently I lay on the chaise, leaning back into it, feeling slightly vulnerable to think of the water just behind, almost beneath, my head. If he kicked the chaise I'd slide right in. Backwards.

He stood at my feet and focused the camera, leaning in closer as it made its capturing noise, once, twice.

'Close your eyes,' he said. I obeyed. *Kssh'k, kssh'k.* I felt even more vulnerable; where was he? Was it a leap of the imagination to feel him above me, to sense the aura of his body-heat coming in closer, nosing up against me?

There was another *kssh'k*, then silence. Eyes closed, I waited. When I opened them he had vanished.

I sat up and turned to see him on the other side of the pool, facing me, the camera cradled in a crooked wrist, its broad black strap wound casually around a solid forearm.

I said nothing. Waited.

Then he was coming back to me. 'Lying next to the pool?' he asked.

'What? Just here, on the ground?'

'Ja, maybe ...' He stared at the paving intensely.

'Well, I suppose I could, but won't it look rather odd?'

'Take your shirt off.'

It sounded like half a question, a request, half a simple state-ment: that's what you need to do if the picture is to work, to not look odd. You need to take your shirt off.

'I'm not sure ...' I began.

'It'll make a good shot,' he said with a new, emphatic tone in his voice. 'Just head, shoulders – water in the background. Water's hard to photograph.'

'I'm sure it is.'

I didn't know what to do, but my hand had already moved up my shirt and was fondling a button from its buttonhole.

The shirt (specially selected for what I thought were its photo-genic qualities, its patterned liveliness) was already coming off when I said, 'I'm not much of a pin-up.'

He looked me over with what seemed to be a professional, eval-uative eye. I could feel the sun's heat descending on to my shoulders and back. Thank heavens, I thought, I've been getting a bit of sun, so I'm not all snowy, which is never flattering. Well, not unless you're a Greek god in the first place.

'You look pretty good,' he said in a way that made it impossible to tell whether he was just being flattering so he could get his own way or he really thought so. Surely – the thought sped through my mind – someone with a hunky little body like his, who probably spent most of his leisure hours (when not bonking said girlfriend) at the gym, pumping and grunting. 'How old are you?'

I was on my way down toward the bricks. They burnt my palm. 'Thirty-five,' I said. Now I was on my haunches, thinking that the paving would be too hot to lie on directly. 'How old are *you*? If you don't mind my asking.'

His face was hidden behind the camera gawking down at me. 'Twenty-three,' he said.

Good guess, I told myself, and said to him: 'It's too hot to lie on. I better get a towel or something.'

He said nothing, so I stood up and went into the house. In the bathroom I opened the linen closet and pulled several towels from it: what colour would he want? I also gave myself a severe once-over in the mirror, standing there in black Levis and black takkies, without a shirt on, ectomorphic and muscle-free, asthenic to his pyknic. I pulled myself upright, as straight as possible, trying to unround those shoulders, breathe in that incipient boep. Ag well, I thought, I'll be lying down.

I went back outside, bearing towels in each arm. 'Do you have any particular preference as far as the colour goes?'

'Huh?'

He had been kneeling at the poolside, dandling a hand in the water.

'I'm beginning to feel like a swim myself,' I said. And, as lightly as possible, 'If you feel like it, jump right in. There are enough towels.'

Silently he looked them over as I stood there like an assistant in a fabric shop with swatches draped over each arm. He pointed at a small white one. The dullest possible option, I thought, but didn't comment. Throwing the rest aside, I dropped it on the bricks and sat, then lay, on it.

'No,' he said, looking down at me. 'Don't want to see it,' and he crouched and tucked the towel away, under me, pushing it out of sight. Through the sleeve of his T-shirt I saw the hair of his armpit and in the same instant smelled his sweat.

'Okay?' I elbowed the rest of the towel away, under me, and shifted so that my head rested on the hot bricks. 'Can you see the towel?'

'It's fine,' he said, and straddled me, one foot on the pool's very brink, confident as a cat. The camera's single inscrutable eye shifted a little this way, a little that way. *Kssh'k, kssh'k. Kssh'k.*

I wondered if I should suggest he take his shirt off, too: It's so hot, and I'd feel more comfortable if you also –

Alex said, 'Close your eyes.'

I did.

'And move your head ... sideways, ja, that's right, stretch your neck out a bit ...'

Now he's talking like a real photographer, I mused. That gabble of phrases directing the subject, do this, do that. Next he'll go all fashiony and start moaning, Oh, that's fab, oh yes, yes, aaah, wonderful, more, more ...

'Look at the camera,' he said.

I obeyed, but to do so was also to look at his crotch, hovering above me – it was in the same frame, so to speak. And to wonder what those slightly grimy blue jeans hid in the area just beneath the mocking echo of the distended money pouch.

'Okay, turn on your side, no, toward the pool ... not so much ... okay ... hold it ...'

This is completely preposterous, I thought with a sudden surge of fear. Worse than preposterous. Serious writer embarrasses himself in major Sunday paper. New novel takes hard look at gay demi-monde; author poses like a sybarite next to his Northern Suburbs pool. I'll be the laughing stock of everyone I know. I will never live this down. *Kssh'k.*

'Okay ...'

He seemed to be done with that lot. He was taking the film out of the camera and – oh dear – putting another one in.

I stood up. 'Is that it?'

'Uh ...'

I waited.

'How about ...' he paused. 'How about naked?'

'Naked?' I must have gasped.

'Ja, you know ... in the pool, maybe.'

'You want to take pictures of me *naked*?'

He shrugged. 'My girlfriend says your work is very naked. So ...'

So you thought a picture of me naked would be perfect, I wanted to supply, but didn't. 'I think not. Shirtless is bad enough. I'm already regretting it, actually. I hope you don't use any of those pictures. Can't you just take some ordinary ones, on the stoep, say, or in the lounge? You know, serious author pictures?'

He looked down at his camera, then back at me. He seemed to be cogitating. For a moment he looked sheepish, then his broad face with the Slavic slash of its cheekbones was gazing directly into mine. I could almost feel a kind of a ray coming from his dark brown eyes, penetrating mine.

'But you ...' he began, then stopped. Collecting his thoughts, perhaps, preparing the utterance. 'You write about all that sex,' he said. 'Cruising, clubs, porn, those holes, what are they called?'

'Glory holes.'

'Ja. Glory holes. Do people really do that?'

'They do,' I said, with perhaps a certain amount of annoyance in my voice. 'All the time.' So the book spooked you? Is this some kind of revenge?

'I just thought ...' Again, the pause. Then the words seemed to come in a rush: 'You know, I haven't had a lot of pics in the paper, they don't always use them, my shots, you know, I'm just a cadet ... I get the wild goosechases, that kind of stuff ... But I kind of feel like I could do some really good ones, you know? Unusual stuff, different stuff, really different ... You know, like you – I really had to beg to get this gig, you know, to take this shot ...'

His hand, the one not holding the camera, described an irregular arc in the air, one that seemed to take in me, the walled courtyard, the pool, the yuccas in their tall pots, the ramrod gladioli, the whole panoply of potential photographs, subjects and surroundings, foreground and background. Suddenly Alex Chambers seemed lost, bewildered, dispirited perhaps. He had some grand eager-beaver idea for some terribly unusual photo that was going to impress his bosses, he had a vision, or at least a drive of some kind, but the subject of the photograph in question – the photographee – wasn't co-operating.

Well, I thought, he'll have to get used to that. Especially if he's going to make requests like this. He probably dreams of being a porno photographer, of working for one of those skin mags, peering up splayed cunts all day. Which is probably where he'll end up.

I was about to say no, to say it very firmly, to say that in fact I thought he'd taken quite enough photos already and I had work to do, the session was over. But then I saw that the hand that had made that arc, which had tried to capture the whole scene in a ges-ture, was at his crotch, grabbing an ambiguous bunch in a tight rapper's fist. And that his eyes were staring straight at mine, their gaze unblinking, the expression on his face incomprehensible.

'I'll have to see them before you put them in the paper,' I said. 'Okay? I want to approve what goes in, okay? Promise?'

'Okay.' The hand was still clenched around some staunch stalk growing there in the darkness of his jeans.

'Is it a deal?'

'Deal.' Now he smiled, a little tauntingly, but with a satisfaction of victory that was clear in his eyes.

I took off my shoes, my socks, my jeans, finally my underpants. I hoped my cock didn't look too shrivelled. Then I turned my back on him and dived into the pool.

I swam a few lengths, not that the pool is very long. Then I closed my eyes and floated there, lolling in the water, thrilling to its cool touch after the sweat of the sun and the burn of the bricks. Sloshing, I couldn't hear the camera's shutter snap. My mind drifted too: what an odd situation; how bizarre this all is. Worth a story in its own right, perhaps. And if I wrote such a story, how would it turn out? How would it end? Do the conjured desires find some kind of consummation, or is there only disappointment? How much of it has been in the mind of the protagonist, unanswered by the object of his lust except in imagination? How does this story end?

After a few minutes I get out, not looking at Alex, and pick up a towel. I dry myself, enjoying the leisurely coarse rub of the fabric across my chest, my head, my groin; towelling my back, I let my genitals swing as if unobserved. I half-expect to hear a *kssh'k*, but there is none. I wrap the towel around my waist and sit down on a chaise.

Now I look at him questioningly. He has put the camera down, in the shade of a yucca. With quick, taut steps he comes and stands before me. He says nothing, just unzips his jeans and lets spring from the aperture a hard cock with a wide red head.

STEPHEN GRAY
WITHOUT WHOM

STEPHEN GRAY (b. 1941 in Cape Town). In 1993 he published *Human Interest and Other Pieces*, including several short stories. His 'Without Whom' first appeared in the Summer 1997 issue of *The Toronto Review of Contemporary Writing Abroad*. Recently he has edited *The Picador Book of African Stories*.

So, she had struck that girl across the face, and then on the back, with the riding-crop, as she quivered in the lift. This must stop as well.

She finished the acknowledgements: a list of half-forgotten benefactors, controlling directors, colleagues, assistants and of course family and faithful friends, some of whom had actually come to monitor first-hand the levels of nutrition in the most deprived city on earth. Not one had picked up and weighed a starved child, though. Now that her report was done, the institute would close. Cutbacks of foreign aid. But here, in this enclave of the famished – bony fingers to split lips, that matt skin texture – what the donors thought of as now chronic Africa staggered on.

She had hit her because she was chubby, with far too much rude, robust health. The daughter of the consul, *for whom* she had gone to so much trouble, after all. Good God!

The shopping lists of her fellow residents had caused it. When she announced she was willing to brave the newly opened route out, they had not been slow to place their orders. The back seat was equipped with the necessary extra tank and the mechanic demonstrated the siphon. Their response was so exaggerated she insisted they produce short-lists. They had all been together about the same stairwell – often without water, fifty-three powercuts so far that year. Some of them were still cheerful people, nevertheless, with whom she shared TV on Tuesday nights. If all others failed, Sylvia's was battery operated. Like her first draft, she had to ask them to cut, delete, hack back their hopes. Alfonso the grocer wanted ... bay-leaves, peppercorns (light to carry); Macdonald (only one item), a printing-roll; Trudi that hair-remover; they wanted Panados (in 200s), water coolers, a toaster with the adaptor. And the doorman, *without whom* her bay-side flat would be overrun and stripped: an Alice band, with painted flowers, for the unruly hair of his now almost marriageable daughter. As the John Orr's department store had closed once the international set quit, trinkets like that were not available.

With the lift out of order again the father of the girl she had slashed had to think twice about climbing to the fourteenth floor. She wondered if she should offer him a towel. She suggested a (personally imported) orange concentrate – yes, also brought back on her trip, through customs without questions, after the usual bribes. The water in the fridge was still cold. She had apologised profusely over the phone; she would apologise again.

She said rather maliciously, 'When you get back to Finland she can always saddle up a reindeer, you know. Maybe help Santa Claus on his rounds. Good shiny presents, for the Third World, too. Put them in the children's socks – not that children here wear socks. At least she could point out to him which pavements they sleep on.'

'But you're right – she is too spoilt.'

'You should see Rina flaunting her plastic hair-band, with such honest pleasure.'

'I know, my wife overindulges her terribly. And so, how much?'

'But they are high-class genuine leather, of course.' She ran her hand down from the pommel of the polished saddle on the chair-arm, went and fetched the girth and bridle. No, he would collect them all some day when the power was back on.

'It was just that …' she said. 'I lost my patience when she asked what good are they *for*. There are no horses left – she said they've all been eaten.'

'This was a bit of unforgivable extravagance on my wife's part, a mere fantasy.'

'Well, you're the one who's paying. I thought it was very ungrateful of your daughter. I just let rip with that crop. I'm sorry.'

'We will use them when we get back home at last, don't worry.'

'I guess I've forgotten what it's like to have normal expectations.'

'I should have beaten her myself, long ago. She didn't even thank you for your great trouble.'

'No trouble at all, I assure you. I am much obliged.'

When the detective came from the financial institution, she alerted the perpetually indebted doorman. The lights were on again, so he tripped them off.

Orangeade. Imported. The ice tray had not refrozen, but the water was cool. The other deckchair still had its plastic on. She was going to bundle it inside when the wind grabbed it out of her hands, took it sailing way over the dilapidated colonial villas, the red trees and towards the cliff-edge.

'I am so sorry,' he said.

They returned to the problem in hand. 'Not the 25th. On that day I had not even left Maputo – anyone can confirm that. My passport has the stamp, you know – as evidence.'

'But it's an *eight*, not a five. That was the Monday. I have the hotel, the news agency – the Sunday and then the Tuesday. That was your great shopping day in between.'

'But how could I be in two places at the same time? – this is not clear at all. Absolutely not.'

He had been over this with her before, and would be going over it again. 'What was that R32 for then, at that moment?'

Finally she said, 'A man like you wouldn't understand. It was for sugar – in cubes. Which is expensive.'

'For sugar.'

'Yes.'

'But we have sugar of most kinds here. That is one of the few things we *do* have, ma'am.' At least he was courteous.

She had been perfectly right about the cubes. When the children with AK47s stopped her at the roadblock, this time she had anticipated them. She just lobbed one box of cubes out of the window. The next burst with white shrapnel. 'Sugar to keep young revolutionaries sweet,' she said.

'But why weren't you in the convoy like when you went, ma'am?'

'I was,' she replied. 'But the others were told to move on.'

'Didn't they wait for you?'

'No, this time they did not – I have explained that to you. Each has to pay his own toll ... Anyway, goods to the tune of ... at Biggie Best. That's your main mistake, isn't it? – floral coverlets. Not my style. Does that sound like me?'

'You may have thrown them out when your car was full, for all I know.' He handed over the summons.

'You'll never prove it,' she said. She lifted her hand from the table, hoping the document would blow away.

'We've been quite lenient, really. It's the others you'll have difficulty with.'

'Which – Mastercard?'

'No, Visa. They will recuperate every last penny.'

She thanked him for the concessions he had made and sent him down.

The phone rang. She guessed who it might be. She was wrong: it was Diners Club. Diners Club had already taken further action. So that her domestic worker, standing there in his new shorts and little else, would not hear her having to plead and wheedle, she slammed the interleading door closed with her foot. The vibration set off the contents of the passage cupboard, coming down like a mudslide in the slums during a tornado.

Previously she had heard what Diners had to say. Only one word was new: repossession.

Later, once she had stacked her spoils and locked them away … bathed, made-up and dressed … although the domestic was off by then, she went visiting Sylvia elsewhere in their block. Their usual Tuesday Brazilian soaps, for which they reserved their sharpest and most enjoyable sarcasm, were not on yet at that hour. Fortunately Sylvia had no client and was all the more welcoming thanks to the surprise.

She exclaimed, 'But you look like – ' she named the ogre of an aunt in the one serial, who gorged chocolates as bulging as her eyes, ruining every plot on cue with her indiscreet, untimely revelations. They both quoted her: 'I have seen what I have seen …'

'And that golden lotus on your lapel, but it is exquisite. Must have cost you a *fortune.*'

'Not so bad, Sylvia. It is only what they call a flame-lily. I liked the workmanship, but the material is not so expensive.'

'They mine the gold there, after all.'

'Exactly, Sylvia.'

Before she knew it, she was on Sylvia's chaise-longue … which she had been avoiding ever since she arrived in this hellhole. 'It's like this, Sylvia, I do not want to abuse our friendship, and I know how draining your patients can be. But I do have to talk to someone now.'

'The first session is always free,' said Sylvia.

'I will not be able to pay you if there are any more. That is a fact of the matter. Another fact – we may as well get straight to the point – is I was thinking of jumping off my balcony. Not into the street – the other way, towards the Russian ambassador's swimming pool.'

'But for all those purchases whose name did you sign? Not your own, I trust.'

'My husband's, of course. But you know there is no longer any legal obligation. In truth, that is why Yunus divorced me – so that he wouldn't have to keep making up the reckoning. That's why I had to get this well-paying job, living off the poorest of the poor, you know.'

'It's the same for me. But he will provide a useful delay, once they've tracked him down. No need to jump yet, either way.'

'Sylvia, you are so familiar with these things. I am much obliged.'

'But what we must not avoid, my friend, is what causes this – this very awkward drive – this overwhelming compulsion – for resistance to break down. And then, all of a sudden, this uncontrollable urge – well, yes, to consume so spectacularly.'

'Shop till you drop,' she said in English.

'Exactly. The same nearly happened to me in Harrod's, when I was over in London. No, it was that Fortnum and Mason's. How easy it would be if you were the Queen of England – you'd just help yourself to whatever you fancied.'

'Charge it to the nation.'

'Well, she has most of the products endorsed by herself, after all, doesn't she?' Sylvia frowned.

Her subject bit her finger. 'It's the TV that gets us like that. We all know it, of course. The more deprived we feel, all the more susceptible do we become. You would have been very proud of me indeed – I had six – no, seven – of those supermarket trolleys, each steered by a little African who would protect it for me with his life. Following me through those miles of shopping centres. No shortages, Sylvia, and no queuing. Not in your wildest dreams can you imagine such a thing. They are like bunkers, to keep the heat and the flies and the dust out – climate controlled. Underground, for security. They call them malls – you can stay overnight even, if you like – bookshops, gambling, health studios, an entire environment. You become lost. You become – absorbed in your dreams. Only when you come out into the parking again are you back in – well, daylight. And do you know I gave them meticais, the usual, for tips. I didn't have any other coins left.'

'And they wouldn't take them, I'm sure.'

'So you start giving them facecloths and other things that they need.'

'I couldn't pay the overtime parking. That is where the bed stuff went.'

Sylvia let her pause and take stock, then redirected her. 'So what is it that causes this madness for us?'

'You put it so sympathetically, Sylvia. Well, I have developed a theory. There is this kind of shark, you see – the slow, silent one. Our bay is full of them, as you are aware. They live deep under-water, cruising very slowly – just enough to get oxygen on their gills. They can sleep in a current for years, the motion of the tide is sufficient. And so they are harmless and forgotten.'

'Yes, but you cannot compare your behaviour with one of those terrible things.'

'Sylvia, look with your binoculars next time a whale dies in our bay, for example. Then you will see what comes over those sharks. Correctly they call it a feeding frenzy. Gentle shadows no more – they are changed into monsters! Now we know what those teeth are for – they propel themselves, they rip, they tear!'

Sylvia poured her friend some more lemon cordial. 'Did you have any good meals at least, while you were there?'

'Oh yes, my dear,' her subject relaxed. 'At a place called the Palazzo. And after that at the Sans Souci. I only considered items you cannot get here at all, which reduced the choice a bit. Then I started at the top.'

'Don't describe the dishes or I will be sick with envy. You crammed every corner while seven little black boys watched you, drooling on the other side of the window?'

'There were only two by the stage of the Palazzo, and I bought them those striped ice-creams in cones. The other was in the evening. Oh Sylvia, what am I to do?'

On that note normally the episode of the serial would end. The following week in life as portrayed on TV nothing would be resolved; a brand-new set of impossible intrigues would begin, that was all.

'I have seen what I have seen,' said Sylvia, tapping her shoe. Once the fifty minutes was over she could no longer concentrate.

'Did I say a shark frenzy, Sylvia? Oh how embarrassing.'

'I beg your pardon?' the psychotherapist answered. Both were acutely awkward.

Sylvia helped her up, put her arm around her. She took a few paces towards the door and turned.

'Ah, but my friend … if only you could have seen it: that salad-dressing shaker you so wanted. It was like a little jug, a flask really. With a very elegant spout. One of those designer glasswares with a slight rainbow sheen. Venetian, I think, with a handle so that you do not get your fingertips sticky. So clumsy. It slipped through my hand. It exploded in a thousand pieces. So lucky nothing else in the shop went as well. After that I could not ask for another one. I am deeply sorry, Sylvia …'

'Of course, if you were a man you'd get away with this whole thing. That is the irony.'

'But men do not make good shoppers as a rule. They are not so easily tempted.'

She should not have left her flat for so long. If she relaxed her vigilance these days, her son would shoot up right in his own bedroom. It was coming to which of them would jump first off the skyscraper. There he was now on the balcony, clutching and pumping his punctured left arm.

'Mario, why didn't you come with me, rather than doing just this all your days? You used to be inseparable from me. The whole experience would have become so different for me, too. We could have gone to a decent nightclub together, seen good entertainment. We could have chosen a film we both liked – there in a cluster they have ten cinemas, and here we have none at all.'

'I do not like American films,' he said.

'They have all kinds,' she replied. 'And what sort of grown-up son leaves his mother to drive through a war-zone on her own?'

'You wanted to get me there to a rehab clinic, that's all. Here I am free to do as I please.'

'That is the cocaine talking, not you. And as I have said before, if cocaine is the only diversion there is for you here, it is the wrong one.'

He squeezed his arm and gave a spasm. 'I can't help it any longer,' he said. 'You should know that.'

'And what would you have done if I had been killed by the rebels? – anywhere this side of the border, dragged into the jungle. You wouldn't even know where I had disappeared.'

He had faced that line of persuasion before. 'Sell up your things,' he replied.

'You callous brute!' she said.

'To pay off your debts,' he added. 'Isn't that what I would have to do legally?'

She looked down at the scintillating beach. Not ten years ago, when she arrived in that deceptive haven, he had played under those palm trees with a bucket and spade. *Happy as a sand-boy* was the expression.

'Where's that saddle and the tack?' she asked, dreading the inevitable answer.

'Ahmed's,' he said. Ahmed ran that front of the pawnshop.

'But it belongs to that Scandinavian girl who can't keep her hands out of your pants!'

'Someone will boil the leather down and eat it,' Mario said. He pushed the deckchair back into the sun, a slight grin on his face. He was still very fetching. She swore she could see his eyes go up into his skull. At least the cocaine kept him out of the saddle of that dreadful, scheming blonde.

The horses have all been eaten, she had said. *I could have eaten a horse.*

She returned to the final report she was so reluctant to conclude. She hadn't paid the rent either, that month. It was time to finalise and depart.

My God, she hadn't expressed her gratitude to the Ford people. And to the Rockefeller Foundation. *Without whom.*

Then she added Sylvia's name out of firm, kind friendship. Out of spite she deleted her ex-husband's, and her son's – he was vomiting now in the bathroom as the power went off on her screen.

CHRIS VAN WYK
MAGIC

CHRIS VAN WYK (b. 1957 in Johannesburg). His 'Twenty Years' Experience' was a favourite in earlier editions of this anthology. His new piece, 'Magic', has not previously been published. For his story 'Relatives', included in the anthology *Crossing Over*, he won the Sanlam Literary Award for Short Fiction in 1999.

A Magic Show
Date: Tuesday the 2nd of February
Place: School Hall
Entrance fee: 20 cents
In aid of: the Seaside Fund
Come One. Come All!

The Seaside Fund took a hundred Joburg children down to Durban every summer for one whole school term – three months. It was hard to qualify for this free train trip to a school on the beach called Transhaven four hundred miles away: you had to be all of the following: starving to death; not wearing shoes to school, even in winter; never bringing lunch to school; and coloured. Most kids, including myself, were only one or two of these at any given time.

Kendrick Appollis was chosen in the year we were in Standard Two. He was all of the above, plus he never had a hanky. He was a third-year Standard Two boy and his mother had been in a bus accident and couldn't work – in case there was more space on the form.

If poor Joburg children went to the coast, I wondered, when I was a little older, where did the poor children who lived at the coast go? Later I also wondered how a term of schooling was supposed to help these poor children. The old people claim that a dip in the sea takes away all the bad luck. But after the three months by the sea these boys and girls came back to school and back to square one, going barefoot with runny noses and begging sandwiches off the haves during lunch breaks.

Anyway, I asked my mother for twenty cents for the magic show. Whenever I asked her for money, she said, 'Otis you really think money grows on trees, don't you?' To which I always wanted to reply, 'If I did think that, I wouldn't be asking you for some, would I? In fact you'd be asking me because I just happen to be a better tree climber than you.' But of course I didn't because that would've been the same as saying, 'Don't give me any pocket money for at least a year.'

She actually wouldn't have given me any money for the show, but I reminded her that when the school showed Steve McQueen in *The Great Escape* she didn't have twenty cents for me. In my eleven years on Earth we had established a kind of fiscal discipline: I could ask for money only for every other school function.

So I got the twenty cents, a grubby little thing with the old prime minister's face on it (who had been knifed to death in Parliament and was dead and buried) that she disinterred from a corner of her purse. Ma handed it to me with a reminder that it could've bought two loaves of bread, but what did I care. Bread appeared and disappeared in our home every day, the Magic Show came once a decade.

We filed into the school hall under the swishing cane of Mr Kelly who, if he wasn't beating us up, was treating us to a dose of his very smelly breath, the perfect atmosphere for his yellow teeth to rot in.

There were no chairs in the hall. If we all sat on the floor they could get in thirty or forty more of us. So we sat cross-legged in rows from the Grade Ones in front to the Standard Fives at the back. This was supposed to have the same effect as a movie theatre where everyone could see over the heads of those in front. It worked up to a point. And that point was me: I sat behind a boy who was in his third year in the same class so that, while his brain was learning the same stuff over and over, his body was growing bigger and bigger. Now today I would spend the best hour of the year trying to look past those same ears his teacher accused him of not having – yes, it was old Kendrick Appollis.

But let the show begin!

Three men came strutting onto the stage, laughing and shouting. One was beating a drum, another blew a whistle and the third man sang a merry tune. We liked it, we liked it. The singer stopped singing and told the two players to shut up so that he could speak to us.

He waved a big golden bangle at us and wanted to know, 'What's this?'

We broke into shouts of 'Bangle!' and 'Ring!'

Our teachers, sitting on chairs along the sides of the hall, smiled at all the goings-on.

On stage the man swirled a finger at his own brain. This meant we were all mad. We cheered; it was a refreshing change from being called stupid.

He took a scarf and asked us: 'What colour is this?'

'Yellow!' On this we were unanimous.

Then, in dramatic slow motion, he pulled the scarf through the ring. It turned green and we, row upon row of Xs went OOOhh. Instead of paying attention to what he was doing, he was looking at us and with mocking bewilderment said, 'What's the matter?'

We pointed four hundred fingers at him and shouted, 'Your scarf is green!'

He said, 'What?'

'Your scarf! It was yellow, now it's green!'

'I beg yours?'

'Green!'

Only after cupping his ear was he able to hear.

He looked down at the scarf, but by then it was yellow again.

He conferred with his two friends and they all agreed: we were a crazy bunch. Try getting a magician to call you mad. I tell you it's the funniest thing in the world.

There was more magic. He took a cake tin and pointed out a girl two rows away from me. She pointed to herself just to make sure. The magic man said, 'Are you not Belinda Brown?'

'No, sir,' she said.

'Then you're the one I want,' he said.

Wow, did that joke get us slapping our knees and rocking our bums with laughter!

The girl got up, a little red in the face now, dusted lots of invisible fluff from her gym and stepped onto the stage.

'What do you see in this tin?' he said. She looked inside, looked up at the magician.

'Stones?' she said, as if she wasn't too sure. But with a magic man who could blame her?

'Show them, tell them.' He handed her the tin of stones. 'Rattle them.'

She showed, rattled and told.

What was this guy going to do?

'Watch,' he said.

He placed the tin of stones on a table and, as soon as his back was turned, his friends covered it with a sheet. But no sooner had they done this than he yelled at them to 'Mind your own business! Who asked you?' and told them to take their stupid sheet off his tin of stones. Only now it was: a tin of sweets! Mints, toffees, nougat, coconut. And he gave it all to the girl who was not even Belinda Brown!

He repeated this trick with a tin of mud, which he turned into a chocolate cake, which he handed to Mrs Petersen, one of the Grade One teachers.

I went home that afternoon wondering why he couldn't just have made tins of sweets and chocolate cake for all of us. God knows we had enough stones and mud on the school grounds just waiting to be turned into something tasty.

Well, whenever I think of that magic show, I think about my Auntie Leonie.

Hardly a week after the show, just as the talk of magic was beginning to disappear, Ma gave me some news.

'Auntie Leonie's coming to visit us today.' This was a Saturday.

Auntie Leonie! She was my mother's youngest sister. She was a replica of Ma, except that she was taller and wore glasses. Like Ma she was beautiful. Even before I was ready for school she showed me how to hold a pen. Of all my mother's ten brothers and sisters, Auntie Leonie was considered to be the cleverest because she had gone as far as Standard Eight. Ma and everybody else, it seems, had dropped out in Standard Six, the beginning of high school. It must be all that studying that led to the glasses. Auntie Leonie was twenty-two years old.

'And she's bringing her new boyfriend.'

'Oh really!' That was all I was allowed to say. Something like, 'What happened to the old one?' would've been regarded as ougat.

In our little two-bedroom township house in Riverlea there was much preparation – shining the three front steps, wiping the sticky marks off the front gate, dusting off the coffee table in the lounge. Then Ma sent me to the shop to buy a family-size Coke and a Fanta. And a packet of Bakers Romany Creams and Choice Assorted biscuits. Usually all we got was one bottle of coldrink and a packet of Choice Assorted which were about seven cents cheaper than the Romany Creams – and then my siblings and I fought over the lemon creams – of which there were only two in every packet. (The Bakers Man can be so stingy, yes the Bakers Man can.)

Auntie Leonie and her new boyfriend arrived in the afternoon.

They walked in and, from our kitchen, I listened to the adult ritual of how-d'you-do's in our tiny lounge. 'Arnold Rhoda,' I heard my father say. 'Related to Peter Rhoda who used to play centre forward for Gladiators?'

'My older brother!' I heard Arnold say. And then all four adults burst into polite laughter as if being the brother of Peter Rhoda was a funny thing.

'Where's Otis?' I heard Auntie Leonie ask. I smiled in the kitchen and got up to have a sip of water so that I could look busy when she came looking for me. Seconds later Auntie Leonie was in the kitchen with her boyfriend. I couldn't believe what I saw. Arnold Rhoda was a short, stocky man – even shorter than my aunt. And in every other way different to what I had imagined. Dark of complexion, a full crinkly beard, big white teeth. His small brown eyes glinted with a mischievousness I usually only saw in someone my own age. A hand popped out from a fawn corduroy jacket to shake my little hand. I shook his hand and smiled back at him. I liked him, from the word go. Auntie Leonie could see that I liked her new boyfriend and beamed behind her big round glasses.

But this was only the introduction.

After the biscuits and tea and coldrink, it is usually the time when children have to disappear. This is when adults talked about who's pregnant, who's still not married, who's pregnant *and* still not married and so on. But Uncle Arnie called for a pack of cards and Ma knew it was safe for me to stay.

He made me pick a card. This was an old trick. I had seen it done before. I picked the three of diamonds and put it back in the pack. He shuffled the pack. He stopped. He thought hard.

'Is this your card?' he held up a two of clubs.

'No.'

He threw it face-down on the coffee table. He showed me another card. Again he was wrong. (This was not how the trick went.) He flipped that one face-down too. He showed me yet another card. This Uncle Arnie was so wrong, he wasn't even getting the colour of the card right. Now there were three wrong cards lying face-down between us.

'But why do you say no, no, no, when your card is there?' (lying face-down on the table).

'But Uncle Arnie ...' I turned to my aunt, who merely arched her eyebrows behind her glasses. Ma laughed, Da looked bemused.

'That's where your card is,' the short man said, pointing to the three wrong cards.

'It's not.' I had known him long enough to put a little bit of indignation into my voice. This short bearded new boyfriend had shown me three cards and none of them was mine.

'Okay, what was your card?'

'Three of diamonds,' I said triumphantly.

'Well, check those cards,' he said, pointing to the three on the table.

I turned them up and there was my card, the three of diamonds! My face must've looked quite a mixture of amazement and disbelief. I had been tricked. But I could see that my parents had been tricked too. Only Auntie Leonie appeared unfazed. I asked Uncle Arnie to do the trick again. This time I watched his every move; even when he put his cigarette in the ashtray and put down his glass of beer which Da had poured for him, I kept my eyes on that pack of cards. But again he tricked me.

And again, and again.

His magic was not confined to cards alone. He showed us how to get a twenty-cent coin out from underneath an upturned bottle – without lifting up the bottle. Then he made that same bottle (the family-size Fanta which was now empty) stand without support in a corner of the lounge – halfway between the floor and ceiling. He also guessed correctly the number of matches in a matchbox just by shaking it near his ear – seven times in a row!

A year later, my aunt was Mrs Arnold Rhoda. They had a son and she was pregnant again. Uncle Arnie had acquired a house for them on the corner of the street we lived in and identical to ours. This was unheard of in those days when the waiting list for houses was so long that people who got married usually only got a place of their own when their eldest was in high school. I heard my father say, 'Arnold,' in admiration. 'I tell you that one's got connections.'

I was still very fond of my aunt. Whenever Ma sent me on my daily errand to the shop for bread, I popped in at her place to see if she wanted something from the shop too. Auntie Leonie still liked me. But she seemed always too busy washing nappies, hanging them out on the line in the bleak and tiny backyard, breastfeeding one baby, feeding another with a spoon, changing nappies. Sometimes so busy that she couldn't even remember where she put her purse or what she needed from the shop or to ask me if I had passed standard whatever. The years went by and she just kept on having babies.

Whenever I walked past their home on Saturday afternoons, Uncle Arnie was at home with his workmates and other friends who had come to visit. Always they would be drinking. The brown quart bottles of Castle and Lion, and Richelieu brandy, and Mainstay Cane Spirit, were a familiar sight on the coffee table. Music on the turntable – El Ricas, Trini Lopez, Johnny Mathis and The Flames – familiar sounds.

Another sound that grew familiar through the years was Uncle Arnie's favourite word for my aunt: 'Bitch.' Used in the following ways:

'Bring the steak, bitch. How long do we have to wait?' 'We' was himself and his buddies.

'Bitch, more money for beer there. And move that fat arse of yours.' This was meant to be a joke but his friends never laughed as heartily as he did.

'Bitch, the fucking child is crying, go and see what's wrong, Jesus.'

Or just: 'Ag, fuck you, bitch!'

Auntie Leonie didn't have another name for him. Arnie was what she always called him.

One night – no, about three o'clock in the morning, there was a knock on my parents' bedroom window. I woke up and heard my mother opening the squeaking window, and my aunt's voice, also squeaking, with fear. Her children were crying, in her arms and around her legs.

'Ag please, Jean, tell David to come. Arnie's gone mad down there!'

I could hear Da shake himself awake. He put on pants, a cardigan. And slippers! I was disappointed by the slippers. You couldn't kick a man with that. My father went out into the cold, barking night to see what Uncle Arnie was up to down the road. My father was an ex-Gladiators goalkeeper. He was tall, athletic and knew how to kick and lash out. But not tonight it seemed. Wide-awake now, and eavesdropping, I pieced together the story. First from Ma and Auntie in the kitchen where they drank a cup of tea and tried to get my little cousins to stop crying. Then about half an hour later when Da came back and told her to try and get some sleep – on the couch. It was okay, Arnold was sleeping it off.

He and his mates had finished two bottles of brandy. His friends had staggered off home at past midnight but he wanted more liquor. He demanded five rands from my aunt. She wouldn't give it to him – 'Because I just did not have,' she told my mother. He beat her up. The noise of her screaming woke up the kids and they all cried in a fearful bundle on the bed. He took a bottle of paraffin from the bathroom, went outside and splashed it all around the house. He tried to light a match … 'That's when I grabbed the children and ran up here.'

There was more Saturday night/Sunday morning banging on the windowpane. Lots more tears. Sometimes Auntie Leonie walked about with a black eye for days.

One day she decided that enough was enough. Uncle Arnie came home late one Friday night, drunk. He knocked up my aunt. She opened the door. He stood there, swaying from side to side. He had a friend with him. Somebody Auntie Leonie had never set eyes on before. A woman who could not have been a day older than twenty, in Levis too tight for her and a tatty, skimpy blouse out of which her breasts popped. A mixture of cheap perfume and day-old brandy fumes fluttered from her. She also swayed and, apart from an intermittent giggle, said nothing, showed no embarrassment or awkwardness for what was happening or about to happen. I don't know how my uncle put it to my aunt, but he told her that Carol, his friend, would be sleeping in their bed with them tonight.

Then, the story goes, my Auntie Leonie used Uncle Arnie's favourite word.

Auntie Leonie didn't say much else to anyone after that. But together with my mother, they planned the Great Escape. Auntie Leonie decided to save some money, borrow some, sell some of their clothes for a few more rands. A few weeks later she went to Park Station, bought a third-class ticket to Durban (children under seven travel free) where she would start a new life, without Arnold, without another man.

The day came. One Friday morning Uncle Arnie got up and went to work. This was the day when his wild weekend began and Auntie Leonie's nightmare started: Friday late afternoon until the wee hours of Monday morning.

The coloured people themselves had named Friday 'Bushman's Christmas'. It was the day most coloureds got their wages and when a kind of frenzy was ignited. On Monday morning many would not even have fifteen cents for bus fare to take them to work. But what the hell; on a Friday afternoon when that first drink cascaded down your throat and splashed down in your stomach, its first effect was to make all Mondays disappear from the calendar – from here to eternity.

The Uncle Arnie weekends were not unique in Riverlea. Take for instance the Lunds and the Radcliffs opposite us. Mr Lund had married Mr Radcliff's sister and Mr Radcliff had married Mr Lund's sister, so they were closer than most families. Plus they lived next door to each other. Unlike Uncle Arnie and Auntie Leonie, these two couples drank together as a merry foursome, alternating their homes as the venue. They drank, joked, fried meat, drank, sang and became maudlin. Then an argument would erupt, usually from something minor: a spilled drink ('d'you know what the fucken stuff costs?'), the words of a song ('it's: Regrets I've had a *few*, not a of *of you*'), because one of them stayed in the toilet too long ('have you passed out on the toilet seat again?'). The guest couple then went outside and smashed all the host couple's windows, all around the little matchbox house, with half a brick each. The host couple would then stagger over the low wire fence and give the house next door the same treatment: tit for tat, butter for fat.

But back to the Great Escape. As soon as Uncle Arnie left for work, Auntie Leonie sprang into action, with an expression of resoluteness that had last been seen five or six years ago in her premarital days.

She washed the kids, she packed three or four suitcases with essential things, she filled a Tupperware box with cheese and tomato sandwiches for padkos. She came to say goodbye to Ma – I was at school, Da was at work. Ma gave her the train tickets that she had kept hidden for her. My aunt left the key with a neighbour – to be given to Uncle Arnold when he came from work that evening. Another neighbour, Mr Jardine, a pensioner, drove her to the station in his old Anglia.

Durban. A new life. Without Uncle Arnie and his drinking and swearing and beating and trying to burn the house down and trying to have three-in-the-bed sex. There were good dressmaking factories in Durban and an old schoolfriend who was also now living in Durban was looking out for a job for my aunt. For now she stood on Platform 14 in the centre of suitcases and bags with zips that didn't work and a child who was hungry, another who was thirsty and one that wanted to pee. The train came. And out of the blue, like the Jack of Spades in one of his card tricks, there was Uncle Arnold.

This was such a shock for my aunt that she cried and said, 'D'you blame me, Arnie? D'you blame me?' taking off her glasses and wiping them on the hem of her dress, putting them on, taking them off … How had he known she was leaving him? There was another surprise: he whipped out … his own ticket to Durban and got onto the train with her and the kids.

They've been living in Durban for thirty years now, in a slum called Wentworth. Uncle Arnold got work on the docks refurbishing ships. Auntie Leonie worked as a seamstress. They had three more children. Every Friday Uncle Arnie comes home drunk and beats her up. He still calls her a bitch and she calls him Arnie. Apart from the fact that they all have a Durban accent, nothing much has changed; they're regarded by most people as just an ordinary coloured South African family.

DEENA PADAYACHEE
HEAVY CEREBRAL METAL

DEENA PADAYACHEE (born in Durban and practises as a doctor there). He made early appearances in *Staffrider* and in 1992 put out his collection of short stories, *What's Love Got to Do with It*? 'Heavy Cerebral Metal' first appeared in *Tribute* in May 1995.

The events that I am going to tell you about occurred many years ago when Mr Nelson Mandela was still on Robben Island. In fact, it was in 1980 when our provincial hospitals were still segregated and it was axiomatic that all black hospitals were still overcrowded and understaffed.

A nattily dressed young man strode boldly into my medical cubicle at the busy public hospital as if he owned the place. I usually attended to shabbily dressed South Africans, often broken both in spirit and in health. He seated himself at the battered wooden table which served as my work desk and greeted me. There was a piece of shiny stainless steel sticking out of the side of his head. I thought that I had seen it all during my years in Casualty: knives, axes and all kinds of evil-looking weaponry in human chests, limbs, stomachs and every part of the human anatomy. Often one had to attend to lips, cheeks and ears hanging by the proverbial thread – bitten by ravenous human animals. But this metallic object was one for the record books.

'That's the tip of an umbrella, doctor,' he explained in a matter of fact voice.

'You must have a headache?' I asked sympathetically.

'Oh yes, doctor! What a splitting headache. This thing in my head hurts.'

'It must,' I replied.

I led him to the couch as he continued speaking: 'But then again, that's women. Nag, nag, nag! They're one huge headache.'

At least the speech area of his brain appeared not to have been affected. His speech was not even slurred.

'But we can't survive without them,' I replied. I had finally tied the knot the previous month. It had been a very difficult decision as, even though the lady is a lovely person, I value my independence and solitude.

I kept my expression deadpan as I proceeded with my examination. My comment appeared to make no impression on him.

He was a real teacher – he just didn't stop talking: 'You see, there's this woman – we teach on the same staff; we had an argument; well, actually' – a shadow of guilt passed across his face for a millisecond – 'she's very pretty and I've been trying my luck with her for a long time now – you know what I mean, trying to get her into the sack. My friends had been teasing me, but I was getting nowhere.' He glanced at the sweet little nurse outside the cubicle and gave me a knowing look. 'So, when I got her alone in the classroom, I tried to embrace her and to kiss her. Just a little love, that's all. But she pushed me away.'

'She's married?' I asked, trying to salvage his delicate ego.

'Yes, and she keeps telling me that my wife is her friend. As if her husband is that careful!'

His tympanic membranes appeared healthy.

'Then she tried to lecture me about ethics and morals and setting an example to the kids. You know how these women go on – always thinking that they're right – never listening to what we *men* have to say.'

I nodded sympathetically. He continued prattling away as I put the stethoscope into my ears and I had to stop him. Don't people know that you don't really hear them when you're listening for heart sounds? He seemed to have a great need to explain what had happened to him and vindicate himself.

I had barely finished my cardiovascular and respiratory assessment when the words began issuing from his mouth again like lava. I proceeded to perform a thorough neurological examination.

'Well, she became abusive and hysterical, when I mentioned that she was very friendly with her Head of the Department. She called me all kinds of names. She seems to have no respect for us *males*. I just couldn't take it any more. So I slapped her. Nothing much – just a little slap.'

'Like you give your wife now and again?' I enquired with just the right tone in my voice.

'Yes, but I only do that now and again. But my wife, she understands that we *men* need to do this sort of thing. And she can take it!'

He shook his head at the memory of his resilient spouse.

'But the younger generation – they're not as tough as we were.' The teacher didn't appear inebriated, he really didn't.

'Where did this happen?' I asked, as I tested his tendon reflexes with my patella hammer.

'Oh, in an empty classroom. No one saw us; at first,' he added as an afterthought.

'She's young, this teacher?'

'Yes, but she's one of the cheekiest. They're all the same: temperamental and full of mood swings. And if they have some education, they get so bucky!'

I nodded sympathetically. Where have all the soft, sweet women gone? Gone with Juliet to other pastures?

'Yes, women are not like women any more. Just a teeny-weeny slap, that's all she got. But she carried on like I'd raped her or something.'

I decided to keep my face expressionless, even though it was difficult. I just thought of my mother-in-law in a foul mood.

'Anyway, all hell broke loose.' He shook his head. 'Ladies aren't ladies any more,' he repeated. The heavily pigmented man didn't flinch and elicited a negative plantar reflex on the sole of his foot with the sharp end of my probe. His feet did not smell.

He continued, 'Well, she screamed and shouted something awful. Said I had no respect for a lady's dignity. There wasn't anything dignified about the way she was screaming. But then she swore at my mother: now, you can do anything you like but nobody messes with my mother. *Nobody*!'

Somehow, I kept from grinning.

'Anyways, I blasted her – one hell of a tight shot and she ended up on the floor. I used to be boxing champion of my class,' he mentioned proudly. 'I hadn't lost my touch,' he boasted. 'Ja, the little witch didn't look very dignified on her backside. Then for good measure, I let her have it. One tight kick on the side of her big bum. I was a *good* soccer player in my time.'

He smiled happily at the memory.

I looked at him reproachfully; I really did.

He remonstrated, 'These little girls mustn't try to provoke us big, strong guys. They like to use words the way you doctors wield scalpels. If they want us to treat them like ladies, then they must behave like ladies. I mean when Poland messed with Germany, she got beaten solid. Women mustn't mess with us men.'

I decided not to comment that imitating fascists wasn't the best way to create a good impression with anybody. He looked like an aggressive fellow, and many doctors have been abused and even assaulted by patients whose values are rather different from ours.

'I walked away then: I didn't want to look like I was gloating or something. But then the little coward grabbed her umbrella and stabbed it right into my head ... when my back was turned. *My head!*'

His pupils contracted nicely in response to the bright light of my torch.

The teacher shook his head sadly.

As I handed him the note for an X-ray of his skull, he thanked me ever so politely and disappeared, his expressive cologne sweetening the air in my musty cubicle.

PHASWANE MPE
BROODING CLOUDS

PHASWANE MPE (b. 1970 near Pietersburg-Polokwane). He began as a contributor to *Staffrider* in 1992, has a cluster of stories in *Unity in Flight* (2001). He first published 'Brooding Clouds' as the unrevised 'Clouds' in *Imprint*, No. 5 of Summer 1995, and it is now part of a sequence of stories with the same setting.

It is the beginning of autumn, the season in which the people of Tiragalong, a tiny village not far from Pietersburg, tend to look younger because of the nourishment they get from their abundant harvest. It is autumn, but this year the fields show no signs of life. Mealie plants are already grey, grey like ash. Trees have lost their leaves, which turned sickly yellow before their time. Grass is dry already and there have been several veld fires. The nearest river is so dry livestock go there only to look at the cracked clay where water used to be. Even the word 'livestock' is misleading, for there are merely collections of bones in the shapes of cattle, sheep and goats.

Everything is dry. One does not need the help of a sangoma to predict that, toward the end of the season, when harvest time knocks on the doors of the villagers, there shall be nothing to reap. The rains take some pleasure in not relieving this tiny village. The old men, sitting under the trees whose shades are no match to the scorching sun, complain that the gods have turned their backs on them.

Makgolo is one of the oldest women in the village. Tonight she is alone in her hut. She sits with her legs stretched out before her. Her eyes stare vacantly at the fireplace. The fire has been out for quite a long time. But Makgolo does not notice. She rubs her hands together like a person who has just warmed them up a bit.

Tonight she has no children to tell stories to. A dreadful thing happened yesterday. Although children love her stories – she tells the most beautiful stories in the village and its neighbourhood – they shall not come to listen to her anymore.

Her stories begin, almost always, like this: 'Long, long ago, when stones were still soft and edible and trees could walk ...'

Who does not want to know what happened in those good old days? Children are fascinated by her stories, stories of witchcraft and ordinary lives, of poverty and abundance, of wars and peace. The children give very little heed to the moral side of her stories.

But Makgolo has no audience tonight. She whiles the time away by drawing patterns in the air with her failing eyes. The thickening darkness in the hut sharpens the bright edges of her mental pictures. She is the solitary watcher of her own art. She has to be alone. Has not the boy, Thusŏ, come running in the heat of the afternoon sun to warn her to fly away on her broom? He overheard a group of youngsters who called themselves 'Comrades' talk about Makgolo.

'She is a witch,' they said, 'and can fly on a broom. What is more, she has sent lightning to strike Tshepo.'

Tshepo was a young man of promise, coming from a poor family. His father was killed in Alexandra for reasons unknown to his family and the village. His mother did not even own a fowl. The mother and son lived on lice, as the villagers would say. But her brother, who, although not really wealthy, was far better off than herself, assisted in the education of her only son.

For his part Tshepo did a lot. His mother had said to him when he went to commence his studies at a university: 'Son, our elders might have been defeated by whites. But they were not utterly stupid. They always said to us, "Bask in the sun when it still shines." Tomorrow it may shine on others and leave you in the cold. So, my child, go to the university; and do your work when you get there. The sun shines. Go bask in it. Think about your mother at home. And show some gratitude to your uncle.'

Tshepo kept these words in his heart. His mother was not the sort of person who gave sermons. When she did, it was with utmost love and warmth. After her words, Tshepo felt warm liquid flood his eyes. He turned round quickly to hide the tears, for he was not circumcised for nothing. He did not cry when that old man cut the foreskin from his penis with agonising slowness. He liked to relive the experience in his memory. It was worth reliving. After all, he did not cry! Not many boys could boast that. But there he was now, his tears betraying him before a woman.

His mother saw them. She came nearer, embraced him tenderly and kissed them dry.

At the university Tshepo worked hard. Although he failed to complete the requirements for his degree in record time, he managed to get it with an upper second-class pass. It was on the day he received his sparkling results that the fatal lightning struck him. There was nothing one could really call rain. Just black clouds, brooding for a long time over the village. The people, seeing such ugly clouds, feared a devilish storm after the drought that had done enough damage already. Blinding lightning tore the black clouds mercilessly and rumbling thunder backed it up. But rain, no! Only a few drops that left the land as dry as a bleached bone. The clouds dragged their feet away when the blowing horn mournfully announced Tshepo's death. On receiving the message concerning the calamity that had befallen her son, Tshepo's mother choked with grief. Thus mother and son took leave of the village of Tiragalong in order that they might go to live in the underworld.

Makgolo had not always been an outcast. She was once a respected member of society. Things changed quite late in her life, with the death of her husband. The husband, after years and years of having deserted Makgolo, suddenly returned home.

All the years he had been away Makgolo had had to fend for herself without an assistant. She fared quite well. She was not one of those people who simply sat on their hands. She put her hands, and all her physical strength, to tilling the land and producing enough food for herself. Even children who came to hear her stories were offered a mealie, a melon and other products of her labour. The other reason she was able to cope was simply that she had no children of her own. When the husband left her for good – until his fateful return, that is – she was without a child.

During the time that the husband was gone, Makgolo, in fending for herself, secured a more caring man. This man, Kereng, in addition to looking after his large family, did whatever manly deed was necessary in Makgolo's compound. And people did not see this as bad, nor did they begrudge Makgolo his help.

'How could she do without the likes of him?' they said. 'Her man was surely irresponsible, or else how could he desert such a wife as Makgolo?'

The problem, really, was the man's return. He looked healthy on his arrival. But within a few days of his return he developed a strange illness. Makgolo, bitter that he imposed himself upon her as head of the family he cared little to build, and regretting that those worthy of such titles were denied them, refused to take the man to a herbalist. It was too costly, she said unashamedly, to take a man there, more especially a man who had deserted her for that long. Staying by himself all that time – and it was rumoured that he worked in the mines in the south – the man must have saved up a little and could take care of himself.

So he was left to die within two weeks of his return. Thus a solid ground for rumours was laid.

Gossip, to the effect that Makgolo had bewitched him, began to do the rounds in Tiragalong. She did not want to lose Kereng, they said. So, naturally, her husband had to be removed from the face of the earth. Others said that it must have been Kereng who had killed the husband, because he was not prepared to lose Makgolo, who was obviously a much better partner than his own wife. Yet others said that if, indeed, it was Kereng, then it was because Makgolo had spiced his food with I-am-the-only-one, a love potion that makes you love a person so much that you would be prepared to destroy whoever happens to come between you and the loved one. Because men were not generally known for dealing in witchcraft, it was in the end obvious that Makgolo had done it.

When Kereng mysteriously died from a similar disease, the truth finally revealed itself. For who has ever heard of a witch, or a wizard for that matter, who bewitched themselves? Hard times followed for mothers, who were at pains to stop their children from visiting the witch. But parents were parents; their interests were not one with the interests of their children. These children could not be told the full story about Makgolo. They repeatedly failed to understand their parents' desire to deny them the chance to listen to Makgolo's stories and to benefit from her open-handedness. Children went on visiting her. As nothing frightening happened in the village after Kereng's death, their daily rounds to her hut were not disrupted seriously.

With Tshepo's death the youth felt that Makgolo was having it too much her own way. Her childlessness was no excuse for making her neighbour to become childless like her. Tshepo's mother was too good a woman to deserve this harsh treatment. It was high time that she had a rest while her son provided for her. Besides, where was the village going to get another fine chap like him from?

Tshepo had made a name for the village by going to study in the south. He was going to teach at the local school. No! Children could not be deprived of proper education simply because of the jealousy of this old witch.

The youth of Tiragalong called a meeting. In that meeting they decided that the village be cleaned. The youth were not going to sit back and watch while their efforts to bring progress to the village were threatened.

'But let us seek directions first,' one Comrade suggested. 'Do we really want to necklace wrong people unwittingly?'

Most of the Comrades agreed that that was a wise suggestion. Representatives were accordingly sent to find out from bone throwers in some distant villages, in which they might find truly great art of bone throwing. Before that, however, money was collected from every homestead in Tiragalong. Bone throwers, like everyone else, had families to feed. On their return the representatives gave their report. Indeed, Tshepo was bewitched by an old woman, to the east of his homestead, they said. The descriptions of this woman could only point to Makgolo, they said.

The few who could have spoken up for Makgolo, who saw nothing to prove that she was a witch, who failed to understand how dead bones could tell anything trustworthy about anything and anyone, were afraid to do so. The thought that they might be said to support her because they were receiving lessons in witchcraft from her was enough to pull them back from defending her. Such an accusation would have meant that whatever step would be taken against witchcraft and its practitioners would also be taken against them.

Makgolo sits alone in her hut. Her eyes are lifted to the roof of the hut. Through the tiny holes in the roof she can catch faint glimpses of the evening sky. Or maybe faint stars, as it is too dark for her to see the sky. The roof itself, and indeed the stars as well, would have been invisible in the darkness. Only, she looks at them through her mind. The thatch is so dry it has turned white like her hoary hair. Thatch burns easily. If those Comrades should come ... Oh, their song is audible already! Fear seizes her. The freedom songs become louder. The Comrades are approaching fast. Makgolo's fear grows with the loudness of the songs. 'They say I am a witch ...' Her mind is engrossed in these words. And she imagines that the songs are about witchcraft.

'They say I am a witch ...'

Makgolo does not understand the songs. She cannot understand the songs, for they are sung in Zulu. If she knew Zulu she would realise that the language of the songs is bad Zulu. They are singing political songs, songs that freedom fighters used to sing in the apartheid era, willing new, hopefully democratic governance into being. The Comrades sing in bad Zulu because they, too, are strangers to the language. But they do not think much about the un-Zuluness of their freedom songs. What matters is that they should cleanse their village. They shall sweep into the roaring flame of their rage all the scorpions in the village. Witchcraft shall be no more!

'They say I am a witch ...'

Makgolo's thatched hut catches fire of her own imagination. Her screams are not of the imagination, though. Her screams confirm to some of the Comrades that she is already being haunted by bloody conscience. Before they can even touch her.

Witchcraft shall be no more!

The police will soon come to investigate, as usual. The Comrades will have fled their village for fear of Mankweng police, who are known for kicking a tsotsi until it does mischief in its pants. Two of the Comrades are on their way to a neighbouring village. They too have fled their own village.

'You know, I wanted to cry "Stop!" to the crowd. I simply could not stand the smell ...' the first Comrade breaks the silence.

The other agrees that the smell of the burning necklaces and petrol was no doubt extremely offensive.

'Absolutely. But it is neither the tyres nor the petrol I meant. I was only talking about the smell of her roasting flesh ...'

The second Comrade tries to stop him. He would rather not hear more. But the first Comrade is not to be silenced.

'Was she really a witch? Did she send lightning to strike Tshepo?'

'Who knows, Com?' is all the second Comrade offers.

The first Comrade heaves a big sigh. Then follows another profound silence.

BLOOD DIAMONDS
MAUREEN ISAACSON

MAUREEN ISAACSON (b. 1955 in Johannesburg, where she is currently books-page editor on *The Sunday Independent*). Her collection, *Holding Back Midnight*, was published in 1992. One of her stories closed *The Penguin Book of Contemporary South African Short Stories* in 1993 and another opened *At the Rendezvous of Victory* in 1999. 'Blood Diamonds' appears here for the first time.

Will that be all, Madam? She has exchanged her scuffed heels for a pair of Kurt Geiger pumps. The hallways of the shopping mall shine like floor polish and everything gleams. She enters a dress store where they wrap the clothes you buy in white cardboard boxes lined with tissue paper as fine as moonlight. The dress is made of pure linen.

A new woman walks to meet her in the tall mirror that caresses her curves and softens the lines the harsh Highveld sun has drawn into her cheeks.

She has left behind the woman whose reflection she scans so briefly in the cracked mirror at home. Home is the biggest house in the settlement on the dry hill where the pigs snuffle and goats scrabble among the stones.

The sales assistant murmurs sweet nothings. Sibongile's new Vixen lipstick accentuates proud lips. Gentle music confuses her senses.

Credit, Madam? Sibongile's plastic bank packet is bursting.

She needs to look beautiful tonight because the elders have instructed her, 'You must look like the queen that you are.'

It is twenty years since she became the traditional leader, the Nkosikasi of her people; for twenty years she has been listening to the wise counsel of the elders. Soon after she arrived, as the wife of Njabulo, to be the chieftainess, as she was called at the time, she discovered that her husband had a child with another woman. Divorce him, advised the elders. She would remain the Nkosikasi and they would remain her full-time advisers. They promised to make her happy. Does she not have the house closest to the water urn, money for lights and a mobile phone? Does she not drive a

Toyota Corolla? Does she not have a television set to inspire dreams?

She dreams of running water in a bath with golden taps and a shower from which water falls like rain. She has seen pictures of such luxuries in magazines and she dreams of white paint and open spaces. She remembers the green fields and the mountainside she knew as a child. As long as she is obedient, the elders will continue to turn a blind eye on her midnight antics with Mandla.

Thank you kindly, madam.

The salesman pockets the additional thirty per cent salesman's tax he has charged Sibongile.

Before she left home she arranged for the slaughter of a goat for tonight's banquet. In a large supermarket she fills a trolley with baking ingredients, she buys four crates of Coke and a carton of potato crisps.

She must hurry back to the people who have good cause to love her.

She has shared her good fortune and she has listened, for twenty years, within the cold walls of this town, to the cries of the elders.

The move from Magersfontein took place before her time. But whenever she leaves her home she observes that the green farm they were forced to desert still clings to the banks of the river where the cattle once drank.

She has heard stories about the white men who arrived on horses and whipped the young women and men. She has heard their names, Smit, Basson and Petrou. She has heard the old women cry in pain as if the whips had only just rent their flesh.

The people tell repeatedly how the men on horses brought papers to the leader of the people. The papers said the people must move by the end of the week or they would lose their possessions.

Their leader was taken to prison far away in Pretoria and nobody was allowed to visit. The people packed their goods on to waggons and began the slow trek across the mountain to a place the people always referred to as 'the new place' at the other side.

Three years later, a packet was delivered to the leader's wife. In the rumpled brown paper bag addressed to Sonti Radebe were the clothes that she had once washed and ironed. Attached to the frayed shirt was a message saying that her husband was to be buried at eight a.m. the following day. How were they expected to travel to Pretoria in that short time? There were no explanations. Nobody dared ask questions.

The men erected a gravestone over a patch of dry earth. Her husband's body was buried with three others in the prison cemetery.

'The new place' is only twelve kilometres away from their real home.

The rocks break in the sun and the wind carries the sins of the past across the town like a virus. The wind carries tuberculosis and bitterness to the people who were forced to pay for this land when they were removed from their own.

They have finally paid the bank loan they were forced to take.

Only the spirits from the liquor store can wash down the dust that sticks in the throat. Friday afternoons the drinking begins. It lasts until Sunday morning, when Reverend Philemon takes the pulpit and speaks about the will of the Lord. For years now, he has repeated his sermon: the Lord has plans for us. Who are we to question his ways? In the Lord we will find redemption.

The liquor store is the only source of entertainment, a cynical gesture that marks the entrance to similar villages across the land. Patience is rewarded when the new government installs a postal service with forty neat little boxes on the hillock next to Sibongile's house. Soon there will be running water for all, they say. The old people listen dully to the youngsters who bring news of a changed world outside. Many have not ventured out of the village for years. They hear that Nelson Mandela's legacy is to be continued by President Thabo Mbeki, who still remains a mystery to the world.

This week the old people with the sunken eyes sit up when the youngsters walk in, cheering. Something has happened.

The home they left twelve years ago now belongs to the state. And diamonds have been discovered on this land!

What does this mean? There is a possibility that they will be able to move back home! It means they will receive money from the land they were forced to leave and they are entitled to the money that they paid to live in the new place. It means they are entitled to the diamonds! They will be rich. Tourism! Sibongile will open a restaurant.

Money! The children will go to school.

Tonight is the first of many meetings that will be followed by banquets such as the one at which Charles Hurt says, 'What is the function of the chieftainess?'

'Nkosikasi,' she says.

'Nko... well, what is your function?' He does not know anything about her people except the happy issues of retrieval that they possibly face. You must be very happy, he says.

She says it is important to sleep where the ancestors sleep. Even though our leader has been buried in Pretoria, the ancestors remain the most important issue.

Hurt says he has recently read a story in a newspaper about a man who was directed by the voices of his ancestors to chop up his baby. The man forced his wife to carry the baby and hold him as he sliced it up; first the head, then the limbs. He then forced her to carry it on her back.

What is the importance of ancestors? he asks.

Sibongile smiles and looks into the distance.

They can hear you, she thinks.

A young woman who is from a commission for gender something, asks, How can you allow the men to tell you what to do? She says she will come back to see her with some of the women in her group and they will explain the meaning of liberation to her.

After a year a judge in the constitutional court passes the verdict.

The land belongs to Sibongile's people!

An architect plans a new village in consultation with the young leaders.

Sibongile is consulted about her home. The architect shows her photographs of beautiful homes generated with solar and lunar energy; swimming pools are painted black and ivory, set in landscaped gardens circled with aloes.

Sibongile indicates the baths with the taps of her dreams and marble floors. She has her eye on a mini roman villa with jacuzzi and adjoining rooms, just like the president's.

A year later her new house is ready. The gender woman has brought her women's group to teach Sibongile how to demand her rights. She discovers that there is enough money in her account to build another house, in the northern suburbs of the city adjoining the farm.

She wants everything the president's wife has.

Is she not an important person among her people? Has she not always shared her privileges?

Government officials and diplomats from countries she has not heard of seek out Sibongile.

She tells them of the hardships of the past in the language of the elders. She hires Winnie Madikizela-Mandela's dress designer. She makes new friends. Michael Jackson comes to visit her in her beautiful new house. Diana Ross joins them and later Madonna arrives. They teach her how to dance, American style.

One night a gang breaks into her house. They ask where her employer keeps the money and the key to the safe. They stuff a dirty sock in her mouth to stifle her cries when they rape her. Each takes his long, ugly time with her. They lock her in a dark cupboard with her many pairs of shoes and coats.

It is only the next day that she is able to escape.

She moves inside of herself. Now she is a sad slow woman with a dull heart and bruises that will not heal. She hires a twenty-four-hour security system. She buys two German shepherds. She hires a man to train them to kill intruders. There are no more parties. Her people are too afraid to visit her. When new friends visit there is nothing to say. She leaves this house and moves back to the new village where her other new house with gold taps imported from Saudi Arabia stands empty.

Sergeant Dlamini finds her in the old dry town.

'Come now, Nkosikasi,' he urges.

'You ask about my heritage,' she says into the blank night, as if addressing a press conference. 'Here is my heritage. Although I was poor and although we suffered, and the old people choked on this dust, it was where my dreams were born and kept alive.'

She moves back into her old house that overlooks the empty village even though the land no longer belongs to her people. She pays the government a fee to use this land, which they have declared unlivable.

Every week the young people bring her supplies.

On the other side of the mountain, her story has been woven into folklore.

K SELLO DUIKER
WHEN YOU LEAST EXPECT IT

K SELLO DUIKER (b. 1974, resident in Berea, Johannesburg). With his first novel, *Thirteen Cents*, he was awarded the 2001 Commonwealth Writers Prize for Best First Book, Africa Region. A short story of his called 'Giant' is included in *In the Rapids* (2001). 'When You Least Expect It' has not appeared before.

'Truth,' I answered.

It was an unusually hot and moist summer night. We were sitting around a table in a small two-bedroom flat that I shared with Themba in Yeoville. A crate of kamikaze Black Labels was near us. The girls were looking tipsy and were giggling. They were from Cape Town and we'd met them at the swimming pool this afternoon. I was feeling drunk myself but desperately tried to act sober. Clear-headed as a pilot, Themba watched us, half smirking at the rate at which we were getting drunk while he wasn't. We were topless, except for the girls who still wore their bras. I noticed that Lerato kept eyeing me.

'So have you ever been arrested for anything?' Lorain asked with a piercing look.

I felt momentarily sober. The others must have seen the expression on my face so I decided to tell them the truth.

'Twice,' I said.

Themba looked at me as though to say: be careful where you're treading. You don't want to fuck up a potential lay. But I was drunk and I knew that if I tried to lie it would be unconvincing. Besides, I was a little weary of Lorain who'd told me earlier that she was a third-year Psycho student. There was something about the way she looked at me that made me a little paranoid, as though she were scrutinising everything I said and forming rash opinions about me.

'For ganja.'

'You naughty boy,' Lorain teased me. 'And did you go to court?'

'No. Charges were eventually dropped. Don't ask why, long story.'

'And the second time?' Lerato asked, pouting a little.

'One question at a time, guys,' Themba rescued me.

'It's my turn,' Lerato said, confidently taking the bottle and spinning it.

The spinning motion made me a little dizzy to watch, so I focused on Lerato's breasts. The bottle stopped and pointed to Lorain.

'Truth or dare?' Lerato began.

'Truth,' she said triumphantly.

'Have you ever had an STD?'

'No,' she disappointed us.

I excused myself quickly and went to the bathroom. The lino was dirty from the previous night's drinking session and the bath still had Themba's wet washing from this morning. It gave off a dank, fetid smell like a high school locker room. After taking a leak I washed my hands in a grimy sink and looked at myself in the mirror. I looked pissed, a wreck. There was no way that Lerato was going to sleep with me. I closed the door and forced my fingers down my throat, my head half-way in the toilet bowl. A nauseating brown stream quickly poured out. I wrenched my stomach till I was sure that I would walk out feeling more sober. I cleaned the mess, flushed and rinsed my mouth at the sink.

'You fine. We were beginning to worry,' Lerato said when I returned.

'Weak bladder,' I improvised.

'As long as that's the only weakness in that department,' Lorain said.

I smiled nervously, performance anxiety looming at the back of my mind. Lerato put on some lip-balm with her small finger, her eyes fixed on the others. I suspected that she knew that I was staring at her. She looked ravishing – I suppose as ravishing as given the effects of four quarts of kamikazes.

'So who's next,' Lorain said eagerly. I could see why Themba had his eye on her. She was the feisty type who probably liked to initiate sex. Themba liked his women upfront and a little coquettish. I took the bottle and spun it. It pointed to Themba.

'Dare,' he said nonchalantly.

I remembered what he had said. Don't frighten them away with silly dares. Remember we want them to stay the night over. And don't ask me to kiss Lorain.

'Tell us what you sound like when you come,' I said without thinking. Perhaps I wanted to rattle Themba a little. He was looking far too sober and in control.

'What?' he said with disbelief, grinding his jaw with irritation. If the girls weren't there, he would have sworn me. You're fucking up my strategy, he seemed to say with his eyes. Wait till they're drunk.

'So?' Lorain egged him on.

'Fuck it. I'd rather drink,' he chickened out and poured himself a glass that he had to down.

As the evening grew deeper we began opting for more truths than dares, confessing intimate things about ourselves like whether we had ever had a threesome or when we had had our first sexual experience. The girls eventually got drunk. But it was Lorain who made the first move. She leaned over and kissed Themba. After that it didn't take long for us to couple in separate bedrooms.

In the morning I woke up with a hangover that felt like my brain was haemorrhaging. Lerato was not beside me. I stumbled out of bed, curious about where she was. My eyes were sore with fatigue as I walked into the sunny lounge. Themba was sitting on a chair, his head in his hands.

'Don't worry, you're not the only one,' I consoled him. 'Have you seen Lerato?'

I sat next to him.

'Have I seen Lerato?' he said sarcastically.

I was searching for the TV remote control when he asked me what I was looking for.

'Where's the TV?' I suddenly realised its absence.

He didn't say anything.

'And the video?' I said getting up. 'Or my cellphone. And the ...'

'Don't ask about the CDs,' he added.

'Not the CDs too.'

'At least they left the stove,' he said, his eyes quietly angry.

We had one kamikaze left to kill and enough shame and embarrassment to keep us celibate for the rest of the summer.

FARIDA KARODIA
A HANDBAG IN THE BOOT

Farida Karodia (b. 1942 in the Eastern Cape). A recent collection of her stories is *Against an African Sky* of 1995. She divides her time between Johannesburg and Vancouver BC, where she used to live in exile. 'A Handbag in the Boot' appears here for the first time.

Carla hated Hillbrow. It was run-down and congested. A disgraceful symbol of the downward spiral of inner-city Johannesburg. Who would have thought that this once trendy area had now become the armpit of Africa? Across the street a man was urinating up against a tree. Her lips curled in disgust.

She really hated coming into town.

'All these bloody one-ways,' she cursed, turning left onto Kotze Street. She had taken a wrong turn earlier and was hot and impatient. She turned off the radio. In this part of town one had to be alert.

Thank goodness she'd had the foresight to lock her handbag in the boot. Her cellphone was concealed under the armrest and she wondered if it might be visible from the outside. Car hijackings were common, but even more common were robberies of the smash-and-grab variety.

She did a quick check that all her doors were locked and the windows shut.

The light was taking ages to change.

Jesse was twelve years old. He was one of the hundreds of kids who hung around street corners begging. On the pavement next to him lay a flattened plastic bottle with its lethal contents of white pasty glue. He was working the corner of Kotze and Edith Cavell when the BMW pulled up at the robot.

The woman in the car was attractive. Judging from the car and the amount of gold jewellery in her ears and around her neck, he shrewdly assessed that he could tap her for a few rands. She was wearing several gold bands around her right arm. Not the thin cheap bracelets one bought at Game, but chunky ones, heavy with gold. One could distinguish the quality from the depth of colour. Although she was wearing sunglasses, he could see a youthful softness in her face which was quite pleasant.

The woman hadn't seen him yet. She was looking straight ahead. Then he was right at her window. He watched as she impatiently tapped the steering wheel with her scarlet nails.

Through the corner of her eye she saw him. Startled, she turned. Jesse scrunched up his shoulders and slipped into 'begging mode', his hands held out in a gesture of supplication, and an angelic smile on his face.

Her glance rested on him for a few seconds and then she turned away, returning her gaze to the robot.

The robot was still red. There had been problems there all morning. The light took almost five minutes to change to green. A long line of traffic had already assembled behind the BMW. He tapped on the window. She waved him away. He smiled again, knowing that the smile would be the last thing she'd remember.

She was anxious about him hanging around the car. The threat of being robbed – windows smashed in an instant, or worse still, a gun held to her head – was a very real one.

Jesse could tell that she desperately wanted to get away. He could actually see her desperation as she wished the light to green so she could speed away to the safety of the northern suburbs.

But the robot remained red.

'Damn,' Carla muttered. The child was still at the window, his hands held out to her. She did not have any money with her. Her handbag was locked in the boot. Carla glanced at him again and then quickly averted her eyes.

Whatever you do, don't make eye contact, she told herself.

He had a lovely smile. He was a pretty child with a mop of un-kempt black curls and even in that brief instant – not wanting to make eye contact – she had noticed his even white teeth. But it was the smile that tugged at her, the sweetest smile she had ever seen.

'Please, please, Madam,' he said with a grimace of such childlike appeal that she felt her heart skip a beat.

Although she couldn't hear him through the closed window, his expression was more eloquent than any words might have been.

A car hooted for her to get going, but the light facing her was still red and there was no break in the flow of traffic in the intersection.

He saw the look of relief on her face as the light abruptly changed. Carla gunned the BMW and pulled away. She glanced in the rear-view mirror and saw the child standing there, still smiling at her.

There were just too many street children around. Where did they all come from? she wondered. Her husband said it was a sign of things going to pot in the country. There were too many unemployed and their ranks were swelling each day.

The ranks of the beggars had swelled too. Youths, old men, young men, old women and women with children. Always on the corner of William Nichol and Peter Place was the same young man, his sign impertinently pushed up against the window – a piece of cardboard on which was scribbled, 'Please Help. No job no food three days. Hunkry. God bless.'

He'd been there for more than six months already with the same sign. She'd heard on the radio that one of the motorists had offered him a job, but that he had declined. Begging was clearly more lucrative than working for a living.

She remembered the euphoria after the elections when drivers had actually doled out fifty-rand bills to beggars. Six years down the line, the numbers had increased, each of them having staked their territory.

Carla turned onto the M1. She'd forgotten about the construction work at Corlett Drive and cursed the delay as three lanes of traffic merged into one. She turned off on Grayston and stopped at the light. Right in the middle of the road stood a woman, holding a toddler by the hand and a baby on her back. As the cars stopped before her, she held out her hand almost tentatively with a shy smile. The woman was still obviously a novice. It wouldn't take long, though, before she'd have the required expertise, playing on the guilt and sympathy of white motorists.

She wondered briefly what had happened to the fellow in the wheelchair who used to occupy that spot. She hoped the woman's grip on the child's hand was firm. The toddler could quite easily release its mother's hand and wander off into the traffic. She shuddered at the thought. The woman looked directly at her. Carla smiled apologetically.

Her handbag was locked in the boot.

Carla turned into Sandton Drive. She thought about the woman in the middle of a busy intersection and the tousle-haired boy with the sweet smile. The two combined to create a disturbing image.

She thought of the squashed plastic bottle lying on the pavement. Had she not watched a documentary about drugs and street children she might never have known what those plastic bottles contained.

Carla felt guilty. The image of the boy's smiling face at the window had left her with an uneasy feeling. What if he had really been hungry?

She dismissed the thought. He probably wanted the money for drugs, or for more glue. What if he was hungry? The doubt took root, nibbling at her, following her. But the boy's face haunted her. That smile. The dark curly hair. The even white teeth.

She could barely focus on her driving, hitting every amber light on her way home. She tried to expel the image of the boy with his dirty face, his hands stretched out in supplication.

The gate was partly open as she turned into the driveway. The security guard must have heard her car. She didn't like the idea of him opening the gate before being able to identify the car. What if it hadn't been her? She was going to remind him on no account to open the gates unless he was able to identify the car and driver.

She took her mind off the boy and the woman by focusing on the gate and its pre-emptive opening. But the boy's smile returned. If only she'd had some money in the car with her, but she couldn't assist him because her handbag was locked in the boot.

She built on this thought, expanded it as she waited for the garage door to close behind her. The boy might have been some kind of point man for a group of thugs. She might have become a perfect target for a mugging.

That night as she lay in bed in the darkness, listening to her husband's even breathing, the guilt continued to gnaw at her. She tossed and turned and resolved to go back there the very next day to find him and to give him the few rands she had begrudged him.

In Hillbrow Jesse's friend Monica, an older girl, was preparing for her night out on the streets. She survived by selling her body in order to support her drug habit. But Jesse had come into her life and she had grown attached to him. The two of them were as close as siblings. She always looked out for him.

Monica had been raped twice in front of Jesse. It was a hard life surviving in the streets of Johannesburg, but infinitely preferable to being at home where they were both abused. Jesse's mother regularly had her arm broken and, when his stepfather didn't get enough satisfaction from battering his mother, he turned on him. Jesse had burn marks all over his body where cigarettes had been ground out. His one side was slightly deformed from a broken rib that had not mended properly.

The hunger was a nuisance. But the glue eased the pangs. Made one light-headed. Kept the heart pounding. Deadened the pain. Left one in a pleasant state of euphoria.

No cares. No worries, man.

He was hungry.

He told Monica he was hungry. She promised she'd bring him something to eat.

At eleven o'clock, she was still not back. Jesse took the cardboard strips and blanket from where they had stashed them in the alley. He carried them back to the drainage ditch, opened the cardboard strips and spread them on the ground. Shivering with cold, he crept under the blanket.

In Sandton, too, Carla was lying awake, thinking about her unborn kids, knowing that they would want for nothing. It would only be the very best for them. The boy's face surfaced again, grew in proportion until it devoured and obliterated all other thought. She tossed restlessly. Next to her, her husband slept peacefully.

Tomorrow she was seeing her doctor. She had not told her husband yet that she might be pregnant.

DENNIS VENTER
BEARING BREASTS

DENNIS VENTER (b. in Johannesburg in 1967). He was educated in Natal and moved to Cape Town in 1986. 'Bearing Breasts' is his first story to be anthologised in South Africa.

The Court A Quo

The Convicted: Carmen Lynne Craven. Adult female. Convicted of Public Indecency in terms of Section 3 of The Indecent Exposure Act number 45 of 1967, as amended, in the Cape Town Magistrate's Court, January 1995.

The Court Officials: Magistrate Frikkie Crouse presiding, Johannes Smit for the state, Deborah Clarke of Clarke and Associates for the accused.

In mitigation of sentence: This was Ms Craven's first offence and several character witnesses painted a picture of a well-adjusted personality with solid roots in the community. It was given inter alia that Ms Craven is a part-time counsellor for Lifeline and a founder member of W(AM)AR, to wit Women (And Men) Against Rape.

The Sentence: A fine of five hundred rand (R500.00) or two months in jail. Due to first-offender status, half the sentence was suspended for two years.

The Facts

It was the day. No more excuses, no more delays. Glance at the book on the nightstand. *Feel the Fear and Do It Anyway.* No normal person would do it, the thought hovers like a gnat swarm. But didn't the same doubt trouble the Suffragettes? Didn't they think, 'tis insane and absurd to fling oneself in the path of galloping mares?

Maybe their motivation was different, maybe fighting for the end of subjugation, the right to be heard in government forums was more important, more noble.

But what of these motivations:
- The maintenance increase was denied. He pleaded poverty, the magistrate barely blinked, postponed the matter sine die. 'That's indefinitely,' legal counsel explained, still expecting payment.
- Passed over at work again. The old-boy network, spread like pinstriped varicose veins throughout the body of business.
- The resentment in the kids' eyes: Your veggies, your home-work, you are *not* going like that! But his weekly visits take them in buoyant spirits to the Waterfront, to heavenly sweets and big-screen motion pictures. Not bad for the oh-so impoverished.
- The men's toilet. Queues a non-thing in the two-stall, ten-urinal substructure. On the other side, straining women stand with twisted limbs. Waiting, sodden tampons having to linger, while men pack away their equipment and get on with their lives.
- Friday nights, *ER* perpetually giving way to the goddamned Super 12.
- And Graaff's Pool. Every morning, Graaff's Pool, squatting in the Sea Point Bay like a bug in blue soup.

It all becomes too much, doesn't it? The little things multiply. Forget the Issues. Forget the blatant discrimination of every day, the violence and abuse. It's the multiplication of the small. The trivialities, like bunnies, they mount.

So it's the day, today. Steaming hot. Frazzled like a peri-peri prawn. Sweat, not perspiration, not aglow. Sweat. It runs down cheeks, dampening hairline. At the back of the knees, it drips. Between the legs, moist, like a sponge.

Below, in the street, in the heat, people stream. Holidaymakers aplenty, drawn by the December sun. Men dressed in shorts, draped in towels, torsos from tanned to tepid gliding, wobbling or muscling by.

And the womenfolk? Skimpy clothing, flesh in sight. It's Cape Town, the height of summer. For there to be no flesh, now that would be wrong.

But wait. There's something different, not that subtle, obvious as BO – tops in evidence. The womenfolk are all wearing tops. Full, skimpy, virtually none at all. But all. All there, all kitted out in society-dictated street-wear.

And in Graaff's Pool, a reserve for the use of men. In Graaff's Pool, they strip away mankind's habits. They render themselves naked, lounging like albino lizards on concrete steps, their skins blushing beneath the voyeuristic sun. In Graaff's Pool, surrounded by grey walls, ensuring privacy so that there are no bothers, no glares, no petty police patrolling for overexposure. In Graaff's Pool. For men. Only for men.

The Appeal

The Court Officials: Judges James Smythe and Elliot Pieters presiding. Advocate Charl Vorster for the state. Advocate Wilma Kruger instructed by Clarke and Associates for appellant.

The Judgement: handed down on 3 April 1996 by the honourable Judge Smythe, Judge Pieters concurring. 'Were it this court's decision to make, the finding of the court a quo would be upheld. To argue that women should be entitled to bare their breasts in public because men are so entitled is asinine. To maintain that to punish a woman for such conduct is discriminatory is stretching the definition of discrimination to an absurd degree. It is the accepted norm that females be covered. There are establishments, yes, where in this lax modern age it is deemed appropriate for breasts (and more) to be exposed. But those shiny-pole places are hidden away, downtown both literally and morally, away from our children's eyes. Public nudity remains improper, and this court is thankful that it does.'

Bushy eyebrows waggle like constipated caterpillars, distaste as obvious as day.

'However, Appellant claims that the section is discriminatory and as such is unconstitutional. And when it comes to constitutional questions, this court has no choice but to refer such matters to the appropriate forum – to wit, the Constitutional Court. It is sincerely hoped that said distinguished forum will exhibit a prudence befitting its status and will treat this matter with the disdain it deserves.'

The Outcome: The decision of the lower court suspended pending the Constitutional Court hearing.

The Facts (continued)

See the ordinary building, on Sea Point Main Road, it's railed, jailed balconies staring towards Graaff's Pool. See its tinted front doors, blinking in the sun. See them swing open, like saloon doors before big bad Bill. See the lady walk from the building, into the street, into the heat. See her turn right, towards the beach, towards the sea. See her looking straight ahead, her eyes fixed on a spot six inches above and six feet beyond. See the shocked expressions, the gasps of old crones, their hands darting to their quivering mouths. See the faces of the kids, amazement engulfed by giggles. See the eyes of all, drawn to the woman's naked torso, homing in on breasts doing their best (after time and two kids) to point firmly ahead. See the young men ignoring their hitherto idolised companions, see them stare with envy and delight too. See the ice-creams stop midway to mouths, the conversations freeze, the smiles, the lewd grins, the expressions of joy as young men whoop their pleasure and lust.

See Spot run, joe&jennypublic. See Spot run.

The Legal Advice

Pay the fine or do the time. Or ...

The plan from the beginning. When talk of the new South Africa became reality. When the irrepressible Nelson was released into the land, to embrace the people to sing the ubuntu song like only he could.

The plan from the beginning: there will be an ultimate rule, and we will call it Constitution. It will rain down justice on all the people. Killer and kid alike, man and muffin will be governed by its wise rule. Both Nelson, and you and ET too. Where best to fight the battle? Where better than the forum that uses nothing but the big C as its god and Guide?

And so, legal consultations were endured, all for the good of the cause. The advocates, the attorneys, the training-to-be clerks, advising on rights, technicalities and occasionally warning about costs. Take a deposit. Legal dogma. Always take a deposit.

But costs are a worry no more. They've all boarded the band-waggon. Women Against Discrimination, Women Against Sexist Pigs. The WADS, the WASPS, even the indomitable Beau Brummell, he of naked-family fame, have stood up in firm support. They're all on board, funding Carmen's Cause like Union Bosses – with small percentages of monthly membership fees. Paying for the food the kids now eat, after the suspension from work (this is not the image the company wishes to portray!) and the new Labour Law be

damned. Paying for legal counsel, between them forty years' experience. The attorney's satin pumps. The junior counsel's glittering
rings. And the senior counsel. The dream team king. Paying for the
removal of his directionless hair, seeming to slip with obstinate
frequency from his once well-covered dome to his now drooping
earlobes.

The mag crt. went like a three-day-itch. The high court stepped
down, reluctantly, petulantly. And the eleven Keepers of the
Constitution came forth to deliberate. Having read the headlines
like 'The Beauty and the Breast', 'Who Gives a Hoot(er)' and
'ConsTITutional Cravings'; having seen the demonstrations, heard
the heated debates, watched on the News the amateur footage,
constantly replayed – Carmen L Craven strutting the street (nipple-
stars suitably positioned for safe-family-viewing, while bums and
babies are reported dead and Bosnians are blown to bits). They
gathered, the judges, like a cabal of elders, and justice, they trum-
peted, was their quest.

The Closing Argument

In an irregular move, delivered by the Appellant herself:

She approached the podium. Her papers shook. She cleared her
throat. Fleeted a glance at the eleven poker-faced law lords. Her
voice cracked, overwhelmed by the urge to giggle – scratch that –
cackle. She regained composure. Began.

'At the turn of the century, in Britain, a civilised and enlightened
nation from where a great deal of our laws and customs have come,
women could not vote. They could raise children, support their husbands, be nurses but not doctors, never doctors. Judges too were
men, only men, because a woman's place was the home.' She looked
up. Her eyes sought those of the female judges. Spotting no obvious
support, they flitted back to her notes like punch-drunk butterflies.
'Times have changed, but so much remains the same. Until but a
few years ago, in our country, women were considered the depen-
dants of men. They required their husbands' consent to do anything
of consequence. They adopted their husbands' domicile, regardless
of their intent. They were like minors. Minors in the eyes of the law.'

Voice stronger now, face flushed, not so much with fear, but
with belief. It is a good fight, this fight. God willing, she'll make it
right.

'That's changed. Another form of discrimination has been re-moved, three hundred years down the line. Thank you legislature, thank you for giving little me this freedom.'

Warning! Alert! Whoop-whoop! Instructing attorney shifts uncomfortably. Junior counsel dips head behind box briefcase. Senior counsel, the great one, tugs absently at a newly sprouted lobe-hair. Sarcasm, they warned, is not appreciated. Judges, like schoolyard bullies, enjoy only to dispense. Calm down, Carmen. Be calm.

Carmen inhales, drops notes to the podium and addresses the judges reasonably. Reason, it will triumph. Ergo, triumphant will be reason.

'Five years ago, I could go onto a certain beach. My char couldn't. She was of an inappropriate skin colour. I could catch a particular bus, my char couldn't. I could go to a particular cinema, my char couldn't. That was a form of discrimination which took years and years to be struck down. Today, the law says I may not take my shirt off in public, the law says he may. Fact. One person may do something, another in identical circumstances may not. That's dis-crimination. Pure and simple. Whether this honourable court agrees or not, it will remain discrimination. Paint it with whatever social brush you like, call it whatever convenient term you wish. Fact: it is discrimination.'

Warning! Red alert! Double whoop-whoop! Don't take them on. Overachievers, accustomed to subservience, egos like South African Rugby bosses, the justices will crush you flat. Bow to their infinite superiority, do so with the law on your side.

'M'Lords and Ladies, irrespective of the decision here today, I will in all likelihood never again walk the street in a topless state. I will never again do what some people have called crazy irre-sponsibility, others indulgent exhibitionism and still others an act of selfless bravery. I have no desire to do so. It's uncomfortable, I am not blessed with a small chest, my physique requires support. Nor do I particularly like the looks, the stares and glares. But I should be allowed to if I so wish. I shouldn't face fines and jail time for doing the exact same thing that my neighbour Bob can do, with sun-burn his only possible sanction. That is just not fair, m'Lords and Ladies, and fairness being the ultimate goal of this honourable court, it is humbly submitted that it has no option but to find Section 3 of The Indecent Exposure Act number 45 of 1967, as amended, to be discriminatory.' She looks up at the judges and nods. It is done. 'Thank you, m'Lords and Ladies, for giving me the opportunity to be heard.'

The Facts (continued)

Don't sit in judgement, be her. Take her place, walk in her naked feet.

You have planned the route. Religiously. Along Main Road for two blocks, down into St James, past the flats and the SABC and into Beach Road. Cross the strip of park to the promenade. Right towards Mouille Point and at the Putt-Putt your destination is reached, your goal is achieved. If you get there. You doubt you will.

You approach the glass doors. Beyond them, everything glooms through the tint. You reach the doors, close your eyes, rest your brow on the cool glass and take a deep breath. *Feel the Fear and Do It Anyway.* You suppress the ice that cracks inside. You banish thoughts of what this might mean to you, your children, your family back home. You have considered it all to death, it is something you just have to do.

One final breath, then you push open the doors. Firmly, now, there is no turning back. You step into the glare. The sun caresses your skin (*'Hello my pretty'*). You exhale, turn to the sea and start walking. You don't look at anyone, just ahead, six feet beyond. Still, you feel the stares that stroke your nakedness like calloused fingers. You hear the shouts and laughter. You sense the movement of heads snapping in your direction, conversations halting mid-sentence, then starting up again in hissed whispers or hoarse cheers. You move on. Your destination has been planned. You have to make a point, it is your duty.

Be her as she walks with upheld head through the gathering, gabbling spectators. Be her as young tearaways run alongside, staring at her like an X-file oddity, as people pickled in screw-top wine exhale their fetid breath on her, as the sun and eyes and scandal burn into her reddening skin, as the story crackles like bush fires and the boys-in-blue come from wherever it is they lurk, ready to protect society from the evil that is at hand.

They come at you, the Kitskonstabels, like dark at dusk. Their expressions are bemused as they suggest you cover yourself. But there is steel beyond the veneer. You push yourself past. Rough

cotton scrapes your skin. A hand grabs your arm, pulls you. You
rip yourself free. A stray fingernail scratches a trail across your
wrist. They babble into walkie-talkies, like foreign kettles boiling.
Still you move. But for not much longer. The yellow van screams
up. They secure you, one on each arm. You do not fight, you are
too afraid. One of them throws a jacket over you. It smells of stale
smoke, of musty bachelorhood. They manhandle you into the van
while the crowds cheer or jeer. It is cold and hard inside. You expected nothing less.

Be her.

As the van pulls off, speeding you like a Banana Republic
President towards a meeting of men. As you breathe in a ragged
sob, pull the jacket together in front of your offence and fail to
experience the elation your fantasies promised would be yours.

The Deliberations

They came, the Kings of Constitution, they came forth, as is their
duty, and deliberated thusly:

It's no joke, too many people take it as such.

There's the possibility of floodgates.

Where to draw the line? Tops now, bottoms when?

Protect the public – but from what? Is a breast a beast?

Yes, but where to draw the line?

Let social conscience dictate the lines.

But one person's conscience is another person's caper.

That is beyond control. Fact, the section is discriminatory. Fact,
the sentence must be set aside.

But what about floodgates?

Nothing to be done about that, let the public build their own
damn walls.

And so, in the end, reluctance succumbed to inevitability. Section
3 of Act 45 of 1967, as amended, declared discriminatory. The decision of the court a quo set aside. Carmen L Craven, the accused,
the convicted, the appellant, set loose on society again.

The Public Reaction

It's a sad, tragic day.

It's cool. I've got absolutely no problem with it.

It's unbelievable. The sins of the flesh. The whores who go bare will be punished!

It's no big deal. It's how life was before enforced colonisation.

It's a famous day for democracy and liberation in this country. It has struck a blow for all women, feminism burns bright, the sisters, they're doing it for themselves.

The End

Now …

Drive along St Peter, drive along St Paul. Witness examples of Carmen's selfless legacy.

- The carwash places where bare-topped varsity girls earn spare cash, soapy breasts squished against windscreens, while men squat in cars, drooling like asylum fools.

- The shop windows, from Truworths to Travel Agencies, filled with cut-out cuties, their naked nubs pointing to product. Because, hey, sex sells.

- The brazen ones on their street corners, the payee-women who come, some sans teeth, but all bearing breasts, baring breasts, both regular and extra large.

Then be her again, Carmen L Craven, as she drives fully clothed down St Peter and onto St Paul, as she stares at the wares, at the way they're waved and waggled, like rand-a-bag vendors and their plump, overripe fruit. Be her as she squeezes her eyes and contemplates what her actions have wrought, as she wonders at the irony of it all, and thinks back to the quote that once made it all worthwhile: It's a famous day for democracy and liberation in this country. It has struck a blow for all women, feminism burns bright, the sisters, they're doing it for themselves.

KEN BARRIS
CLUBFOOT

KEN BARRIS (b. in Port Elizabeth, resident in Cape Town). In 1988 he published his first collection of short stories, *Small Change*, with Ad. Donker. He has been an associate editor of *New Contrast*. 'Clubfoot' has not been previously published and was written as a response to J M Coetzee's novel, *Disgrace*.

He watched his mother as she worked. Her hands were chapped, the flesh was pale. The light coming in through the window was stark, and bleached her face and arms almost the colour of milk. She was cleaning a galjoen, scraping off the scales with her sharp knife. The scales sprang into the air, rasping off in silver-grey showers. The kitchen stank of fish blood.

He longed to talk to his mother. He knew she wouldn't answer. Her mouth was a healed gash. She was a creased milky body that breathed and moved and spoke only when necessary. He closed his eyes and tried to enter her flesh. He wanted to move her arms, see through her pale eyes. He wanted to live inside her where, perhaps, it was warmer. But she remained solid and distant, and he remained where he was on the kitchen chair, kicking his heels softly against its wooden legs. He could taste the whiteness; it was like eating chalk or sand.

The sounds coming from outside – the teasing wind, the scream-ing gulls, the sea – combined with the scraping of his mother's blade. They twisted together into lines of music, briefly caught, something he might sing; then they were sounds and noises. The scraping stopped altogether. The fish slapped onto the board, he heard the cold water tap running. He knew it was the cold tap because it sounded different to the hot one. Then came the pad-dling of her hands and the smell of Sunlight soap.

He opened his eyes again. To his surprise, his mother was watching him. As usual, he couldn't read the expression in her eyes. He looked away.

'It's cooler outside,' she said. 'Come, we'll walk down the beach.'

Silently, he shifted off his chair and limped to the door. They stepped down onto the white sand, the scraggy grass. Light knifed into his eyes, and his foot hurt more than usual. He sat down on the step.

'I don't want to go,' he said.

The flesh around her eyes seemed to soften. She said, 'I'll carry you the first bit.' She knelt down, turning her back to him. He climbed onto her back and wrapped his arms around her broad shoulders, his legs about her hips. With a grunt of pain or weariness, she straightened up and walked down to the sea.

He pressed his face into the back of her neck. There was the jogging of her stride and the milky odour of her body. The breeze coming off the sea tugged at her hair; it brushed against the side of his face. Then his mother walked into the sea, and stood ankle-deep in the surging water. She let him down. The icy shock was a relief to his foot. They stood together looking at the horizon, holding hands.

'It's getting too cold,' he said.

Reluctantly she turned away, and they began their walk down the beach. He crouched over a large stranded jellyfish – a pudding of flesh almost a metre across – and the mob of whelk boring into it.

'Is it dead?' he asked. 'They're eating it.'

'I don't think so,' she replied. 'I don't know.'

'Can it feel?'

'I don't know. I don't think so.'

He picked up one of the whelk by its conical shell. With nothing to attach itself to, the sucker squirmed about blindly. He put it back on the jellyfish and watched as it began to dig into smooth clear meat. He thought: it must have a mouth in its foot to do that. Then he straightened up and limped onwards. Pain curled through his foot and shot up the muscles of his lower leg. He turned back, and looked at his mother.

'All right,' she said, 'we can go back.'

But they stood still for a while. There was no one else on the beach. They were alone with the white light, the noises of sea and wind, the long converging lines of the shore. Am I alive or dead? he wondered: is my mother alive or dead? Can we feel? He heard his mother's voice say: I don't think so. I don't know.

It was a hot morning. He sat staring at the patch of light falling in through the open door. When he didn't blink for long enough, chimeric colours emerged from the rectangle of light and drifted across it. When he did close his eyes, their lids stung pleasantly. His mother was working in the kitchen and humming. It was a wordless song about being tired, and wanting things she didn't have, and about having things she didn't want.

He turned back to the rectangle of light. He could feel its heat on the surfaces of his eyes. It was a dangerous desert, and he was flying safely in a boat above it.

He was distracted by the noise of an engine beating irregularly. It approached the cottage and pulled up with a rich squeaking of springs. His mother fell silent, and a door creaked open. They waited. Then, as the visitor's shadow fell across his patch of light, the reek of unwashed flesh entered the cottage.

It was hard to see the man who stood at the door because of the glare behind him. He was tall and had long, wild hair. He cleared his throat and asked, 'Would this be the home of Caitlin Turner?'

The boy scrambled to his feet. He looked around, to see his mother coming. She dropped the plate she was holding – it broke with a dull sound into two uneven pieces – and then she stood quite still.

'Caitlin,' said the visitor, 'Caitlin – it's been …' His voice tailed away, and he started again, almost pleading: 'It's been a long time.'

She bent down and picked up the pieces of the plate. She straightened up and said, 'I suppose you'd better come in.'

He came in then, his smell overpowering the small room. She looked at him in dismay. 'God, Arthur, you're a mess,' she said. 'How on earth did this happen?'

He gestured lamely, let his hand fall. 'I don't know,' he replied. 'One thing after another … I lost control, I suppose, quite badly.'

As if driven by the same spring, their heads turned to the boy.

'Is he the one?' asked the old man.

She nodded: 'His name is Luke.'

The man and the boy studied each other. There was something wild about his face and eyes, his skin was brown with ancient dirt, his fingers were long and bony; they trembled when he raised his hand and scratched his chin. The boy was frightened.

'Luke,' said his mother, 'this is your grandfather, Arthur Turner. You can call him Arthur.'

The old man grinned desperately, showing gaps in his teeth. His eyes were moist. He advanced on Luke, holding out his hand. Luke shrank back, and his grandfather stopped.

'I suppose not,' he mumbled. The grin had vanished. 'It's all too much for him.'

Luke limped to his mother's side. Half his fear was her speech, her voice: usually when she spoke, it was as if she moved through deep water, or was caught dreaming in a heavy rain. Now it came out too smoothly and tasted sour. The old man had changed her into a different mother.

Her hand went down to his shoulder and stayed there. The grandfather filled the room with uncertainty. He seemed to be casting about, trying to find his bearings.

'Caitlin,' he said, 'I suppose people have told you that he is frighteningly beautiful.'

'People around here don't talk. They don't talk to me. But I know that he is.'

Her hand tightened on his shoulder to protect him from dangerous ideas. Again, there was a terrible silence. Then his mother said, 'I suppose you'd like some tea.'

'I don't suppose you have any brandy?'

'There is no alcohol,' she said bluntly.

'Ah well. Tea then, thank you.'

They moved into the kitchen where there was a worn table and four chairs. Caitlin opened both windows as wide as possible and the back door. She lit the gas and put the kettle on the ring.

'I'd forgotten,' Arthur Turner said, 'how charming this place is.'

She made no reply and kept her back turned as she gathered what she needed. He made no further attempt at conversation until the tea was ready. All the while, a mist of pain built up in the air. Luke knew that it wasn't his own, though he could feel it.

Caitlin poured for her father and her son, and then for herself. The old man took a sip and grimaced: 'Rooibos tea,' he said, 'of course.'

Caitlin watched him expressionlessly, and waited. He took another sip. 'It's not bad, really,' he said hastily. Still she said nothing.

He abandoned the attempt to communicate with her then, and his eyes roved about the room, picking out details aimlessly: the two-plate burner, the small paraffin fridge, the blue shelves, the patchy distemper, the stacks of chipped plates, the forlorn etching of Bird Rock in Port Elizabeth. He sipped his tea, and she sipped hers; perhaps a century passed in this way, while Luke studied the grain of the table surface, as he had many times before, the waves of dry brown colour that converged and then shook themselves free of each other and marched in endless ranks from horizon to horizon.

When he had finished his tea, Arthur put down his cup with a trembling hand. At last, he said, 'No quarter given, Caitlin. I should have expected it. I'm sorry, I made a mistake. I was stupid to come back here.'

Caitlin's shoulders hunched; she leaned forward and asked, 'What was a mistake, Arthur? Coming here like this, or staying away for five years? I'd really like to know.'

'I didn't come here to fight with you,' he replied, rising, his lower lip trembling visibly. As he did so, his chair fell over backwards; they winced as it crashed. 'I'm sorry,' he repeated, bending over to pick up the chair. He straightened up, his face white under the grime. 'I will leave you now. But please bear in mind that it was you – it was your decision – it was you who refused all contact, afterwards, after it happened.'

His eyes strayed to the boy. It appeared that he wanted to say something to Luke, as a struggle of indecision passed over his features. Then he turned round and left the kitchen heavily.

Luke's mother remained hunched in her chair. 'That is true,' she mumbled, not to Luke; but she remained where she was.

The door of Arthur Turner's car slammed. Then there was a prolonged silence. The car door creaked open again.

'I think he's coming back,' said Luke.

His mother looked at him mutely, her expression a mixture of dull anger and relief. Luke turned away.

Arthur returned. 'It won't start,' he said lugubriously. 'I suppose it's the battery. Can I borrow your car? I'll try to get the damn thing out and take it in to Lambert's Bay. I'm sorry, you're stuck with me for at least a day. But I'll sleep in the combi.'

'Don't be ridiculous,' said his daughter. 'You can sleep in here.'

He stood where he was in the doorway, silent and proud.

'Providing,' she added, 'that you have a bath.'

'Very well,' he replied grumpily, and came in. 'But there's no point in cleaning up until I've taken out the battery, is there?'

'I suppose not.'

He sat down at the kitchen table, his ripe smell filling the room. The stink reminded Luke of rotting seaweed. He wondered if his grandfather came from under the sea too.

There was a great deal of splashing, and a song. Arthur Turner had come back from town late that afternoon with a skinful of wine. He sang about jermin officers crossing the rine. Luke came to the blue-painted doorway – there was no door – and watched his grandfather labour to clean off his own filth. The soap didn't lather easily in this hard water.

Arthur stood up in the bathtub. He was painfully thin, except for a sagging little belly. His skin was an ivory colour; his penis was darker, a thick blind earthworm the colour of cooked liver. His ribs stuck out and there was a huge scar down his chest. The scar was shiny pink-brown skin, with florid stitch marks on either side. Luke wondered why he had been cut open and what had been taken out. The water in the bath was brown.

'They drank the women and kissed the wine,' sighed Arthur Turner and staggered where he stood. 'Careful,' he said, 'careful.' Then he sat down and eased himself back. 'Oh God,' he said. It sounded to Luke like a sob. Arthur rested his head against the back of the tub, breathing heavily, on the edge of snoring. Luke thought he might be asleep; but then he peered over the rim of the tub at Luke.

'You don't say much, do you.'

Luke looked down at the floor.

'You might find this hard to believe, boy, but I dreamt about you once. You had no face.'

Luke raised his hand to his face. It was still there. There was a strange hissing sound, which frightened him; he realised that his grandfather was laughing.

'You can understand that missing face,' said the old man. 'Your mother kicked me out of her life before you were born. What do you think of that?' Old Turner splashed water about and snorted. 'She's like that, you know,' he said. 'She can be obtuse. She becomes an obtuse mess in moments of great crisis. Mass, I should say, a doughy but unyielding mass of silence. It has an almost religious quality, you know, a religious mass. You can't really penetrate that, can you? It's baffling and tormenting, and of course utterly demoralising. To suffer in silence; to turn the other cheek – it's an abuse of power and a bloody lie, my boy, but I suppose you know that, better than most. Oh yes, you're an expert yourself.'

Luke felt the weight and pressure of the words. He didn't know what they meant, but he liked 'obtuse' and 'tormenting' and 'bloody lie'.

'Obtuse or not, she kicked me out.'

He looked up at his grandfather; Turner's eyes were focused on him now, glittering cruelly.

'I don't suppose you've met your father?'

Luke shook his head.

'Has she ever told you about him?'

'No,' replied Luke, his first word to his grandfather.

'Of course she hasn't, with bloody good reason too.' He lay back in the tub again and muttered tiredly. 'But she should have done something about your foot. She's let you down there, old son. Not my business, of course …'

Luke stood up and limped out of the bathroom.

Arthur called him back; he stood silently in the doorway.

'Has she ever told you?'

Luke shook his head, not knowing what question he answered. His grandfather rose messily out of the tub and seized a towel.

'She should have told you. She should have told you that you're good looking. No, you're more than that: you are an astonishingly beautiful child.'

'She didn't tell me that,' said Luke. He turned round and limped off to his room.

There was a tarnished mirror above his work table. He climbed onto his chair and knelt on it to look at his reflection. A solemn brown face stared back. He was slightly plump, with full lips, dark eyes and curly black hair. His grandfather was wrong. It was an ugly face; the image made him feel mildly sick. But he forced himself to look at it, and after a while the figure split off from himself and became a picture of someone else. He thought he could see that other person grow older, and become a dark strong person, grow into a life that wasn't his own. He preferred then to look at the space behind and around the image. He peered in at the sides of the mirror, both sides, trying to see more. It was a clear world that he couldn't get into – everything in it was hard and clean and real. It was a better world.

Luke went out into the sun. The light was harsh and made him squint. He wandered round the side of the house to where his grandfather's car was parked, a decrepit Volkswagen bus, orange and white. He slid open the middle door and climbed in. He paused, stopped by the dangerous smell of human flesh, mildew, petrol, burnt oil. But he didn't mind the smell that much because it was steep and vertiginous – he could position himself in it, float at a certain level – and his curiosity drove him on.

It was brutally messy inside. Worn blankets, clothes, cooking utensils, a gas stove, jerry cans, food tins lay on the seats and on the floor. A pair of boots, a bloated pack of Vienna sausages, scores of books, sections of rubber tubing, an old portable typewriter. Luke didn't know what the latter was, though it interested him greatly. He pressed down on one of the buttons – marked E – and a grey arm rose up from the middle. He tried a different button, and the same thing happened. He lifted a small silver lever, and part of the device ratcheted noisily and swiftly to the side, giving him a great fright. He left the machine alone, consumed by anxiety that he might have broken it.

Under one of the middle seats, he found three yellowing type-scripts, the paper blistered by exposure to moisture and sun; but then the world swam, revolved once and landed with a definite, inaudible thump. It was too hot in the bus, the stink had become unbearable.

Luke realised that this was Arthur Turner's house. It was a travel-ling house. He realised that his grandfather was a different kind of person from his mother and himself. He was a wild man who lived in a rich and violent mess, and didn't care about many of the things that his mother cared about so terribly much. At a level deeper than thought, Luke welded together composites: his grand-father was a type of man animal, an everyday savage; he was turtle and hare at once.

He stumbled out of the bus head first, fell onto the white sand and straggling seagrass, and somersaulted, and lay on his back. The earth and air outside were fresh, and he grew solid again, bit by bit.

He went back into the house. Arthur Turner sat at the kitchen table. He looked different, now that he was clean. His skin was pale, his limp grey hair fell across his forehead. Now his grey eyes were tired and shrewd. There was a cup of tea before him and an untouched slice of toast.

'Do you want this?' he asked, pushing the plate towards Luke.

Luke silently took the toast and bit into it.

'Don't tell your mother,' said Arthur. 'She's trying to feed me up, but I don't eat breakfast.'

Luke didn't reply; he was too busy with the toast.

'She thinks I'm too thin. I'm not too thin, I'm too old. In fact, in my view, your mother's too fat.' He interrupted himself, quite irritably. 'Don't you ever speak, child? You're depressingly like your mother. I wonder if you can speak at all.'

Luke swallowed, and said, 'I can speak.'

Arthur raised an eyebrow and took a sip of tea, ignoring the boy's answer. At last he shook his head, dogmatically, and said, 'I don't think so.'

'I can speak,' insisted Luke.

'I tell you what. If you finish that toast and pass the plate back here, and don't tell your mother you ate it, I'll confess that you speak all the time.'

Luke dropped the remaining toast on the floor and stared imperiously at his grandfather.

Cruelty flickered in Turner's features, in his eyes. 'I can see your father now. In your face, in your demeanour. But you don't know your father, do you?'

Luke was trapped. He didn't want to answer; but if he didn't, he would again be accused of being unable to talk.

'I know my father,' he said. It wasn't true. He had never seen his father.

'Of course you do,' nodded Turner grimly. It was clear that he didn't believe Luke. 'I know your father,' he said. 'I came to know him surprisingly well, despite our brief acquaintance. He gave me this.'

He pulled his lank hair aside and leaned forward, to show Luke the tail-end of a livid scar on his scalp. Luke stared at it in confusion.

'It was a brick, boy. His instrument of choice. I tried to stop him, but I went down all right.'

The old man straightened up, his mouth the same bitter gash that was his daughter's mouth, and let his hair fall.

'I was conscious, most of the time. I saw it, I saw most of your getting. But I couldn't move.'

He smiled then, in horrible satisfaction. It was unbearable for Luke. The room had gone dark and he didn't know why. He found it hard to breathe; he didn't understand his grandfather's words at all.

'That brick summed up everything,' said the old dry voice. 'It was his personality. You see things clearly when you're on the floor, broken and bleeding. The imprint of his personality, I should say. There is a relationship – in such moments – that surpasses explanation.'

The old man shuddered, pulled himself back within his own skin. He glanced at Luke, apparently surprised to see him there. He looked down at his teacup.

'Perhaps,' he said quietly, 'that is why you have so little to say.'

Luke's face had pulled into a rictus of weeping, but there were no tears. He limped out and disappeared back into the blinding white light.

Luke stood on the rocks and watched as a fisherman killed an octopus he had caught. He forced his gnarled brown thumbs into the bell of its head, hooking his fingers underneath, into the roots of the tentacles that struggled about his wrists; then he turned the creature inside out. It vibrated fiercely and went limp. Luke stared at the fisherman's hands, at the mangled animal hanging from them. Both were brown and mottled, iodine-stained. They were of the same world, shoreline monsters too ancient and violent to bargain with or to understand. A final convulsion ran down the tentacles.

His mother tugged at his arm and they picked their way through the series of rock pools, onto the beach. They walked some distance. The sky was calm now, this late in the afternoon. Acres of pale green light above the horizon, fading to mauve, long silver sheets of light on the earth. They came to a halt and stood ankle deep in that mirror. The cold bit right down into the bones of his leg, but eased the duller, chronic ache of his joints.

'Is Grandfather a fisherman?' asked Luke suddenly.

'You should call him Arthur,' replied his mother. 'I would prefer that.'

'I want to call him Grandfather.'

His feet sucked into the sea mud as the water withdrew. His mother smiled angrily.

'But is he a fisherman?' insisted the boy.

'I don't think so. I doubt he's caught a fish in his life. What makes you ask?'

Luke thought of the octopus and made no reply. Instead, he asked, 'Why does Grandfather stink so much?'

'He doesn't anymore, Luke. He's had a hard time, I suppose. Things went wrong for him a long time ago, badly wrong.'

Luke fell silent, wondering why things going wrong would make a person stink. Perhaps something had gone wrong with his bath; perhaps he couldn't find the soap.

'He used to be a professor,' she said, more to herself than to Luke. 'A professor of aerial perspective.'

Luke glanced up at his mother. She smiled down at him and said, 'He lost his own, you see, lost it entirely.'

They waded out further. A particularly big hillock of waves rolled in, wetting Luke up to the middle of his thighs. He jumped, sucking in his stomach, shuddering.

'He taught people how to draw the sky, and the clouds, and the light in the clouds. He gave lectures on how to paint distance and light.' Her eyes were moist. She said, 'He gave lectures on many other things too. And he was a writer.'

Luke understood none of it, but everything made sense: his grandfather was a mystery.

'He never thought he was good enough,' she added. 'Or perhaps he thought he was too good. I've never worked it out. In any event, he copied another writer, and so he got into trouble.'

'Aren't you allowed to do that?'

'No, you're not. And then he started drinking more and more.'

'He drank until he fell asleep,' said Luke. 'Like last night.'

She smiled again and tousled his hair, and he jerked his head away.

'Perhaps we should go back,' she said. 'The tide's beginning to rise – I don't want you to walk too far on the soft sand.'

She took his hand, and so they began the long slow walk back, the boy rolling as he limped.

'Grandfather saw my getting,' said Luke.

Caitlin stopped, and looked down at him sharply.

'What does getting mean?'

She started walking again.

'What does getting mean?'

'Getting means where you come from,' she replied, walking too fast for him now. He struggled after her. He still didn't understand, but knew his mother too well to push for a clear answer. Besides, he could feel the giant waves of silence that radiated from her stride, from the set of her back. There was something about his getting that upset her badly. Perhaps it was his grandfather's fault, perhaps it was his own: he knew he shouldn't have spoken about his getting.

The light failed as they walked. His loneliness mounted up, until it battered at him like an onshore wind. He knew he would have to wait for her, perhaps several days. There could be no bargaining with her rage and fear. That was one of the most important rules of the world.

A southeaster gale built up, stacking up its violent energies in wearying succession, one upon the other. Gusts tugged at the roof and knocked the old sash windows, swirled without hindrance through the front and back doors. Fine drifts of sea sand built up on the floorboards and the mat, grit got into their food and ended up between their molars. It was a bullying, swaggering wind, a contemptuous wind. Luke hated every long minute of the storm.

The Turners sat at the kitchen table eating supper. The bare bulb seemed weaker than usual. The sound of the gale, its presence, dimmed the light. They ate snoek and brown bread and apricot jam. Arthur Turner chewed, his face a mask of distaste.

'If you call this fish a snoek,' he said, 'it acquires local colour. It becomes a regional delicacy.' He took another forkful and chewed ostentatiously. 'If you call it barracuda, it becomes a marine predator. Now that is an anomaly.'

The word 'anomaly' pressed down on this small company of three generations: Luke felt its viscous weight pouring down over the table.

'Every kind of predator is forbidden as food, except marine predators. Do we eat eagles or butcher birds? Do we eat crocodiles? Do we eat leopards? But this is merely a snoek! – an incomprehensible word! – and therefore edible. Does that make sense to you, Caitlin?'

'Snoek is not barracuda,' she replied. Then, with great articulation: 'I don't know why you think they are the same.'

'Christ, they look the same to me,' said Arthur Turner. 'Thin pointy fish with big toothy mouths.'

'All fish are predators,' she said dully, and turned her attention to her plate.

'Well, exactly,' he rejoined, but she ignored him.

Wind battered at the house, the light grew more dingy. Arthur Turner lifted his two-litre bottle of red wine with difficulty and poured himself another glass, his raised elbow trembling. He turned to Luke and said, 'Would you like some wine, my boy?'

Luke shook his head. Caitlin looked up sharply, but again said nothing.

'A wise choice, Luke,' said the old man. 'This stuff is terrible.'

Her silent rage filled the room. Arthur pushed his plate away, half the fish uneaten, and hunched over his glass of wine. Luke fiddled with his food, Caitlin chewed methodically. The wind blustered.

'The atmosphere in here is so thick,' said Arthur querulously, 'you could cut it with a knife.'

His daughter ignored him.

'So damned awkward,' he complained, as if to himself. 'So damned difficult.'

'And whose damned fault is that?' she snapped.

'Oh, mine undoubtedly. Everything here is my fault.'

Her anger redoubled at his sarcasm, and burst loose: 'You come here – I haven't seen you for *years*! – you practically *abandon* me and my child – you offer my son wine without consulting me – how do you know I approve of that? – and you expect, no, you virtually *demand* conversation when it suits you. Jesus, Arthur!'

Luke thought his grandfather would respond angrily, but Arthur seemed to fold over the wine, to shrink into his shabby jacket.

'I don't suppose it would help to remind you again,' replied Arthur, his voice dry and calm, 'that this was your decision. You've refused to see me for years. You know it perfectly well, Caitlin.'

'I'm not going to discuss the matter further, not in front of Luke. God knows what it will lead to, or what you'll say in front of the boy. I certainly can't trust your discretion.'

'Caitlin, you might hate me for saying this, but you will have to tell the boy one day where he comes from. These things always come out, and when this particular thing does come out – as inevitably it will – both of you will regret your silence. He will resent it to the day you die, and long after.'

'That proves it,' she retorted furiously. 'I cannot trust your discretion at all – you've already said too much.'

'Very well then, I shall have nothing further to say.'

He hitched his chair around, with difficulty, so that he no longer faced her. He sat in crumbled dignity and glared at the corner of the room. Caitlin's fingers drummed on the table, then stopped. They flattened out. Luke wanted to laugh wildly at the sight of his mother's pale, broad fingers spread out on the table.

Later in the night, Luke dreamt that his mother and grandfather still argued. Their voices raged through the thick wall, through the wind, almost merging with the wind. You've neglected the child horribly, said one voice. A clubfoot can be rectified these days. You can ignore the fact that it mars his beauty – but think of the pain of every step that he takes! It is shameful!

Christ, do you think I'm unaware of that? protested the other voice. I was broken at the time – I'm sorry, that's the only way I can describe it. I had no support, I still have no support; and I still am a broken personality, whatever you think of me. Besides, how dare you preach to me! If anything is shameful, it is you – practically telling Luke that he is the child of a rape.

The argument raged on, rising and falling. He thought he heard tears in his grandfather's voice, while his mother's was harder, grinding into the attack relentlessly. Arthur Turner's voice raised itself in a final wavering protest – an old man's helpless rage – and then, mercifully, Luke fell asleep.

He walked down the beach for a very long way. He didn't get tired as he usually did, and his foot didn't hurt. Sometimes he splashed his way along the icy water of the littoral, sometimes he pressed on through hot soft sand, above the tideline. It was a hot morning, but he felt comfortable. He was at home on this beach. He had walked along it and explored it ever since he could remember. Light seemed to spear through him, but not the heat; as he walked, he became a citizen of white light and salt air.

He saw a dark smudge in the water some distance away, obscured by the glare: a dark body lay in the wash of the tide, gently rocked by the action of the waves. Perhaps it was a human body. He thought at first that it might be his grandfather – it seemed to be a man in a shiny dark jacket – but as he drew closer, the illusion of human form fell away. He realised at last that it was a dead seal.

It had been gashed open and its intestines and other organs were visible. Luke squatted down to study them. A cloud of flies buzzed around the exposed innards, whelk swarmed through them, their conical pink shells swirling rapidly as they dug into the guts, halting and reversing like small, startling mechanisms in a living clock. Luke studied this everted palette, astonished by the tubing, the sacs and bladders, the mixture of pastel colours and bitter gore. The eyes of the seal were open. They stared blindly up at the sky;

the drying film over them reminded him of his grandfather's eyes. He questioned the seal: are you my grandfather? Do you know my father's name? Will you tell me that secret?

The seal's flippers were undamaged. They rested beside the cadaver like dull mechanisms of rubber, not animal parts at all.

He straightened up and walked further down the beach, much further. The glare had grown more extreme, so it was difficult to make out details beyond the immediate shoreline. He stopped eventually and retraced his path. It was a very long walk. Perhaps because of the nature of the light, he missed the seal on his way back; perhaps it had been removed by the action of the tide.

There was no sign of his grandfather on his return. The bus had gone, his belongings too. Luke's mother was in a bad mood, clearly reluctant to talk about this departure or explain anything to him.

'Arthur left while you were asleep,' she said. 'I don't think we'll see him for a long time.'

'Why did he go?'

'Why did he come?' she snapped, and that was her last word on the subject.

You made him go away, Luke thought dully. He will die soon and I will never know my father's name. He sat on the front step of the house for a long time, lifting handfuls of coarse white sand and letting it drift though his fingers.

Luke watched silently as his mother built a coffin on the sand in front of the cottage. Perhaps it was for his grandfather. She used materials that came from the sea: driftwood, shark egg pouches, oars of kelp, mussel shells, fish bones. She was an inept craftsman and the coffin kept falling apart. Then she would leave it for days on end to spend her time hanging up fish to dry under the north-facing eaves of the cottage. They were called harders, silver fish about the size and shape of herring. As they dried, their silver skin grew bronzed, eventually turning a dull brown. Soon the whole north wall of the cottage was fringed with harders. For months on end, Luke and his mother ate nothing but salt fish.

She returned to the coffin, packing broken seashells into her weaving of kelp and driftwood. It was more like a basket than a coffin, a dry black tangle of organic matter. It smelt of salt, urine, rotting seaweed. As she worked on these two things, the coffin and dried fish, she began to change. Her pale skin gradually turned the colour of stained ivory; yet it retained a smooth texture, despite the wrinkles that grew around her eyes and mouth and under her chin. Her skin was badly wrinkled silk. Luke knew that this change had something to do with the wind hunting through the coffin, probing her sighs, the shuffling whisper of her movements, the long speechless nights they shared. The wind dried her out like the fish hanging from the eaves. There was a lesson for Luke in this dream, one that lasted into his waking years. It demonstrated the importance of skin: to whom it belonged, how smooth it was, its colour and texture and how it breathed.

Early one evening, the man returned. It was his first visit that year. He was a short, muscular man with a surly face and scar on his cheekbone that came from a knife fight. As usual, fear inflamed the child, and he was unable to speak; it was wiser not to speak. His mother also regarded the intruder silently. There was something prayerful in her expression.

'I want meat,' he said. 'Meat and food.'

She took sausage out of the fridge and began frying it. The man sat at her table and waited for his meal. He knew she did not keep beer in the house.

Luke kept very still, his eyes on the floor. Occasionally he would look up and track his mother's movements. Ten minutes passed in silence, except for the sound of fat hissing and bubbling. The rank smell crowded the room, battering at Luke's senses. Then his mother scooped the sausage into a plate and set it down before the man. She served him bread and jam as well, with thick layers of margarine on the bread. She made him tea, with four teaspoons of white sugar, then sat down before him.

Her normally pale face was milky now; he chewed his food vigorously, looking at her from time to time through his surly eyes. Luke began to tremble. In the distance, faintly, he could feel rage and fear. Was it his own? He didn't know; he didn't dare speak or approach his mother. He could only watch her, mutely drink in her presence. But she was not there. Caitlin Turner was not his mother. She was a white sack of nothing. The man at the table had sucked her away from inside and hidden her.

Only once, he turned and stared at Luke, for a long time. The child quailed. Then at last he turned away.

Presently he rose and stretched across the table, taking Caitlin's wrist in his hand. Luke couldn't understand the expression on his face – was it loathing? was it anger, or desire? – he had a cold, dull, brutal face.

His mother rose meekly and followed the man into her bedroom. They left the door open, so Luke clearly heard his voice raised, though he couldn't understand the man's language. He heard the wet stinging slap of flesh on flesh. Then his mother said, 'Wait,' and she returned to close the door. After that, the sounds were muted but still audible: the nauseating percussion of his blows, the noise of their coupling, her mewling.

Luke huddled in his own room, his face turned to the wall. His body ached, his face burnt, he trembled with fever. The pain grew worse and worse. I am an octopus, he thought, thinking of the strong hands of the fisherman he had seen on the rocks, his brown thumbs.

The man was gone by the time Luke came out of his bedroom the next morning. His mother stayed in her room all that day. It didn't matter, as he knew she wouldn't talk, and he felt too sick to eat. She came out towards evening and limped to the table, older now than her own father. She sat down, unable to break the silence. Her lips were fat, overripe, split. There were new colours on the palette of her face, shades of indigo and yellow, crimson and taupe. Her silence deepened as colours bleached out of the light, making the colours on her face deepen too. I am here, said her silence. Nothing can be done. This is the cost of my life here, and of my motherhood. I make no choices: my life and death are indistinguishable.

SHEILA ROBERTS
A KIDNAPPING

SHEILA ROBERTS (b. in Johannesburg). Although in 1977 she emigrated to the United States, where she teaches creative writing, she makes frequent return trips to her home country. Her evergreen story 'Coming In', in the original edition of this anthology, was later collected in a volume to which it gave the title, *Coming In and Other Stories* (1993). It has been replaced here with a brand-new work, 'A Kidnapping.'

Gerda

I never thought Louise would neglect Solly the Chimp as if he were just an old coat of fake fur. But she did, too weak at the time to think straight. Now, six months later, she is still in such grief that she moans that her throat is choking on Solomon's blood and his last screaming breath. I never thought I'd see Louise Williamson, always the one full of puff and handy muscles, lying flat on her back with her dirty boots on the quilt and holding a flannel over her face.

'Get up, Lou,' I said. 'You'll lose pay and seniority points if you don't get back to collecting samples for the lab. Liefie, I'd go with you, but I've got to head up Polokwane way. Another farmer has been shot and the gangs have slashed his cows. Damn them to hell! We need …'

'I want to die, Gerda.'

'Get up, Lou! You've got to!' I brushed the face-cloth away, took her by the shoulders and heaved her up. For a moment she looked at me with eyes like two small gun barrels, but then the old Williamson heat left her face and she obeyed.

Louise used to be tough. We started our courses in Nature Con-versation and Game Ranging together in '92 when we were both twenty-two and both from Port Elizabeth. But, figure this, there we were, one straight Babe and one Dyke among a troupe of twenty-three white boys, three black ones and two camel-jawed supervisors, who lived in their own worlds of pock-marked egos and filthy language.

For safety's sake Louise and I *had* to join forces, even though she was English-speaking and I was a boere-meisie – so to speak. I was tall, near six feet, and my body and limbs were strong. I was the kind of frizzy-haired Bitch-never-say-die with whom the supervisors didn't plan to arm-wrestle. Louise was maybe five-foot-two, with a limp white ponytail like a feather duster and skin so smooth and clear it reflected the light edging into our tent of a morning, helping me to wake up. She was strong but she *looked* delicate. Added to which, she was so pretty that she had the supervisors walking with stiff legs and fat throats any time she was around them.

During our first stint of fieldwork, they drove us out in open trucks to the campsite at Makatwana. This was a beaten-earth clearing surrounded by thorn-trees. For the next eight weeks we would be living in tents and eating tinned food and what we could scavenge from the veld and underbrush, which during the day thrummed with heat and during the night snapped and creaked coldly and echoed with the sounds of animals.

We immediately discovered that Roux, one of the supervisors whose god was cruelty, had put Louise and me in a tent with Hans, a big shaven-head student from Tukkies, someone who should've been our natural enemy, for he was from upcountry while we were from the coast. After the first night of our clumsy shyness, he turned out okay and made a point of not staring. Sometimes, feeling silly, we teased him. I would say, 'O, watse reuk is dit, Hans?' And Louise would say, 'But at least the smell keeps the lions away, Gerda.'

'So you two dolls think you don't … don't … break wind too? I hear you when you're asleep, believe me, I do!' Then the three of us would gargle in our laughter.

That first night, once Hans was asleep, we lay awake to whisper in the owl-fluting darkness under the coughs of the jackals how we'd always wanted to be game rangers, since we were little girls, how we hated the cities, and how *we* would help our country out of the ecological and murderous mess it was in.

Before they took us deep into the bush, we had to learn to shoot with .30-30 rifles. My family has always been hunters and I was already trained, close to being a crack shot. But Louise was having a lot of trouble, not only because of the size of the guns but also because of not knowing how to control the retort against her shoulder. Roux wouldn't let anyone help her. So after the second time of seeing her face tighten in pain and hearing Roux calling her a pathetic little pussy, by mistake-on-purpose I shot to tatters a blister beetle crawling on a branch near his neck. He jumped like a rabbit and nearly fell. I dawdled over. 'Jammer, *Mynheer* Roux,' I mumbled. Then I picked up the papery and toffeelike tatters of the dead beetle and silently apologised to it.

Our first assignments were to monitor the quality of water in all the holes and streams. Then we had to check the flora for parasites and nematodes. After that, they took us by truck further into the bush in search of the wild dogs that had been tagged the year before. We were to check them. Louise and I and the others were also to help fit radio collars onto the young ones so that they could be checked in the future. First we'd shoot pacifiers into them, and then as they lolloped over, run to give them a quick medical once-over and, if they were clean, fit on the new device.

It was on the drive to track down untagged wild dogs that I saw how goddamn callous ou Du Toit could be to Louise. We came upon a dead wild dog lying under some brush. You could see the poor thing had been dead for some time because the abdomen was very swollen. Our orders were, of course, to establish the cause of death. Instead of sending one of the experienced black game rangers or even one of the new guys to slit the paunch, Du Toit said, 'Hey Lou-Lou, let's see what sort of a surgeon you'd make. Get your knife and cut!'

'Let me do it, Supe, let me try? It's something I've always wanted to do,' I begged, dancing in front of him.

'Shut up, Gerda. You'll get lots of chances. Go, Louise!'

One of the guys hissed, '*Shee-et!*'

Louise approached the corpse, knife ready. She hesitated, then plunged it in just under the breastbone. The distended skin immediately exploded outward and intestinal juices umbrellaed over Louise. She stepped back, fists at her eyes, gasping. I jumped to her and tried to wipe her face with my shirt-tail while one of the guys, as quickly, splashed water from his bottle at her eyes and used his handkerchief to wipe her off.

'I told you, *poese* are not *meant* to be in this line of work,' screeched Du Toit. 'Had the little fool any sense, she would have first tied her scarf high over her nose and mouth to protect her eyes as well. It's in the textbook. Is nobody not *reading* their *donderse* textbooks?'

He stood there ranting while Louise, without instruction, turned again to the gaping carcass. She did as the textbooks said. She snipped off a segment of intestine and placed it in the sample box she carried around her neck. Then she caught some of the stomach acid and blood in small vials. Pulling up and cutting a string of rotting intestines to expose the liver, she threw them to one side, unaware that Du Toit had come up to observe her follow-through.

'You bitch,' he hissed, kicking dog-guts off his shoes. Louise took no notice of him. Her mouth had taken that flat Williamson line which meant she was close to turning and planting a punch in Du Toit's throat, even if it meant getting sent down. When the intestines and juices were analysed back at the base, it was established that the dog had died of rabies. Oh God, were we in for a heartburning *then*! We had to return to that area and track down all the uncollared wild dogs and any of the collared ones we could observe that were frothing and ailing, and we had to shoot every one of them. The mingling of gunshots, yelling and yelping; the stink of hot metal, cordite, dog excrement and blood, made us groentjies crazy and we screamed along with the dogs, leaping after those that tried to get away. Some of us just kept on shooting wildly at boulders and tree-roots even when all the dogs lay dead. Then we dragged the creatures by their mangy, spindly legs to build a pile of carcasses ready for incineration. How the stench followed us back to the camp! It was in our clothes and hair, up our noses and down our throats. Jolting along in the truck back to the tents, Louise and I, standing close, sucked at our cigarettes as if our own execution was at hand.

Fieldwork was not all blood and guts, though. One experience that left us first years high and amazed was with a small herd of elephant that we had to pacify and mark. Ag, to see how those huge beasts tottered and then rolled onto the dust, just like boats being dropped into water from a high dock, the sand rising in splashes upwards! I thanked God that none of those elephants was infected and that we could insert little monitors in the skin under their ears and then push off, knowing they would awake, stagger upwards like heavy grey sails being erected in wind and go moving drunkenly on their way.

Soon we broke camp and moved northward outside South Africa proper to the borders of primate territory. Our supplies were running low (they plan this, I'm sure), and we had to live off the bush. There were days when we had to limit our water intake so severely that we could only dribble khaki liquid at night instead of having a good pee. The nights up in the hills were colder too, and Louise and

I would both get into my bed. When Hans frowned at us under his eyebrows, we made kissie-kissie noises at him. 'This is not a hoor-house,' he tried to say. We just laughed and said, no, it was a *poor-house*. And I cuddled Louise into me and she fell asleep, her head at my shoulder, and I crooned, *Little luvva, my big little small little luvva*. Not that Louise was my lover during that time, though of course I wanted her to be; and then later she was my little beminde.

I was beginning to realise as job followed job that nothing you study in Zoology at university prepares you for the realities, pre-pares you for the shivery realisation of what your own body might contain and how many visible and invisible things exist able to gnaw at your bones, bring pain to your tissues and cripple you. In different ways we were as vulnerable as the undefended packs and troops and prides of beasts, trying to survive on a terrain that was lush with food when the rains were good, and was like a death camp prowled by poachers when there was drought.

By now we were all getting thin from poor rations. Louise would go into shivering fits even though the sun beat down strong enough to stun the lizards, and at night we were both riding the black-mares. All I could do at that time of hunger, as we chewed on wild celery, tree-gum, bits of bark, hawthorn berries; sucked on stones; and fried up saucepans of flying ants, was to get Louise to reminisce about the surf rising at Humewood Beach and the waves trans-forming themselves from smoke that thundered into lace shawls on the sand. I also pointed out to her that they weren't planning to kill off all us hotshot Zoology students from the best universities.

It'd been slow-travel, reaching the camp of the primate researchers. As we moved we had to keep constant watch for the game pits dug by poachers. Once, poor old Hans nearly tripped an elephant trap, which was a bloody great 100 -kilogram log and a heavy rusty spear slung precariously over the trail. Had he touched the liana nearby, the trap would've been triggered and the log would've taken off his head and shoulders while the spear sliced his body down the middle. 'Jeesuss!' was all he could say. 'Oh Jeesuss, my God!'

Louise

When we reached the camp where the primatologists were work-ing, I began to feel better. They had lots of food and they shared with us. It was like magic amongst the deep green foliage, the flame and butter lilies and the newly hatched painted-lady butter-flies to go tracking with them in search of the Vervet and Samango monkeys and their bean-baggy tiny young. We'd head out at night to spot thick-tailed bushbabies, following their haunting wails. Those that we trapped, we sedated, examined and tagged. I loved the work. We'd all seen videos on primates during lectures, but the reality of their supple aliveness among the swinging branches, the brilliant innocence of their eyes and the deftness of their hands all hooked love into my heart. All I wanted from life at that moment was to pick up and hold one of the little newborn ones, perhaps a Chacma Baboon. But it wasn't easy. The mothers, with tight worried eyes and lifted snouts, would lope away with their babies hanging under their bellies, and the males would stamp, beat their chests pok-pok-pok and bark at us.

A special treat for me was when I was permitted a quiet tour of the young chimps the primatologists had rescued from the vol-canic disaster at Goma. They were housed in the hutments in large comfortable cages and were treated with calm, loving expertise. Then I wanted one of those babies badly, more than I wanted a new-born Chacma. I made and unmade plans over several days.

But I got my way. A couple of nights later when we climbed down the rocks from the primatologists' enclosures on the way to our own tents, Gerda noticed that my field jacket looked very fat and funny. 'What loot've you got there, Louise?' She smiled, think-ing I had food.

'Shshsh,' I said, showing her. The little one was still sleeping heavily against me from a mild tranquillising shot.

'*Holy shit!*' Gerda exclaimed. 'You stole a chimp from the pri-matologists! You're going to be expelled from the programme, Miss Louise Williamson!' She grabbed my shoulders.

'Be *careful*, Gerda …' I knew that I sounded like some little girl who thought all she was doing was bringing home a stray cat. 'Maybe not; maybe I can hide it.'

'How are you going to feed it? And what if the primate-workers realise that there's one missing? Listen to me, Louise, you could go to jail!'

'I also stole one of the bottles with a teat that the workers use,' I said, feeling determined that I would *never* give up my little ape, 'and I'm going to give it diluted condensed milk and real milk and some of my fruit. You'll see, everything will be okay, Gerda.'

'You're finished, domkop. You're out of here. In no time they'll discover what you've done …'

'Hush,' I said, 'and don't worry. I opened all the cages and a window. I made it look as if there had been an attack by poachers.'

'Ag, so you are prepared to let some innocent black guys take the blame? I no longer understand you, Louise *Williamson,* jou gemene klein teef!'

At that moment Hans followed us into the tent. His eyes looked as if he had thyroid trouble when he saw the baby I was cradling at my breast.

'Louise, what nonsense are you fucking with now?' he demanded.

'Hansie, I want to keep him,' I pleaded.

'Oh, so it's *Hansie* now, Louise?' sneered Gerda. But I ignored her. He looked down at me and I opened my eyes wide and pressed out a couple of tears. I think I even managed to blush.

'Ag Hansie, please help me. It's not as if I *wrenched* him away from his mother or anything. He was stuck in a cage, playing with his tummy and looking sad. To make sure that he wouldn't be upset, I gave him a tranquilliser shot, but not a heavy one.'

'Fokken ongelooflik!' hissed Gerda.

'Well, I can be his mother now. He's my babe, my little luvva babe.' I ogled Gerda.

'Ag so, just when the poor brat is feeling secure and is resting in his cage, what happens but a beach-bum broad from Port Elizabeth kidnaps him,' said Gerda, sucking the mucus to the back of her throat. 'I won't stand for this shit!'

'Okay, okay,' said Hans. 'I'll help, as long as I'm not involved. As far as I'm concerned, I know nothing about this business. I'll swear it in a court of law, Louise, no matter how nice you are to me.'

My baby in arms, I went to kiss the big guy on the cheek, almost as if *he* were father of the child. Gerda was watching us jealously and I knew that the saliva at her back teeth had turned metallic.

In spite of the hard secret job we three had taking care of Solomon (for that was his name) until the fieldwork was over, with the help of some of the others and with more tranquillisers than were good for him we kept him quiet and hidden here and there when we were on duty. A couple months later, Gerda and I walked away from Du Toit, Roux and all the guys. Solly, padded with towels and clothes and well-asleep, hung on poor Gerda's sweating back in her kitbag, while I had her stuff tightly packed in mine.

Gerda and I would be graduating together, and so together we took jobs in the semi-desert terrain of the Karoo, where we and a couple of geologists with students would do regular tests on ground-water subsidence; the effect of pollution on the scrub; and would check on the shrinking herds of small mammals. We would also be eradicating the prickly pear bushes when time allowed. We already knew that people from the Barolong villages were migrating ever deeper into the desert proper out of fear of a retaliating group of dispossessed farmers joined by some White Racists from the north. Our crowd of ecologists, sometimes linked up with an army brigade and a couple of doctors, would track after the tribes for their protection and, of course, for medical reasons.

Gerda and I had rented an abandoned wooden house at a railway siding where the trains stopped coming through, and we paid workers to put bars on all the windows so that Solomon wouldn't get stolen or go scampering off when we were at work. Solomon was by now our child, our dearly hairy beloved, part big diversion, part big dilemma. We tried without success to put those new nappies on him, the ones with Velcro fasteners. Later he could manage the toilet by jumping up and standing on the lid, and then we had him in khaki pants and shirts, but whether pants or whatever, he didn't care for clothes and for some months would simply undress himself as soon as he was dressed, and if we got impatient with him and tried to force the clothes back on, he would screech, skip widely and then crap in his hands, and throw it at our shuddering retreating bodies. Then, one day, he just became accustomed to keeping his clothes on. In the evenings after dinner, we'd play madcap rugby with him in the backyard, or games of tag and hide-and-seek, but as he grew stronger he would tumble us down, and Gerda and I often had scraped elbows and knees. One time I hurt my ankle and he knew it, because he came and licked it and sucked the sore bone, hissing something that sounded apologetic, I swear it. So, for the next few weeks, I sat on the back stoep wall and let Gerda tackle him while I kept score. No matter who won, we all had beers afterwards.

The area around about was so depopulated that it was all right for us to go walking, with him swinging between us, along the red sandy paths winding through the thorn-tree scrub and the milk bushes. Sometimes the geologists, enjoying a smoke out of doors, would wave at us. They thought Solly a joke and Gerda and me not proper women. But they were mostly too busy to be interested in us. In time, Solomon pretended to smoke an occasional chocolate cigarette (that was when I resumed smoking to try and cut my eating), and he'd lick at a teaspoon of cherry brandy in a shot glass when we'd let him. He slept in the big bed with us every night, or part of the night, anyway. Not that we always slept well. He had very active dreams and his nails and fur would be a torment as he turned over and tossed. When Gerda and I threw him out of bed, he'd bark, throw angry somersaults and menace us with his toddler chest-pounding. He'd settle himself among cushions on the floor but be restless and muttering. Then he would swing and lope around the room, or his hard-encased fingers would sneak up under our covers to pinch at our feet and legs. I would yell, 'No, Solomon, no! Go to bed!'

'Ahahahah ...' he would call, as if copying me.

As Solomon grew, he hated being left alone in the small house when we went to work. He'd tired of toys, of balls, old tricycle wheels, his little trampoline. But not the ropes Gerda had attached to the overhead beams holding up the roof. *Oh baby, leap and swing, rotate and swing, upside down, right way up, swing, swing, swing, then bounce, back on the bed, round bare tummy pumping. Jump again and swing, one arm, two arms, cough and droop. Ah baby, again and again.* Yet at times we would come home to find the whole place undone, as if he'd been hunting frantically for his kin or crawling in search of the softest leaves of the undergrowth.

I persuaded Gerda to apply for the graveyard shift. She would go out at midnight with the trackers to follow the spoor of the farmers or tribesmen. Then at dawn I would go out into the veld to check the pollutants settled over the scrub and trees from the trucks grinding hurriedly through in the cool of the night from one dead-end town to the next, or from the poisons blowing in from the paper factory at Loskop. As the weeks passed, I found myself sauntering over to the men's camp in the afternoon when Solly was dozing; for an hour or two, to be Desdemona to a certain Major Tanner's war stories. Also, selfishly, I now had Solly's attentive eyes only on myself at our dinner of his melons, bananas and radishes, and mine of two grilled cheese-and-tomato sandwiches and a chocolate milkshake. He would get playful and mush my sandwiches or throw fruit skins down the front of my shirt, and I would reproach him by patting his hands and making him look at how well I was handling my food. Then he would behave and I would kiss the corrugations of his head and nose. Eeeeeing, he would kissie up to me too. Before bedtime, I would try for a quiet moment with cardboard and paints. Sometimes he would splash paint seriously on the cardboard; other times he splashed it on me. I would get cross and smack his hand, whereupon he would tackle me in fun, forcing me to play the game *Row, Row, Row your Boat*, which was where we put the soles of our feet together, grabbed each other by the forearms and rocked and pulled backward and forward. I would have to clench my neck backwards in effort, but I always ended up pulled onto Solomon and rolled about by him, his thick lips slobbering on my cheeks. In the morning when Gerda got in deadbeat and grey-faced from her dreadful night, I would give over the bed to her where she would lie face downward and, for a while, allow Solomon to groom her thick hair, pulling off the midges and seeds and twigs, his fingers also sensitively roaming in search of lice under her arms and in her ears. Then she would wriggle and insist that she needed to sleep, needed *badly* to sleep.

Gerda

When I say the sky fell I don't mean a nut fell on a hen. I mean the anger of Louise and me fell like hellfire on our heads. Then we entered a Nomansland where soon we were staggering around in dust. In only a matter of days our lives went dry.

We'd been living at Gamtoos for over a year and had also graduated. One Sunday evening we were sitting quietly. I was reading a book Tanner, one of the officers, had lent Louise for a laugh, a book about gymnastics progammes during the Third Reich that he'd confiscated from a Skinhead. I was enjoying the illustrations of fatly muscled Germans in striped bathing-suits that covered their chests and came down to their knees. I looked up, wanting Louise to scope their thick, waxed moustaches, when I realised something. Strange. Louise Williamson was no longer the thin little Babe I used to sing *Luvva little luvva* to. She looked as if her bones and muscles were pressing against her smooth suntanned skin. Her breasts had grown and her stomach was half a musk-melon under her khaki combat trousers. How could I not've noticed before?

'Hey, Solly,' I said. He looked up from a picture book he'd been trying to make sense of, turning it this way and that, upside down, sideways. He raised his eyebrows at me and lifted his upper lip. He was comfortably reclining in a big cushion and I was sorry to disturb him.

'Sol,' I repeated, 'kyk na Louise. She's gone fattish, don't you think?'

He looked at Louise then rubbed his skimpy dry hair. Uncertain as to what I wanted, he put his book down and took a last suck of the chocolate cigarette in his ashtray on the floor. Then he clapped his hands perfunctorily and retrieved the book.

'Gerda, what do you mean, I've gone *fattish*?'

'Well, you have. Look at you! Louise, finally it's caught up with you, the way you're always gutsing your food.'

'I don't *guts* my food, Gerda!'

'Well, why've you put on weight?'

'Because, stupid, women my age usually put on weight.'

My eyes still on Louise's stomach, I put down my book, upon which Solomon closed his and came to sit next to me, clearly uncertain about our hardened voices.

'I don't get as much exercise as you, Gerda. I don't have to go hunting white extremists and tracking down infected tribes-people, for God's sake!'

I dragged at my smoke while Solomon played with my knee. Trying to keep calm, I gazed down at his bald forehead, long eye-lashes, so-obvious nostrils and tar-paper bottom lip. Beminde ou ding, I thought. But he wasn't old; he'd not even been through puberty yet was my next deurmekaar calculation. But what could I have been thinking of?

'Louise,' I said more sensibly.

'What, Gerda?'

'Who is the father?'

'*Which* father? Oh God, Gerda … I … I'm not sure. It's …'

'Ah, don't tell me, it's that Tanner who brought this stupid book over today when you'd gone to Tousrivier. He was clearly hoping to see you, so he brings me a bloody Nazi gymnastics book. Why, I could fold him in two in a bladdy second and put his head up his hol. I'll do more, I'll kill him; I'll fucking kill him and you, you little surfer slet!' I got up to give Louise the slapped face she deserved.

Solly, upset, had started coughing in jerks and rubbing his face.

'You can't put Tanner's head up his hol. He left this morning with the army. They're chasing those black thugs into Botswana. Gerda, it's done, I'm up the pole, so *what*?' I had her by the shoulders then but, God Almighty, you can't beat up a pregnant Babe.

'How are we going to take care of a baby out here?' My voice went high with panic and a feeling new to me – grief. 'You'll have to resign and we'll have to live on my salary, and … you'll leave me, Louise, you'll leave me …'

I cried and ranted while Solomon began bundling up the bed-clothes, tearing off his sweats and ripping at the posters on the walls. He began flinging faeces around, at which Louise rushed to vomit in the bathroom before running out of the house. Then I fetched the brandy bottle from under the sink. Slowly Solly and I calmed down.

So I missed midnight shift and in the morning I woke with a head that seemed to have all my inner organs pulsing inside it. Solomon was sprawled across his cushion, sleeping off either a pain or a premonition. Louise hadn't returned.

Over the next few days when Louise was sometimes at home and sometimes not, and there was no talk between us, Solomon went through the full range of his appealing gestures and broken-hearted screams. He wouldn't wear clothes, but crawled and hunkered into corners or between the headboard and the wall. Keening, he swung slowly from the ropes this way and that, hour after hour. Before going on my shifts, I would take pity on him and go jogging. I would jog and cry and he would jog and howl at the back of his throat, as if calling to his people.

It was something of a relief when the military, knowing me for a sharp-shooter, whether it was with tranquilliser guns, automatic rifles or AK47s, wanted me to go with them all the way to the Namibian border. We would be gone for about four days, they said, tracking down any surviving workers from a destroyed farm near Bitterstroom and hoping to find the attackers. Going was one thing but getting back was another. Bugger it all, because of a dust storm that turned earth and sky into one gritty red moonscape, knocked down trees and erased the paths, we could only labori-ously track ourselves back three days later than expected.

Hellish tired, jumpy and bitter at what I'd seen and done, I dropped off the truck, waved goodbye to the guys and dragged my piece and my sand-infused kit to my house. The place was in darkness. I let myself in easily, the door not being locked, and turned on the light. The destruction hit me like a tree-branch in the face. It was as if that dust storm had entered here and exploded everything. Globs of excrement and splashes of blood were everywhere and the room stank of Solomon's anger and fear. Yet neither Louise nor Solomon was to be seen. I was about to limp back to the trackers' camp when Louise, her blonde hair loose and her face bleak, walked slowly up to the door.

'Louise, oh Louise, my baby, what happened, what happened?' I clutched her to me. 'Thank God you're alive. But what *happened*?'

'You see, Gerda, *you* were supposed to be home three days ago ...'

'Yes, so?' I pushed Louise away and stared at her blank face and stiffened body.

'So that day when you were expected back, Tanner had been given time off and he asked me to go with him to Cape Town, just for the day, you see, to take care of the pregnancy ...'

'And, Louise, *and*?'

'I left Solomon with plenty of food and ... and those new squeagy toys we'd sent for. I thought you'd be home before he ... he could get into any kind of distress, you see.'

'No, I don't see.'

'Being certain that you'd be home, Tanner then decided we should stay the night in a hotel – I was really sick and in pain – and come back the next morning ...'

'So, when you got back he'd got out, he'd run away, is that it? Why isn't everybody out looking for him? Let's go look for him, come on Louise, let's go.' I tried pushing her backwards out of the door.

'Gerda, I am ill and Solomon's dead.'

'Dead? Dead? What are you saying, Louise?'

'Yes ... I'm telling you that he's dead.'

'Where is he?'

'It was too hot, we had to bury the body.'

'*Where?*'

'In the garden. Gerda, please don't shout.'

'Who killed him, Louise?'

'I'm not sure. Poachers, probably. They hacked off the expensive parts. Oh Gerda, it's easy to force the lock on this door. As you can

see, there was a great struggle ...' Her eyes looked insane for an
instant and her small mouth flattened. 'He fought. But they speared
him and ...'

'*What*, Louise?'

Then Louise told me how she and Tanner and some of the guys
had gone scouring the brush and the sand-hills and had found
Solly's corpse. He'd been speared through the heart and his hands
and feet amputated. I began panting and turning this way and that
as if I'd misplaced something. Then I saw it, my rifle leaning
against the wall. I picked it up and pushed past Louise. 'Gerda,
wait for me!' she screamed. But I didn't wait: I went running around
the house and out into the bush, firing wildly. I needed a target but
there was none, so I shot at the sky, at the last birds flying home,
my mouth a wide-open noise. I shot branches off thorn-trees and
blasted shrubs to splinters. I chewed my inner cheeks until I could
taste my own blood in my mouth. When the men came out of their
tents to see what the noise was about, I stood and took careful aim.
I was getting Tanner clear in my sights when I became aware of
Louise next to me, rifle dragging in the dust, her mouth a slash of
pain. She touched my arm softly, and we both stood like that for a
long time, a very long time.

ACKNOWLEDGEMENTS

The editor and publisher are grateful to the authors/agents below for permission to reproduce copyright material:

In the first part for renewals our thanks to:

Es'kia Mphahlele for 'A Ballad of Oyo'

Lionel Abrahams for 'The Messiah'

Yvonne Burgess for 'If You Swallow You're Dead'

Ahmed Essop for 'Gerty's Brother'

Nadine Gordimer for 'You Name It'

Elizabeth Fairbairn of John Johnson (Authors' Agent) Ltd
    for Bessie Head's 'The Prisoner who Wore Glasses'

Sipho Sepamla for 'MaPuleng'

Mongane Serote for 'Let's Wander Together'

Peter Wilhelm for 'Lion' and

Pieter-Dirk Uys for 'God will See You Now'.

In the second part for work newly included our thanks to:

Elleke Boehmer for '27 April 1994'

Rustum Kozain for 'The Tongue'

Rachelle Greeff for 'Tell Him It is Never Too Late'

Peter Rule for 'Eclipse'

Rose Moss for 'A Gem Squash'

Shaun Levin for 'The Good Outside'

Shaun de Waal for 'Exposure'

Shelley Power Literary Agency for Stephen Gray's 'Without Whom'

Chris van Wyk for 'Magic'

Deena Padayachee for 'Heavy Cerebral Metal'

Phaswane Mpe for 'Brooding Clouds'

Maureen Isaacson for 'Blood Diamonds'

K Sello Duiker for 'When You Least Expect It'

Farida Karodia for 'A Handbag in the Boot'

Dennis Venter for 'Bearing Breasts'

Ken Barris for 'Clubfoot' and

Sheila Roberts for 'A Kidnapping'.

Our thanks also to the editors past and present and publishers of particular journals (as mentioned in the contributor's note to each item), where stories first appeared.